It Is What It Is *Chronicles*

BOOK ONE

Living with Feet Too Big for a Glass Slipper

www.lynnetapper.com

Matador
5 Weir Road
Kibworth Beauchamp
Leicester LE8 0LQ, UK
Tel: 0116 279 2299
Fax: 0116 279 2277
Email: books@troubador.co.uk
Web: www.troubador.co.uk/matador

ISBN 978 184876 660 0

British Library Cataloguing in Publication Data.
A catalogue record for this book is available from the British Library.

Matador is an imprint of Troubador Publishing Ltd
Printed in the UK by TJ International Ltd, Padstow, Cornwall

In memory of my darling brother Ian
A true prince amongst men

ACKNOWLEDGEMENTS

I would like to thank all those people I have met who provided wonderful inspiration for my characters. I would particularly like to thank my very own Prince Bad Boy, Baron Press, Lord Lie-A-Lot, Captain Unavailable and Prince Rescue Me, for if not for our relationships this book would not have been possible.

I wish to thank my wonderful family for all their love and support and always allowing me to make my own choices.

For all my friends who have had to endure my endless tales of heartache and woe I thank you for your unwavering loyalty and friendship.

To Mike for providing wisdom and guidance as I navigated my journey as a writer and for reminding me to have fun on the way.

Doreen, you are my very own Fairy Godmother who told me I didn't need anyone else to make my dream a reality.

Monica, you are the supreme Queen of Living a Creative Life! Thank you for helping with the design of the book and for all your inspiration.

For Eagle – thanks for always being there.

Stefanie, my graphic designer for being my angel in Shanghai and creating a book from a story.

I would also wish to acknowledge the joy and inspiration for me that is London, Vancouver, Paris, Milan and Venice – great places, great people, great stories!

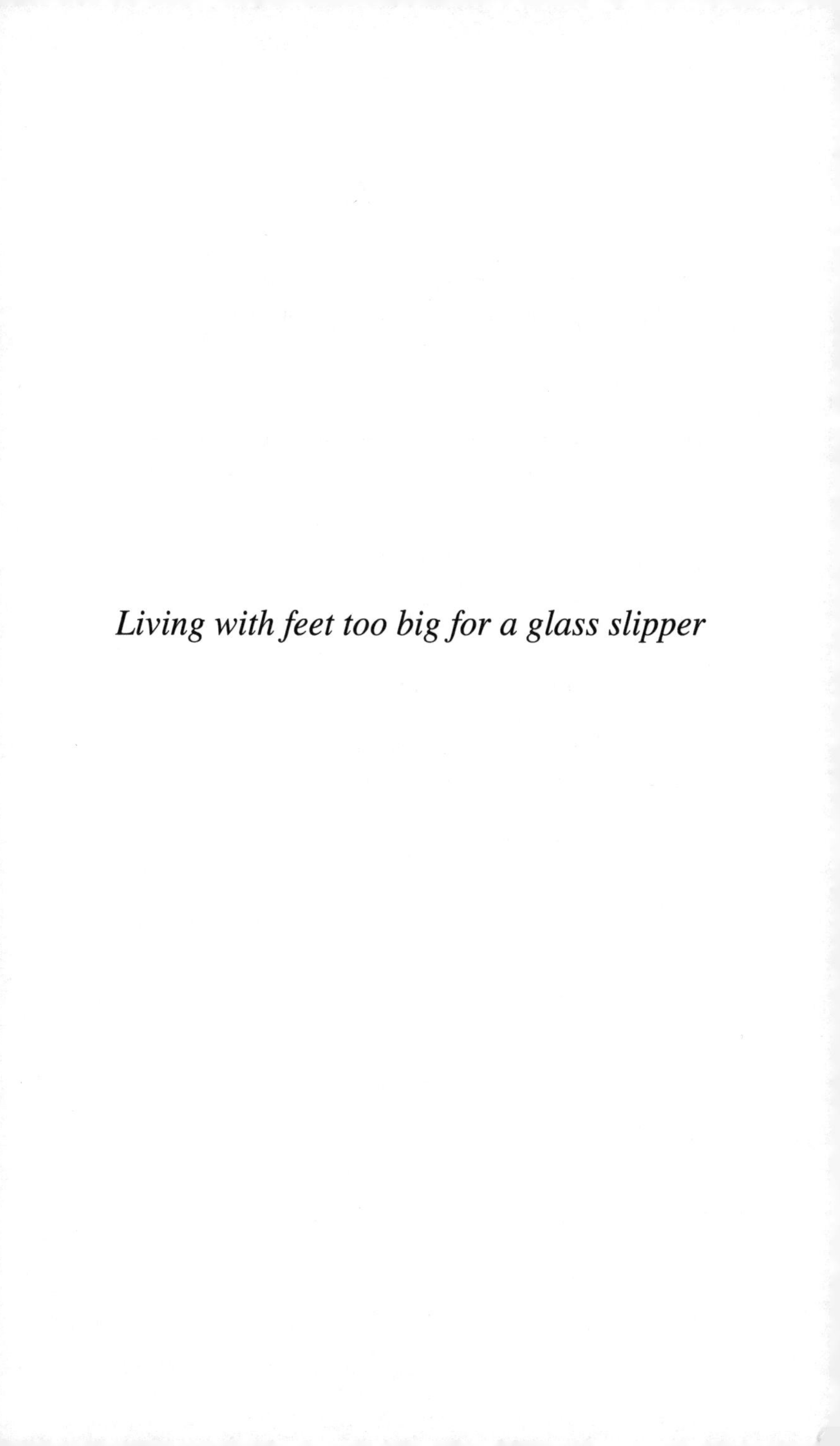

Living with feet too big for a glass slipper

FACT

In the beginning there was happily-ever-after.
Subsequently, people everywhere have lost the plot …

An exaggerated excerpt from *Phineous Blog's Great Guide to The Kingdom* – published in the year, 1178 B.R. – Before Reason.

The Kingdom of It Is What It Is

Wonderful weirdoes will welcome you all,
Performers will bewilder and enthral.
A place full of fickle and frantic folk,
A Fairy Tale Land? That's truly the joke!
A Princess seeks love and is fraught with pain,
From pain comes wisdom and power to gain.
Enjoy the journey as you jaunt about,
Life's great mystery is there to figure out.

1
Princess Innocent

Innocent was born with all the promise of happiness a first child brings. She was the most beautiful of princesses, with glimmering green eyes, high cheekbones and long dark curly locks. Petite and delicate, she was graced with a smile like the sun.

Her parents, King Absent and Queen Appearance, held governance over Look At Me, the richest and poshest Royal Borough in the Kingdom of It Is What It Is – where everything was as it seemed and people were the perfect performers in the game of life.

They were meticulous monarchs who micromanaged all aspects of life in the borough, ensuring that posh principles – or at least the illusion of *poshness* – were maintained at all times. So successful were the monarchs at cultivating the notion that *posh really was better,* that other boroughs sought to emulate their success by importing their posh protocols – sometimes even hiring Absent and Appearance as advisors for quality assurance. The export of poshness became so vital to Look At Me's economy that the monarchs spent most of their time away from Innocent on *royal due diligent duties*.

Innocent's upbringing was heavily influenced by past events. When her parents were children, It Is What It Is had gone through a terrible and tragic war with the neighbouring Kingdom of Capitulation, lasting almost seven years.

It all started when the Grand Duke Diabolical became ruler of the nearby nation. He had been a terribly spoilt child who suffered from visions and illusions of grandeur that his smothering mother had bestowed on him. Lacking stature, good looks, intellect, compassion, common sense, humour and diplomacy, he believed the world owed him a living. Not the brightest lamplight in the street, Diabolical decided that the only way to make up for his shortcomings was to blame others.

He discovered a unique formula for creative coercion by convoluting the truth. He recognized that in the land of Capitulation, where people were always comparing themselves to others, blaming and belittling struck a cohesive cord. He gathered enough bolshie *Blamerites* to bully himself to the front of the presidential queue and took command. He concentrated his cruelty on anyone who was smart, good-looking, successful, kind, intellectual, musical, artistic and happy. The only people who prospered under his iron fist were those who were as nasty and nihilistic as he was.

The people of It Is What It Is were a plain-speaking, practical nation of identities, innovators, industrialists and inventors. Every quadrennial they invited the neighbouring kingdoms to a four day event of friendly athletic activity. The Olympic-size event had everything from jousting, archery, fencing, tennis and marathon running.

As a participating member, Grand Duke Diabolical had been invited to represent the Kingdom of Capitulation. During the commencement ceremony The Kingdom's handsome Minister of Defence the Oracle, Sir Orator, roused the home crowd with his incredible introduction.

Once he had finished, Sir Orator took his seat besides the dower and dire Diabolical. As the Duke got up to speak, he tripped over Sir Orator's foot and fell flat on his face. The crowd roared with laughter as Diabolical's toupee went flying and landed on the tournament tarmac. Humiliated, he picked himself up and swore revenge on the revered Orator and the people who so rudely laughed at his misfortune.

'I will take his kingdom and kick that Orator into the ocean. That will teach him,' screeched the little man to his mother on returning home.

Diabolical mobilized his mighty maniacal forces, determining that It Is What It Is would be in his hands before long. However, he underestimated the resolve of the people, who had always stood up to bullies.

Being the large, lush, and lucrative kingdom that it was, many invaders had attempted integration through invasion. There had been the fashionists who had attempted to spread their fashion ideas of togas and tunics. There had been the righteous religiositists who had attempted to impose their religious rhetoric on the good people of The Kingdom. There had been the politicalists, who had attempted to promote their political practices on the people. There had even been the foodists who had attempted to spice up the blandness of the food.

Invaders had always been met at the border by the Minister of Deference, a Master of the Amicable Arts. He always politely declined their services, but nevertheless extended the offer of hospitality. Usually within a month of being hosted by the amiable Minister, the cold wet weather and bland food seemed too much hard work and the invaders retreated.

Diabolical was a different and demonic breed. He did not do hospitality. When he attended a party, he wanted everyone to be aware of his prickly presence.

It Is What It Is experienced the first bombardment in the south, and for the first time ever, rockets rained down on the royal kingdom's soil. The ensuing years were severe as people endured the horrors and hardships of war. Many great souls were sadly lost.

Like thousands of young children, Innocent's parents were packed off to a place of safety in the quiet countryside. For seven years the children sat waiting for their parents to take them home. Occasional visits broke the long, lonely absences.

With the children tucked away safely, Sir Orator rallied the hungry and weary citizens with superlative speeches spilling with greatness. Unbeknownst to Diabolical, Sir Orator had a secret weapon brewing ... the comfort of a cup of tea!

Teatime had arrived in It Is What It Is a hundred years earlier. It had been introduced to The Kingdom by a great and wise China and Porcelain Tea Set Travelling Salesman from the faraway

Eastern Kingdoms. He had braved the seas to seek his fortune finding new markets.

Recognizing the comfort a warm cup of tea could bring to a dreary, drizzling, damp and dark climate, the salesman cultivated conspicuous consumption and customers for his china and porcelain tea sets and bags of tea. He meticulously market researched The Kingdom, zooming in on the richest Royal Borough of Look At Me. Realizing its influence around The Kingdom, he ingeniously introduced tea bags and tea time to the Toffs, thereby taking the tasty trend to the thirsty masses.

Tea tales travelled tenaciously, translating into thousands of tea sets and tea bag sales. Tea time became a national pastime as even the poorest pauper purchased posh and pretty china and porcelain tea sets. An entire civilized culture of conversation and a *Cup of Char* emerged to define the nation.

Every day as the bombs bombarded the good people of The Kingdom, at 11 a.m. and 3 p.m. without fail everyone would stop, sit or lie down for cover, with a cup of tea. Each sip and slurp strengthened the peoples' resolve by reminding them daily of the civilized culture and cuppa they were fighting to defend.

Thankfully with tea time, tenacity and tactical know-how, both Diabolical and his forces were forced into the sea. As Diabolical began his long slumber with the fishes, It Is What It Is began the long process of rebuilding.

So shocked by the nastiness of the barbaric and bombastic Diabolical that the powers that be looked into how it could have all been prevented. The ruling parliamentary party at the time, The Political Correctness Party dictated a new dictum of decorum, *People Pleasing for Peace*. It was a school of thought that threw light on the influencing powers of pleasing and placating to procure influence and friendship – having a heaving heart became order of the day.

Innocent's Grandparents had been at the forefront of the movement. Consequently, her parents grew up in the School of People Pleasing, where grandiose giving was glorified as a means to gain affection and appreciation. After five years of post-war pleasing, many people found the pace too exhausting and the movement moved on. However, in the Borough of Look At Me they had incorporated the ideology into daily life.

Being the brashest borough in the land, it was the centre of charitable campaigning. The King and Queen oversaw all contributions, ensuring the benefactors gave generously and in return gained gratitude, glory and greatness. They even enacted a royal competition to see who could gain the most commemorative plaques. Appearances were absolute in Look At Me.

In senior school, Innocent carried on this tradition as she mastered the Pleasing Arts. Her classes included *Saving the World 101, Pleasing for Popularity and Platitudes, Prettiness Makes Perfect, Magnified Martyrdom* and *Worming Your Way in the World by Wonderfulness*.

Innocent's favourite class was called *They Like Me, They Really Like Me* where she gained instruction in how to garner male attention through garish giving. She excelled in her studies, but her research was only confined to the classroom as her protective parents had not allowed her to start courting.

By way of genes and guidance, Innocent became gifted in the art of giving. She was always ready to *give* a mandolin recital to the household staff as they were setting up for a banquet or gladly *gave* a two-step dance for the footmen as they were polishing the silver. She was more than happy to *give* singing lessons to the cooks as they sweated over the great ovens preparing meals for over 100 household staff. She *gave* the *gift* of the gab to her lady-in-waiting filling her in on all her school gossip. She was the first person to *give* a performance of a Soap Opera as she often rubbed soap in her eyes as she re-enacted a dramatic scene from an event at school – tears streaming down her face for effect.

Innocent even collected flowers from the gardens *giving* them as gifts to the burly knights who guarded the castle gates, often decorating their suits of armour with daisy and dandelion chains.

She was a princess in every sense of the word and although egocentric – and in the knights' opinion, slightly eccentric – she nevertheless radiated likeability and loveliness.

As well as being an apt pupil in the art of giving, Innocent also learned about loneliness – miserably missing her mobile parents. Although she had friends and family to take up company with, and a household of over 100 staff to entertain, none of her entourage could fill the gap left by her absconded parents.

Absent and Appearance ensured the head housekeeper supervised every aspect of Innocent's upbringing and that she would want for nothing. After enduring their own edgy and difficult childhoods, they wanted to bestow on their daughter a bubble of bliss whereby she would know nothing of the hardships and cruelty of the world. They encouraged her to read the *Fairy Tale Land Press* where happily-ever-after permeated every story.

It Is What It Is was on the border of Fairy Tale Land and Innocent like most girls her age, often read all the Fairy Tale Land gossip about the people who resided there. There was a great buzz about a local girl who had been working as a scullery maid for her step-family when she was swept off her feet by a prince named Charming. She went from climbing the Larder Ladder to the Social Ladder!

There was also a big scandal about a princess who had just married the heir to a great throne, even though she had lived with seven, possibly eight men, all at once!

Innocent spent many a day imagining how her own prince would sweep her off her feet. However, she knew things were a little different in It Is What It Is. Princesses were expected to go out *searching* for their own prince.

Sheltered by her parents, Innocent's only real experience of men was the cartoon hanging on her wall of the giant of the jousting world, known simply as *Golden Poles*. The jiggy, jaunting, juggernaut of a jouster had triumphed at every tournament he had ever been in, knocking knights off their horses and knickers off of young maidens.

His six foot frame had caused a great frenzy among females throughout The Kingdom. His reputation so preceded him that when he arrived to joust in Look At Me, Innocent's cautious parents kept her locked away in the castle compensating with a cartoon likeness. From sixteen to eighteen years of age she swooned over her cartoon idol fantasising about their fairy tale future. It was her first *real* relationship.

She continued living life in both people pleasing mode and ignorant bliss until one day her father and mother told her it was time she moved out of the castle and started searching for her *One True Prince*. It was the tradition of every citizen of It Is What It Is to embark on their *great life's journey,* as soon as they turned eighteen. Innocent was excited about her rite of passage, confident that she was worldly enough to walk without delay into wonderful wedded bliss. After all, she had the looks and charms to find her own Prince Charming and felt cheerfully up to the challenge.

Innocent was called to the great throne room where her parents were waiting with one of their ministers.

'My darling daughter, what a proud day this is for your mother and I. Today is your coming out day, where you will go forth on your great life's journey and leave our great borough to not only search for your *One True Prince* but to also find your own great fortune.'

'I don't understand father, I understand about the prince part, but I thought we were rich – why would I have to go out and seek my own fortune?'

'My darling child,' said the Queen, 'all princesses need to follow their own path in order to reach the riches awaiting them. This is how they eventually get to change their names and become queens – if they so choose. You cannot only rely on a prince to give you that title – you will have to earn it! Every decent prince worth his gold will expect you to already be a queen when he proposes.

Now you must go out into the world and discover what it is you want to be queen of. Alas, so many of the youth today lack the tenacity and courage to eventually change their names. But I am certain with your looks, charm and character you will conquer and complete this challenge.'

The Queen smiled at her daughter's perplexed face. 'Don't worry my child,' she reassured her, 'you will discover this in your own time.'

The King nodded to the minister to step forward. Sir Steady was the Chief Minister of Defence. He was in charge of security and making sure there was no trouble in the land. He was a trusted advisor to many kings, administrators and parliamentarians and had managed to keep everyone secure and safe for the last twenty years.

'My dear Princess Innocent, what a proud day for us all as you embark on your magical journey. The Ministry of Defence has a presentation to make to you, to mark the occasion.'

He held out a small box. The Princess opened it up and inside discovered a beautiful red silk scarf, encrusted with tiny diamond hearts.

'It is from The Great Armoury,' said the Minister. 'Read the label inside.'

Innocent looked at the words on the label: *Love Scarf – made in It Is What It Is – Woven with love and care. Wear it and feel the love. One size fits all. Wash in cold water only!*

'The greatest defence we have in the land of It Is What It Is – is love. The scarf will remind you of this. Let it be your standard!'

'Thank you Minister, it is surely a beautiful scarf and I will be proud to wear it on my journey,' smiled Innocent sweetly. And surely I will be the most fashionable of princesses, wearing it, she thought privately to herself.

'Now you are ready, my dear daughter to start your journey,' said the King proudly.

'You will have the finest horse and the grandest carriage to venture out with. We will instruct the best tailors to arm you with the most fashionable wardrobe money can buy. You will also be given your inheritance early – your own Privy Purse packed with enough gold to allow you to live life as you so choose. Spend it wisely my dearest daughter.'

How spiffy, thought Innocent – a new horse, a fine coach etched with gold trim, fashionable clothes and enough money for me to do anything I want. I will be *the* new belle of the ball. This journey is going to rock polite society! And while she was on a roll she asked sweetly –

'Can I also get a new hairstyle before I go mother?'

'Of course you can my child. I will take you to the royal barberess to tend to your tresses.'

Innocent gave them a dance and a song, and with that, plans for her journey were signed, sealed and meticulously delivered.

THE
DREAM

2
Innocent and Bad Boy

After careful consideration of all her options, Innocent decided to move to the South of It Is What It Is. Any princess who was anybody spent time there. It was the centre of après high school society, where young folk of The Kingdom went after leaving their home castles. There they could mingle and find a match in the endless balls and courtly cotillions.

Innocent checked herself into the Regal Rooms, a ten-star, silver service, Palace Inn. This would be her home for the foreseeable future.

She had arrived just in time. The Great Matching Ball of the season was about to commence. All the eligible princes and princesses would be there. Innocent heard that the competition for a princely trophy would be fierce. She was determined to eliminate any rivals and armed with the latest accessory – a beauty mentor – busily readied her royal self.

She spent the whole day deciding what she would wear. After watching a private fashion parade arranged by her mentor, she finally settled on a racy red robe, with a low-cut bodice and a skirt which exposed her ankles. It was the latest rage which had caused quite a scandal with the senior royals. Innocent took out the red scarf that Sir Steady had given her and deciding it lacked trend-setting style, put it away in the bottom of her drawer. She would not wear it until years later…

The shoes and matching bag she had chosen were from the fashion house of Wear for Status. Upon her feet she wore a pair of the latest glass slippers, all the rage among fashion conscious princesses everywhere. She chose fashion over comfort as she found the glass slippers a rather tight and uncomfortable fit for her broad feet.

She had her hair coiffed and nails painted by a local artist. With a heap of make-up caked over her face, she was ready to make her grand entrance.

Arriving in her grand coach, she walked through the great wooden doors and waited. As she stepped forward the doorman announced her arrival in a booming voice.

'Princess Innocent – from the Royal Borough of Look At Me.'

Innocent gasped. She had never seen so many beautiful young ladies gathered in one room. How on earth am I going to get noticed amongst all this beauty, she thought to herself. Seriously scrutinizing all the competition, she took stock of all the physical advantages she had over each of the young ladies, concluding that in comparison, she stood up extremely well.

Deciding a sophisticated Princess needed a drink in her hand, Innocent headed to the long bar area and ordered a Confidence Cocktail. She was about to take a sip of her drink when a prince approached her. He was so quiet that he had to repeat himself a couple of times before Innocent heard him and looked up.

'Ah–hem, Ah–hem. Hello, my name is Prince Nice Guy, and who – ah – whom do I have the pleasure of addressing?'

Innocent's excitement at being approached by a young man quickly dissipated as she looked upon the Prince. He stood five feet, seven inches in height and wore both a pair of spectacles and a huge grin which he flashed at her.

'Hello, I'm Princess Innocent,' she replied, rather disappointed that he wasn't better looking.

'Great to meet you,' he gushed. 'Have you been here long?'

'I just arrived – it's my first time here. I have never seen a ball-room so packed before and with so many beautiful princesses,' said Innocent downheartedly.

'You are by far the prettiest girl in the room. I noticed you right away.'

As Nice Guy started chatting away, Innocent found her eyes roving eagerly around the ballroom and her mind wandering. She had already decided that Prince Nice Guy was not quite tall enough for her liking and his garments were definitely not in fashion.

'Princess Innocent ... Ah–hem, Princess Innocent. What's your sign?'

Oh are you still here, thought Innocent, wishing he would just go away. 'I'm a Sagittarius,' she responded half-heartedly, now in the throes of planning how she could ditch him.

'Oh I love princesses of that signage! They are always so spirited and sharp-witted.'

By now the perturbed Princess had completely closed her ears to him. She continued scanning and scouting the room, until she spotted a spectacular sight. There, a few feet from her, standing at the end of the bar was the most hopelessly handsome prince she had ever laid eyes on. He measured at least six feet tall, had long brown locks and the most glorious and gleaming green eyes she had ever beheld. He wore fashionable pantaloons which displayed a divine derrière. Innocent was entranced. She had to somehow gain this God's attention. But first she needed to rid herself of Prince Nice Guy, who by this time was besotted.

'Would you like to dance with me?' he asked.

She found her opening for escape and seized the moment.

'Please excuse me my dear Prince, but my betrothed has just arrived and I must go to his side. Thank you so much for keeping me company but I must now bid you farewell.'

'Oh you are betrothed. Forgive me for being so unawares. Alas, my great loss is another prince's great gain.' And with that he bowed to Innocent and disappointedly took his leave. She began to feel bad about her brash behaviour toward him, but laying eyes once again on the fabulous prince a few feet away made the feeling quickly pass.

She came up with a plan to gain this Adonis's attention – she checked herself over in her miniature mirror and gave her mouth a refresh of lip paint. She marvelled at how marvellous she looked and decided that she was far better-looking than most of the other princesses in the room. I will get his attention for sure she decided, and set her plan into motion.

She walked towards the handsome young man and as she brushed passed him, discreetly dropped her delicate silk handkerchief.

He couldn't help but notice and smiled to himself. He'd had hundreds of handkerchiefs dropped at his feet and was always happy to accommodate. How wonderful, he thought to himself, a new challenge …

He scooped up the handkerchief and bowing before her declared, 'Beautiful lady, I believe this belongs to you.' Innocent blushed as he handed her the handkerchief. Momentarily, their fingers met and she felt a surge of electricity race through her body.

As she looked into the handsome stranger's face, she noticed that he was even better looking up close. She fluttered her eyelashes at him and wondered whether this could be her *One True Prince …*

'Thank you,' she replied demurely.

'Chivalry is alive and well and at your service, my dear lady. I am Prince Bad Boy,' he said smiling broadly, thoroughly impressed with the beauty he was beholding.

'Oh, what a naughty name,' she gushed. 'My name is Princess Innocent.'

Bad Boy couldn't believe his luck! 'Well Princess Innocent, would you like to dance?' And with that he took her hand and swept her onto the dance floor.

'Do you like the musicians?' said Bad Boy, pointing to the group playing in the corner of the ballroom.

'They are called Pink Palace and they are the newest and most relevant performers in town. They have a groovy new sound. This is one of my favourite songs, *Royal Lust*. What do you think of them?'

Innocent had never had such stimulating conversation.

'They're simply spiffy,' she concurred, and they continued to dance the whole night away.

She couldn't help but notice how much attention Bad Boy paid to her low-cut bodice and her ankle displaying skirt. For the first time in her life she felt thoroughly grown up.

Prince Bad Boy was twenty-five years old and originally from the Borough of Secrets. His family had made their fortunes in horse trading. By all adept appearances he had come from a loving family, but beneath the facade he had come from a family of *fighters and flighters*. As a child he had often cowered in the corner, as his well-connected and charming father used his fists on his mother.

His terrified mother eventually fled with her son and found refuge in a safer marriage. His father continued his charm offensive, collecting an assortment of weary wives and restraining orders. By the time Bad Boy was eighteen he had accumulated ten half-siblings, twelve step-brothers and sisters, seven step-parents and eight nannies. There were so many people coming in and out of his life, that he often did not know all the names of his step siblings and parents, and did not dare to get attached to affection.

Taking a lead from his father, he developed his own superficial shell and became a Master of The Charming Arts. In fact, under his father's tutorledge he became an even better master. He was so good in fact, that his father often used a night out with Bad Boy as bait for bringing beautiful ladies to his table. Once he had procured a beautiful distraction Bad Boy would often not see him for weeks.

He began his charm offensive on Innocent and she became caught up in a whirlwind of excitement. The Prince called upon her the next day and the next. Within two weeks of meeting they were officially an item. The Prince had to admit that he liked the young Innocent and she began to break through his hard shell. He took up the challenge of educating her in worldly ways. Bad Boy lavished attention on Innocent, buying her bouquets of fragrant flora, garishly glittering gems and the most fashionable robes. He took her to candlelight suppers at the finest eateries and moonlit walks along the promenade. In return she often sang and danced for him.

After three weeks of courting, Bad Boy took Innocent to her first Pink Palace performance under the stars where he introduced her to the pleasures of Hazy Herbal Weed Smoking. As they listened to the sounds of Pink Palace's *Dark Side of the Moat,* the Hazy Herbal Cigarettes swept them away in a cloud of smoke.

It was at the concert that Innocent had her first kiss, as Bad Boy planted his lips on top of hers. She had only ever seen someone kissing once before, when her mother had shown her *that book,* a how-to-tell-your-young-prince-and-princess-the-facts-of-love-making-whilst-maintaining-a-posh-and-dignified-demeanour. It had a brown paper cover with no title, but with its racy illustrations it demonstrated the mechanics of physical contact.

Innocent's mother had shown her the manual on her seventeenth birthday. She encouraged her daughter to ask questions – no matter how embarrassing. Innocent studied the book intensely determined that her people pleasing acumen would translate to the boudoir when the time came. She often practised her kissing on her mirror, determined to get it right.

Now here was the real thing – a pair of princely lips. As Bad Boy leaned forward to kiss her, Innocent adjusted her head several times, trying to get comfortable. When she felt his tongue slip into her mouth, she wasn't quite sure which side she should move to. She wriggled her tongue around furiously, like a fish out of water, determined to get it right.

As Innocent rammed her tongue ever deeper down his throat – still trying to get comfortable – the Prince started to get more even more aroused. She must be more experienced than I imagined, thought Bad Boy, confusing her inexperience for passion.

The next day Innocent's tongue ached, but she felt proud that she had entered the realm of physicality. She was completely enamoured with Bad Boy – convinced without a shadow of a doubt that he was her *One True Prince*.

A week later he asked her if he could be the one to deflower her.

'My sweet, I would be proud to teach you all that I know in the boudoir. Won't you let me tonight?'

She didn't have to be asked twice and eagerly said 'yes'.

She remembered *that* conversation she had with her mother when they talked about her deflowerment day, when she had finally finished *that book*.

'Traditions have changed and princesses no longer need to be virgins when they marry,' the Queen advised. 'In fact, princes today prefer their new brides to be Princesses of the World.

In these modern times, princes are used to having everything done for them and have become lazy. When you do let a prince deflower you, always remember to wear royal protection. Your mother is not ready to become a Grandmama just yet,' and with those words of wisdom, she handed her daughter a box of fine leather sheaths which caused Innocent to blush profusely.

When the time came she retrieved her box, handed them to Bad Boy and as the sun set to the sounds of Pink Palace emanating from the performance grounds below, the virgin was deflowered.

Although the Prince tried to be as gentle as possible, the first couple of times of lovemaking hurt horrendously and she truly wondered what all the fuss was about.

But after several weeks in his arms, she really started to enjoy herself. In fact, she discovered that she had quite a talent in the boudoir and impressed herself at how good she had become. She prided herself that she was a novice no longer! She even learnt to play the sounds of Pink Palace's *Royal Lust* on her mandolin and often gave Bad Boy impromptu recitals.

These marvellous moments continued for months and months. Innocent convinced herself that a proposal from her Prince was imminent, and in her head went about planning her big day.

It was early spring when Bad Boy had some shocking news for his sweetheart as they lay in bed together.

'My love, my father has called upon me to attend a racing event in the East Coast. As the oldest son in the family, he has asked me to take up the reins and help him to ensure the family's Privy Purse remains packed by moving into the new sport of racing. I leave tomorrow at the break of dawn.'

In shock at the heartbreaking news, Innocent failed to notice the faraway look on Bad Boy's face, as he contemplated his trip. He had not seen his father since he began courting her.

'Can I go with you?' pleaded Innocent, unnerved at the thought of being parted from her beloved.

Bad Boy broke from his reverie. 'No my love, it is family business. I will return to your loving arms in but seven days.' Before she had a chance to protest he kissed her longingly.

The next day as he rode off gallantly on his horse, Innocent wept.

As the seven days passed, she became heady with excitement. Convincing herself that he would return with a ring for her delicate finger, she busied herself with her stylist in preparation for the proposal.

'I do hope the ring has rubies *and* diamonds. I love rubies and Mother always says that the two complement each other so well in a fifty carat gold setting. Don't you think rubies would suit my colouring?' contemplated Innocent to her stylist.

When the primed Princess heard a gallop outside her courtyard, her heart skipped a beat and she rushed downstairs to greet her beloved. Once outside, she was disappointed to find a messenger. He handed her a scroll from the Prince which Innocent read, her heart racing –

My darling

Some important business matter has arisen and I will be staying in the East Coast for another week. Missing you and sending you abundant kisses.

Forever yours
Bad Boy
X

Innocent's heart sank. How could she stand being away from him for seven more days? And why was there only one kiss in his correspondence? She began to feel sick.

From that moment on things began to change between Innocent and her Prince. Upon his return, she sensed a distance between them. In his desire to please his father he had returned to familiar territory. Day by day Bad Boy succumbed to type – choosing his comfort zone over his feelings for Innocent. It wasn't long until he was off on the next *business trip*.

When he was home, he seemed less inclined to take her out and his glittering gifts were few and far between. When they did venture out together, Bad Boy would become distracted and would make a point to smile at any pretty princess when they happened to walk by. Within three months of that first fateful business trip, it became apparent to Innocent that Bad Boy had become bored with her.

She began to panic and decided she needed a plan. She drew on her Pleasing Arts Education and made up her mind that she would become even more alluring to him – by losing some of her voluptuous volume. If she could fit into smaller garments he would find her even more irresistible. So she began to skip meals and lived on a diet of berries.

Her diet made her irritable from hunger, but she persisted anyway until the Prince commented.

'Why Innocent, where on earth have all your beautiful curves gone? There is less and less of you to grab hold of.'

She revamped her entire wardrobe and brought garments with the lowest and tightest bodices and the shortest skirts that exposed her entire ankle. But Bad Boy had seen it all before and became even more disinterested, and their lovemaking lessened.

She changed her tactic, deciding to lavish love and gifts on her Prince in the hopes of demonstrating how much he really needed her. Each gift she bought was more exquisite than the last – a new saddle, a beautiful engraved sword of the finest silver, a new suit of armour and six pairs of leather shoes made by the most skilled shoemakers. She even gave him the grand coach that her parents had given her.

Taking advice from her stylist about the in-thing to entice a prince – Innocent learnt the art of massage. At night she would knead the knots in his neck and shoulders after he had been riding all day and bathe his feet in rose petal oil. As Bad Boy melted into the moment of relaxation, Innocent got her Prince back.

'How you spectacularly spoil me, my sweet.'

Unfortunately, her stylist had worked with many a young princess – successfully coaching them on the art of enticement. Some of them found their way into Bad Boy's boudoir and it wasn't long before he resumed his business trips.

The more she did for him, the less time he spent with her and eventually all the princely surprises that she once delighted in, ceased entirely. Gone were the fragrant flora, the glittering garish gems, the Pink Palace performances and the long-lasting lovemaking lessons. Whenever she attempted to sing or dance for him, he left the room.

Innocent felt the Prince slipping through her fingers – like a slippery eel, impossible to hold onto. Her heart heaved heavily with hopelessness.

She finally crumbled when she followed Bad Boy and saw him kissing Princess Easy on what had been *their promenade*. She ran home and threw herself on her bed and wept. When she received a scroll from Bad Boy's messenger she knew what it would say before she even opened it –

Dear Innocent

This last year and a bit with you has been divine and you are truly a beautiful Princess, but I am not the settling down kind and I need room to explore all that life has to offer. I therefore send you a big kiss and bid you adieu, until we meet again, my love.

Yours sincerely
Bad Boy

Innocent wanted to die. She read the message over and over scrutinizing every word and reading between the lines for evidence that there was still hope. Alas, she found none.

She spent a week weeping in her room inconsolably. Every day she would try and recapture the rapturous moments that she once spent with the Prince by retracing their steps. She would frequent the succulent supper eateries he had taken her to. She would attend Pink Palace performances solo, but nothing could ease her sorrow. Music left her life as she stopped singing and dancing – her mandolin locked away in a wardrobe.

After weeks of sadness and solitude she decided to walk to their favourite esplanade seat. As she sat down, her mind flooded with memories of magical moments and she began to cry. She was so involved in her weeping that she did not notice the elegant lady who sat down beside her.

'There, there, ma petite chère, what makes you weep so? Whatever has troubled you so, this too will pass. Take my handkerchief ma belle, and wipe your wonderful eyes.'

Finding her words comforting Innocent smiled, and after a last sob and sigh, wiped her eyes. She could tell by the lady's accent and fashionable attire that she was from the Kingdom of Joie De Vie, just a small journey across the outlying ocean. No women in all the kingdoms looked quite like the Joie De Vien women. They excelled in elegance, had stupendous style, and perfect poise. Innocent's mother had told her that all the women of Joie De Vie, both titled and untitled are taught from birth onwards how to meticulously master the Arts of Supreme Style. That is why they never lost a gold medal when competing in the Miss Princess Olympic Championships.

She had been told by her mother how Joie De Vie was once the greatest borough in the entire Kingdom of It Is What It Is, but broke away due to a dispute over blandness of both politics and food. When It Is What It Is lost its Joie De Vie, many a royal family took flight and fled to the fashionable new kingdom. Therefore, some of its finest families there were descendents of It Is What It Is. Perhaps feeling a royal rivalry, her mother often commented that you could take the family from It Is What It Is, but you could never take It Is What It Is from the family.

'I am Countess Confidence and what do they call you, ma belle?'

'I am Princess Innocent,' she said unenthusiastically, reflecting the low opinion she now had of herself.

'I am charmed to make your acquaintance,' said the Countess extending her hand. Innocent noticed her elegant, long, black silk gloves which extended up her entire arm. She studied the Countess from head to toe. The Princess was struck by the lady's long, blonde, curly locks which tumbled all the way down to her waist and her green eyes which glittered like small diamonds catching the light.

The Countess was thirty-six years young and even though she was a striking woman, what was most remarkable to Innocent was how poised and self-assured she appeared. She was a Countess who demanded attention just by simply being present.

She touched her hand reassuringly. 'What has distressed you so? How could one so beautiful be so blue?'

Blushing she recounted with perfect precision her princely saga. All the while the empathetic Countess nodded her head and smiled.

'Innocent ma chère, it seems to me that Bad Boy's dastardly deeds have done you a disservice. So much so, that you are well rid of that *royal rat*. One so beautiful and charming deserves a king – a doting darling who will adore *you* and is secure enough to possess the capacity to give to you.'

My goodness thought Innocent, she does have a way with words and she suddenly felt uplifted.

The Countess continued, 'My darling child, they will simply adore you in Joie De Vie, won't you venture to our fine shores and grace my kingdom with your presence? I would be most happy to make some useful introductions in our capital city, Nous Parlons Pas Anglais.'

Innocent had always dreamed of visiting Joie De Vie, with their class conscious couture, their colourful cuisine and more importantly the legendary potent prowess of their princes. Maybe this would be the place she would find her *One True Prince*. She turned to the Countess and squealed, 'When can we leave?'

'Oo–la–la, what spirit you possess,' laughed the Countess.'I leave within a week. You will accompany me, oui?'

But before we depart, one more word of advice, petite amie. We need to rearrange your racy wardrobe. Your garments display far too much of your fine wares. In Joie De Vie, we girls are particularly prudish in our presentation. We prefer to entice our men folk by hiding what is on offer rather than by previewing it on a platter. We make them work hard for a glimpse of an ankle. By displaying an air of mystery we keep them intrigued. We seduce subtly rather than sluttily. You understand?'

Innocent nodded at her, slightly embarrassed at her faux pas.

'I will take you shopping tomorrow for appropriate attire for your debut,' reassured the Countess and with that Innocent's journey took a new juncture.

Armed with her new found knowledge of fashion and guided by her new friend Countess Confidence, Innocent felt ready to conquer the world – or at least Nous Parlons Pas Anglais. The evening before her departure with the Countess, she decided to take one last stroll down the promenade. She was wearing her new attire which displayed not a hint of ankle or bosom. Even her hands were hidden by long, satin gloves.

Innocent had never felt such excitement and felt proud for taking such a big step into the unknown. She was positively radiant and felt gloriously happy for the first time in her entire life. As she was contemplating her forthcoming adventure, her reverie was abruptly interrupted by a familiar voice.

'Why, my darling Innocent, how serendipitous to see you.'

She looked up and there before her was Prince Bad Boy.

He smiled salaciously as his eyes scanned over her silhouette. Something about Innocent had changed …

'Why Innocent, I have never seen you looking so spectacularly sexy.'

She somehow looked different since they had parted and he found himself more attracted to her than ever before.

'Oh hello,' she replied nonchalantly.

As they stood facing one another, Innocent became aware that the butterflies he once generated inside of her were no longer present. As she scrutinised his sturdy frame, she no longer found him all that dashing. He had doused the passion she had for him when he deserted her so callously.

Bad Boy was intrigued by her demeanour.

'Innocent darling, let us play catch up. Won't you take your stroll with me now?'

After quick deliberation, she decided that due to his dastardly deeds, the old spark was definitely doused. She was now desperate to distance herself from him.

'So sorry Bad Boy but I need to prepare for my sojourn to Joie De Vie, I depart tomorrow and must take my leave.'

'Sojourning so soon, how sad, then I insist on taking you to dine with me this moment.'

'No thanks,' and turning on her heels she ditched the Prince, leaving him dumbfounded at being dumped for the first time in his life.

She felt elated at being the one doing the rejecting – and Bad Boy felt deflated at being the rejectee.

Princess Innocent was finally free of any princely feelings. With her new found friend, Confidence, she felt ready to take on her next romantic possibility.

3
Baron Booty

When Innocent arrived she immediately moved into the grand apartments that the Countess had arranged for her in the centre of Nous Parlons Pas Anglais. This would be her home for the foreseeable future.

True to her word, Confidence introduced Innocent to Nous Parlons Pas Anglais' polite salon society. An immediate hit, she was invited to join a glittering, gathering group who met on the right bank of the river for breakfast each morning. The group consisted of a vast array of characters from dapper dukes and darling duchesses, deposed dauphines, multi-married marchionesses, chivalrous chevaliers and pearly queens.

There were also members of the bourgeoisie set ranging from captains of industry to master craftsmen, gamblers, edgy artists, shameless and saucy performers, writers of great wit and generals of small stature. A few peasants were also thrown in for good measure along with a chaste troupe of Can't Can't Dancers – devotees of The Touch but Don't Look School of Seduction. The group was rounded up by a boisterously funny woman, Lady Laugh-Out-Loud from the Borough of Look At Me, proving to Innocent that the world was smaller than she had imagined.

She had never met such interesting people in her whole life and engaged in exhilarating exchanges about art, poetry, literature and most importantly, chic couture. Salon society sat well with her, and for the first time ever, she felt sophisticated.

On one such breakfast gathering, she was called aside by Captain Opportunist.

'Innocent ma belle, please come and meet a business associate of mine, a most intriguing gentleman from your own home Kingdom of It Is What It Is. He is here for the summer season. May I present, Baron Booty …'

Baron Booty was a buccaneer of legendary endeavours. He had a rakish smile, permanently etched upon his ruggedly handsome face. His goatee was clipped and neat and he wore the most stylish attire fashioned from the softest leather one could buy. He oozed machismo and urbane cool.

He had chartered new lands, chased pirates and princesses and taken treasures. He was a rascal and a rogue. The Baron was a man who made no apologies for who he was being. He never pretended to be anything other than himself. He loved life and people, and people and life loved him back in return. His wayward ways made women want him and men want to be like him.

Innocent smiled at the tall, muscular, imposing and impossibly good-looking icon standing in front of her. He took off his chapeau and bowed majestically at her feet, exposing a mane of thick, jet-black hair. As he kissed her hand he broadsided her with his charisma.

Baron Booty became besotted with Innocent's outer and inner beauty, and bent over backwards to bestow affection on her.

'Ma belle, won't you accompany me to my castle and spend a spectacular season in my company? I have a small boat in a remote part of my castle moat I would like to show you.'

Despite being who she was Innocent knew that any involvement with Baron Booty, however blissful, would be but a brief affair. She learnt from one of the Can't Can't troupe that he was a Baron sworn to the sea and was allergic to settling down for more than a season.

Countess Confidence, counselled Innocent to consider the Baron's proposal carefully.

'It will all end in tears ma bichette! You know I speak the truth. He will depart after the social season, as he always does and will leave you sobbing with a broken heart. He is a kinder, gentler, Bad Boy. Do you really want to tread precariously upon that territory again?'

Although Innocent agreed that the Countess was probably right, it was her hormones rather than her head that won out in the end.

She decided that since she was older and wiser, she was now sophisticated enough to handle the Baron – much better than she had Bad Boy. Besides she concluded, a season of frivolous fun with a man as exciting as Baron Booty would be well worth the risk of heartache.

'Who knows, he may even come to favour me over the sea!' she assured the Countess, trying to convince herself in the process. Confidence just shook her head.

As soon as Innocent got into his boat, she experienced personal pleasure that she never thought possible. She realized that her previous Prince's pleasing positions were quite below par as she discovered the world of orgasms.

From the first time their bodies intertwined they became inseparable. They were hooked on each other, taking pleasure wherever and whenever they could. They stole moments in the moonlight and became acquainted with all the alleyways in the city. They took their leave behind closed curtains at courtly cotillions.

Baron Booty, the romantic fool he was, always blew a bugle below Innocent's window, announcing his impending arrival. When Innocent heard the *Bugle Booty Call*, butterflies engulfed her and she raced to ready herself for the royal romp.

One time, an old shipping rival had the Baron arrested and locked in the Bastille for plundering his ship. Despite not a shred of proof of perpetration, the Baron was forced to reside alone in a dungeon for two weeks before a royal ransom was paid to the accuser.

The Baron's foot was chained to the wall of the dungeon, which he found most inconvenient. Not letting the clanking chain stand in the way of romance, Innocent had to become a creative contortionist. As she visited the dungeon daily she dabbled in dextrous deeds she never thought humanly possible.

Innocent loved having a captive audience and found her new role as a dungeon dominatrix quite exhilarating. She was thrilled at the double life she was leading; perfect princess by day and convict's lover by night. 'What would they say back home?' she squealed to herself in delight.

When Baron Booty was finally released they both felt rather disappointed that he had been sprung so soon.

Innocent had never known such fun and the Baron had never known such feeling. As she lay in his arms, he often found himself opening up to her about his love of the sea.

'In open water – against a backdrop of a myriad of stars – one learns the meaning of true beauty. When the light of the full moon punctuates the blackness of the night, it reflects upon the sea like a million dancing diamonds.'

'It sounds wonderful. Perhaps you will show me one day,' said Innocent gently, certain it was just a matter of time before he realized he could not live without her.

The Baron smiled as he took her face in his hands and kissed her passionately.

He suspected early on in their courtship that he was falling in love with her but he put the idea out of his mind for fear of spoiling the fun. After all, there was no room for love in his life. The only love he allowed in was his love of the open seas.

As the season came to an end, Innocent convinced herself that Baron Booty would never leave her. After all, their affair had been so full of passion how could he *not* stay and settle with her? She even speculated on the type of ring Booty would give her – after all as a man of the sea he was sure to have a large ruby or emerald floating around – which would look spectacular within a gold setting.

She was sadly surprised when he came to tell her that his ship was in preparation to sail.

'Don't go, or if you truly have to go, please take me with you!'

The Baron gently took hold of her hands.

'My beauty, the sea is no place for you. I am a sole seafarer – a seasonal lover. I am not cut out for a settled life.'

'But how do you know if you don't try?' cried Innocent, desperate to *save* her love from a lonely life.

'My darling I am a coward, I admit it. My father forfeited the sea for the love of my mother. She repaid his loyalty by making a cuckold of him. He spent his entire wedded life in misery and shame. When he could take the humiliation no longer, he threw himself in the river. I swore as a young buck that I would stick with the sea.'

'But I would never do that to you,' pleaded Innocent sincerely.

'I know dearest, but eventually I would do it to you, and a beautiful girl such as yourself deserves far better.' With that he took her in his arms and kissed her.

When she awoke the next morning he was gone. On his pillow was a huge purse of gold coinage and a note which simply read –

Here is a token of my love, use it to enjoy all that life brings you. You are truly unique in a world of mediocrity. If I was not Baron Booty we would live in bliss!
A fool, but forever yours in affection and admiration

Your Baron always
xxxxx

And with that, Innocent sobbed into her pillow, and well into the next social season, with the Countesses' words ringing loudly in her ears.

4
Captain Unavailable

When Innocent finally emerged from her boudoir she was determined to erase all feelings and memories of Baron Booty and his *Bugle Booty Call*. She decided that the only way she could accomplish this feat would be to transfer her feelings for Booty onto another. She had heard that many a prince and princess had successfully romped royally in order to forget and she decided to give it a go.

When Countess Confidence came to see Innocent for a catch up, Innocent told her of her plan to forget the Baron. Confidence shook her head.

'Ma petite, don't you know that a lady can never separate her feelings from a frolic. You will only get hurt all over again. His gain will be your pain.'

'My dearest Countess I know you mean well, but be comforted by the fact that I have developed a shell around my soul which is impregnable. No man will ever be able to gain access to my heart again. I am purely seeking a frivolous romp as a distraction from my distress. It is nothing more than a symbolic two-finger gesture to that *seafaring bastard* who broke my heart!'

The Countess shook her head and drew her fan to her face.

'You know where I will be when it all ends in tears,' said the Countess as she kissed the Princess goodbye. Innocent ignored her warnings as she was too busy mulling over her plans for casual comfort.

She got out her finest gowns and tended to her tresses and set about the task at hand. Taking a leisurely stroll along the banks of the river, where many a royal barge and yacht were docked, she was bound to encounter a suitable rebound.

She walked past a large elegant yacht measuring at least fifty yards in length. Innocent had never seen an object that long.

There standing on the deck was an equally large man in tight breeches, brimming with brawn. He tipped his hat to her as she walked by. She smiled coyly. This was the one to help her forget the old *Bugle Booty Call* she thought.

As if sensing she was available, in a flash the large man had jumped off deck and stood at Innocent's feet.

'Captain Unavailable at your service my lady,' he said, flashing a broad, brash smile.

'Princess Innocent, charmed I'm sure,' and moments later she was swept off her feet and onto his yacht.

Unavailable was a successful import–exporter who roamed around the globe searching for new wares, new markets and new conquests. He lived aboard his grand yacht 365 days of the year and never docked longer than two weeks in one spot. Innocent believed he was the perfect solution for her No Strings Attached Seduction.

The yacht was lavish and splendid and so was Captain Unavailable. He was as well-endowed as his yacht and for the first time Innocent got to ponder the question *does size really matter*?

For an entire week, like the waves they rolled in and out, taking pleasure aboard what they affectionately called their *Love Boat*. The yacht was so plush and comfortable that at first Innocent couldn't decide if she liked the boat more than she liked the Captain. As the days turned into a week, Innocent felt her detachment waning and she started to speculate on what a future with Unavailable and his big yacht might look like. In keeping with the bigger is better theme, she was sure Unavailable would endow her with a big rock for her ring finger.

On their seventh morning together, like a deer sensing danger, Unavailable knew he was about to be hunted. He always found that with the ladies whose company he kept, emotional involvement would always kick in after day seven. The next day, when Innocent came to the boat for another pleasure cruise, Unavailable had vanished.

She cruised for her Captain in the taverns lining the banks of the river but to no avail. At first she began to panic fearing that her beloved had fallen into the river and possibly drowned. But then to her relief she saw him walking towards the yacht.

She was about to run up to him and embrace him in her arms when she suddenly noticed he was not alone and that beside him walked an elegant lady. She convinced herself it was nothing to worry about that the woman was probably his sister. She called out to him. Unavailable looked up and ignored her. He took the lady in his arms and at once Innocent realized she was no sister. With his guest safely inside the yacht, Unavailable walked up and greeted Innocent.

'My dear, it has been a pleasure having you this past week. While you are a great Princess I never hang out for more than a week with the same gal. Life is too short not to taste all the wonderful wares on offer. That is how I conduct all my business and all my affairs.'

He took her hand and with a kiss, turned and walked to his next conquest.

Innocent felt humiliated and hurt. How could he be so cold and so cruel? How could he be so detached? How could she have been so stupid to think she could have a No Strings Attached entanglement? How could she have frolicked so casually? How could she live without that big yacht?

Questions were turning over and over in her head. Worst of all she was almost right back where she started when Baron Booty fled, leaving her in floods of tears.

As if sensing the impending doom, Confidence paid Innocent a visit.

'Ma chère, when will you learn? You must stay away from men with big boats!' said Confidence with a loving smile. She resisted the urge to lecture her broken-hearted friend – after all, she knew she felt embarrassed enough.

A smile broke through from her tear-stained face. Confidence gently touched her cheek.

'This too will pass,' Confidence reassured her. And it did.

Innocent swore off suitors for the next few months. Shortly after Captain Unavailable she had received a proposition from Captain Opportunist.

'My beautiful Princess you are solo and so am I, so why not let us benefit by becoming *friends with fringe benefits?'*

As lonely as she was, she had learned her lesson about cold casual encounters and politely declined the offer.

5
Marchioness Mostess

Throwing herself into socializing with the spectacular salon set, Innocent attended soirées, galas, recitals and fencing tournaments at a frenzied pace. She resumed attendance at the breakfast gatherings, which she had neglected upon meeting Baron Booty.

There she met the marvellous, Marchioness Mostess, who had just returned from a season abroad. She was by far the most glamorous member of the glittering gathering group. She was the most breathtakingly beautiful woman Innocent had ever laid eyes upon. At thirty-five years of age, she looked at least ten years younger. She had long dark hair which cascaded down the middle of her back and provided a striking contrast to her pale skin. She had wide, almond eyes, with long eyelashes which she used to flirt to perfection. Her bee-stung lips always seemed to be puckered.

Mostess beguiled many a man and had an entourage of chivalrous knights, gallant cavaliers, adoring dauphines, performing jugglers and artists. The Marchioness was a muse for many a poet who penned odes and sonnets to her great beauty.

The *Glitterazzi Press* followed her around, prolifically reporting on her every whim and pronouncing her a living goddess. Mere mortals stood in awe of Marchioness Mostess – Innocent being one of them.

She had been married four times already, each husband richer than the last. Mostess never stayed single for long. She was a Master of the Seduction Arts. She lived in one of the grandest palaces and even had her own private vessel equipped with an indoor spa and crew who could service her many needs.

The Marchioness did not count Confidence as one of her friends. In fact she hated her and considered the Countess to be her greatest rival. When Confidence entered a room, everyone took notice. Worst of all, she had one-upped Mostess in the happily-ever-after stakes by marrying one of finest men in the entire city, Count Catch.

Sensing the close friendship between the Countess and Innocent, the Marchioness took a keen interest in the young princess and carefully cultivated a friendship with her. Innocent loved being around the Marchioness and looked up to her.

'If only I were more like the Marchioness, my life would be magic,' pondered Innocent.

Countess Confidence sensing the growing friendship grew concerned for Innocent. She tried to warn her young friend about the Marchioness, who she knew all too well.

'Ma petite, Mostess is the most complicated of Marchionesses. She is the belle of the ball, a man-eater who will stop at no lengths to retain her position as the *fairest of them all*. The Marchioness does not do friendships – only conquests. She sees me as her chief rival and as a dear friend of mine you are no more than one more conquest for her to one-up me.'

Innocent was mortified and offended at the *very suggestion* that her new friendship was fake. She glared at Confidence.

'Countess who I am friends with is *none* of your concern. I cannot believe that you conclude that the Marchioness would only be friends with me to spite you. That is pure arrogance madam and I think maybe it is *our* friendship that is the fake one.' And with a flick of her fan, Innocent fled to her new found friend.

The Marchioness was most happy to take Innocent under her wing and away from Confidence. To secure her position and Privy Purse, Mostess had produced two young sons, whom she had sent away to boarding school. She had always wanted a daughter to pass along her seduction skills and Innocent seemed an acceptable substitute. Besides, being venerated was her favourite sport and it was apparent that Innocent was clearly in awe.

The Marchioness started by taking her protégé to the finest couture houses and instructed Innocent on the colours and shades of successful seduction. She made sure her clothes were tailor-made to accentuate every curve, without being too brazen.

Mostess then turned to the Facial Arts, introducing Innocent to her fantastic Face Physician. He had developed a poisonous potion call *Bowtoxin*, which when spread over the surface of the skin produced an allergic reaction causing the face to swell slightly thus puffing out any lines or wrinkles. The physician had a disclaimer warning that one in two procurers of the potion would swell excessively, and look so hideous, that hiding their face away was the only option.

To please the Marchioness, Innocent tried the magic potion … Unfortunately, she was a *one in two* leaving her beautiful face bloated beyond recognition. She hid away in her rooms for an entire week … Mostess stayed away citing social commitments.

The Marshioness loved throwing glittering sorees, where she could entertain and entice. Innocent became the perfect excuse for the hostess-with-the-mostess to organize a Coming-Out-Ball where she could invite all the young eligible bachelors to her palace in the guise of perusing for a worthy suitor for her young friend. Mostess loved engaging with the young men who she affectionately dubbed *target practice*. They were malleable to her many charms and had more stamina than their older counterparts.

Innocent did not see the hostess-with-the-mostess all evening as she was too busy flitting and flirting through her guests. She kept herself occupied by making the acquaintance of a young gallant knight who was her age and had just left his home castle for his new life's journey.

'I am Sir Lamb, and ready to do service to you madam … ur … ur what I meant to say is I am at your service,' corrected the rather tongue-tied young man. 'Won't you do me the honour of escorting me onto the dance floor?' As he went to take her hand he tripped over his feet.

Innocent smiled and gave the awkward knight her hand. She was immediately attracted to both his good looks and sweet demeanour which reminded her of her own naïvety when she left her home castle.

As each dance turned into another, and another, she was pleasantly surprised at how much Sir Lamb's waltzing improved. With each turn on the ballroom floor he thankfully stepped on her toes less and less. By the fifth dance, he had not stepped on her toes once.

As he twirled Innocent around and around, the dancing duo spent the entire evening talking about their life stories.

The next day Sir Lamb came to her rooms with a bouquet of flowers.

'I had a wonderful time dancing with you. You are like a breath of fresh air. Won't you walk with me along the banks of the river?'

Innocent beamed, Could this be her *One True Prince?* She wondered.

As she and Sir Lamb sauntered along the river bank, she saw the Marchioness sitting outside a brassiere having café and croissants. As usual she was surrounded by an assortment of suitors. Innocent beamed as she excitedly introduced Mostess to her new intended. The Marchioness rose from her seat.

'Sir Lamb won't you sit beside me and tell us all about yourself?' she said seductively as she patted the chair beside her.

From the moment he sat beside her she monopolized his attention, flirting furiously with the young Lamb. When he tried to make conversation with Innocent, Mostess moved in for the kill, distracting him by rubbing her perfume between her blossoming bosoms. She got Sir Lamb into such a state that he could hardly speak. He was about to ask Innocent if she would leave with him when the Marchioness stood up and cried –

'Oh Sir Lamb, I suddenly feel woozy,' and with that she fell into his arms and grabbed him by the orbs.

He sat rigid and erect. It was no use, he was caught in her clutches and if he removed her from his person he would be caught in the most embarrassing, protruding, predicament.

He hoisted Mostess in his arms and got up slowly, careful not to expose himself. He smiled at Innocent, somehow hoping she could sense the position he had been forced into. Before she knew what was happening, Lamb had carried the Marchioness to her carriage and drove off with her. Innocent sat dumbfounded, dumped and duped. Surrounded by Mostess' sad suitors, the Princess swore she would never forgive her.

As soon as Innocent heard the Marchioness had returned, she marched over to her palace to tell her exactly what she thought of her. She knocked furiously on her palace door and stormed past the footman and straight into her boudoir. Mostess was still sleeping when Innocent woke her up with a loud roar –

'I have come to tell you that I no longer wish to be your friend after your brazen and brash behaviour!'

The Marchioness awoke from her slumber.

'Oh Innocent, my foolish child, this isn't about that silly knight, what was his name?'

'Sir Lamb,' Innocent incredulously interjected.

'My darling child – I did you a big favour. He is a boring little fellow who has a lot to learn about pleasantly pleasing a princess.'

'That is not the point!' screamed Innocent, stamping her feet.

'He was my friend, my potential *One True Prince*. We were just getting to know each other when you unscrupulously screwed him and everything else up.'

'Innocent I am bored with this story, let us order a croissant and afterwards go shopping.'

'I don't want to go anywhere with you. You are a heartless hussy and our friendship is finished for good!'

She turned on her heel and was about to walk through the door when she heard the Marchioness suddenly break down in tears.

'O–Oh Innocent you are right, I behaved in the most shameless manner ... I–I don't know why I do these things ... All I know is what my dear Mama always taught me that unless I could capture and contain any man with my charms, I would be nothing more than a useless woman … She told me that my security, social standing and self-assurance depended on meeting these targets. I guess old habits die hard …

Mama's instruction has led me to live life lightly, never committing my heart or soul to anyone or anything. I have become a master of masking my feelings. For the truth of the matter is that I awake most mornings feeling miserable … '

'You miserable?' said Innocent, turning to face the Marchioness.

'But you are Mostess – the hostess-with-the-mostess. People want to either be with you or be like you. How could one who has everything be so unhappy?'

'My dear girl, don't be fooled by the illusion. It is you, not I who has everything. You are young and yet to discover your true path. You can still be Queen of anything you wish. All I am Queen of is unhappiness and pretence. The men who flock around me are in love with my visage. They do not know the real me, as I myself do not know anymore.'

Innocent walked over to the Marchioness and suddenly all the anger she had felt towards her was replaced by pity. The women she had propped up on a pedestal for so long was even more insecure, lost and unhappy than she was.

The Marchioness cried in Innocent's arms for a long time. When her tears dried up she began her first honest conversation with her protégée.

'Do you know what I always wanted to do when I was a child? I wanted to own my own Ye Book Shoppe. I adore books. As a child my favourite pastime was reading. Alas by sixteen years of age my Mama replaced my books with study of the Seduction Arts, a subject she had been forced to endure at the same age by her mother. It was a tragic family tradition.'

'It's not too late,' said Innocent encouragingly. 'After all, you have enough money to do anything you want. You can go out and purchase a Ye Book Shoppe tomorrow!'

Mostess suddenly stopped crying. 'Do you really think it is possible? Why, I do believe you are right my dear child.

Tomorrow I will come and collect you and we can go shopping for a Ye Book Shoppe,' and with that the Marchioness seemed to be back to her old bright self.

The next day Innocent waited and waited for the Marchioness. When she went to her palace looking for her, she was told that Mostess was gone. She had boarded her frigate, spontaneously sailing for a six-month long sabbatical.

'Did she leave a note for me,' Innocent asked the Butler. He shook his head and closed the palace door leaving her standing alone, shocked that Mostess did not even say goodbye. She would never hear from Mostess again and the Marchioness would never again reveal her true self or her weaknesses to anyone.

Innocent realized that Countess Confidence had been right all along and that Mostess had only used her – as a new plaything. She felt deeply ashamed of how she had treated her dear friend, and decided to call upon Confidence to beg for her forgiveness. She only hoped that the Countess would not slam the door in her face.

As soon as she appeared at Confidence's gate, she was greeted with a giant hug. Innocent told her what had transpired with the Marchioness.

The Countess countered the sad tale by filling her in on some of the missing details of Mostess's life.

'As a young girl, Mostess was my dearest friend. That is when she was simply named, Lovely. She was full of light and laughter and got most of her pleasure from her books. Alas, as soon as she turned sweet sixteen things changed forever, as her mother forced her to study The Seduction Arts. She put up a brave fight, but overpowered by family tradition and loyalty Lovely left behind not only her true self but also our friendship. Her mother felt I was a threat to her domination in the field of seduction so she barred me from her life. I still miss my old school friend dearly,' said the Countess, her eyes tearing slightly.

Innocent could not believe that she had been duped once again by her own naïvety. It was bad enough that she made such awful choices in the courting department, but now it seemed that she wasn't too good at picking female friends either.

'Dearest Confidence are you truly as happy as you appear?' she asked, allaying her fear that she had not misjudged this great lady too.

'Blissfully, ma chère,' said Confidence reassuringly.

Innocent smiled, relieved that sometimes people were who they appeared to be.

6
Lord Lie-A-Lot

For the next few months Innocent devoted her time to a new hobby, a love of books and learning. Sir Studious a member of the glittering gathering group was one of the finest intellectuals in Joie De Vie. He bestowed on Innocent a beautiful bound book on fine art. He told her that one as intelligent as she would appreciate it. Innocent felt positively proud as no-one had ever called her intelligent before. She had never considered herself as anything other than beautiful of body and relished the idea of having brains as well.

For the first time she was determined to increase the depth of her dialogue to more than just talk of cotillions and couture. The book had captivated her and inspired a quest to discover all she could on the subject. She was particularly taken by the painters from the School of Impressive Art and visited all the galleries and museums that housed their work.

One morning Innocent visited the Musee d' Magnifique, where one could view the most marvellous, mind-boggling modern art collections in the entire kingdom. She spent two hours marvelling at all the magnificence before her eyes and wished she too could be an artist.

After two hours she decided to retire to the Musée Café, where she could sip a goblet of fine wine and read the book on the collection that she had just purchased from Ye Musée Shoppe. Lost in her book, she was startled when a man interrupted her.

'Marvellous exhibition wouldn't you say?'

'Oh yes,' said Innocent, not looking up, almost resenting the intrusion into her solitude.

'Lord Lie-A-Lot at your humble service,' said the tall, thin, handsome stranger.

'Princess Innocent,' she replied rather disinterested. She attempted to get back to her book but the stranger was persistent.

'So you like Modern Art – how wonderful to find such a beautiful lady with brains to match.'

The next instance he was at her table talking about all the lovely pieces in the gallery. Innocent's demeanour softened toward the stranger as his knowledge of modern art was not only interesting but also impressive.

Captivated, it wasn't until three hours after he had first sat down that Lie-A-Lot looked at his timepiece.

'My dear Innocent how time has stood still while I have been in your presence, alas I must now attend to urgent business. Please forgive me! Would you do me the honour of letting me call upon you tomorrow?'

Innocent was charmed and impressed by his intellect and even more impressed at how intelligent he had found her. She said 'yes' immediately and gave him her calling card.

Lord Lie-A-Lot was a local lodge architect and lover of art. His designs which incorporated both modern and traditional art motifs and masonry had caused quite a stir in the upper echelons of polite society. His services were in demand as everyone rushed to be the owner of the latest *In Thing* in home living. He was a local lord who had made good.

On their first courtly outing, Lord Lie-A-Lot took Innocent to a very expensive eating establishment. It was a discreet place where all guests had their own dining room.

He lavished attention on her. Lost in each other's conversation, they talked until almost midnight. As the clock struck twelve, Lord Lie-A-Lot excused himself for *urgent business*. He ordered a coach to take Innocent home. By the time she arrived home, she had already planned in her head the wonderful life they would have together.

Lord Lie-A-Lot asked Innocent to accompany him on a business trip to the Northern Region, where he promised to show her the great snow-capped mountains. By this time Innocent was in love.

They spent hours by the roaring fire, talking incessantly about myriads of subjects and marvelling at the breathtaking scenery.

They had spent eight loved-up days in the Northern Region. So spectacular was their time away together that Innocent assumed that he would now desire to spend every waking moment with her. She imagined that he had already designed a ring for her, decorated with an original matrimonial motif created especially for *the occasion*.

It wasn't long after their return that she became frustrated that his work took him away from her so often. He had not even had enough time to take her to his permanent palace a few miles from the centre of the city. Often she had to settle for rushed rendezvous in his offices.

On a rare evening out at another discreet eating establishment, they were spotted by Countess Confidence and her husband Count Catch. As soon as Lord Lie-A-Lot saw the elegant couple he whisked Innocent away before they had even started their meal.

Innocent was perplexed at his behaviour, but he reassured her by stating that he simply refused to share her with anyone.

The following day, alone in her boudoir she received a visit from Countess Confidence. It seemed the two lovers had been spotted the night before.

'My dearest Innocent, I felt compelled to come here today. You are still in some ways such a child, and I felt it was my duty to offer you my guidance.'

The Countess' choice of the word *child* rankled Innocent and she felt herself getting annoyed.

'Lord Lie-A-Lot is already locked in wedded bliss.'

The words rang in Innocent's ears like the great cathedral bells that rang throughout the city. She was frozen and couldn't move or respond to what her ears had just heard.

'Just what I suspected,' exclaimed the Countess, catching Innocent out. 'I knew you were none the wiser!'

Everything the Countess said after that went in through one of Innocent's ears and out the other. By the time she left with

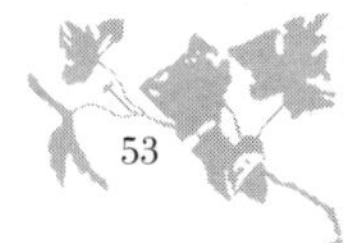

offerings of optimistic prospects for the future, Innocent had a blinding headache.

'It can't be true,' she screamed out loud and immediately dispatched her messenger to Lie-A-Lot's office with a note which simply read –

Come at once. I know your secret!
Innocent

It didn't take long for Lie-A-Lot to arrive with protestations of love:

'You are my one true love.'
'The union with my wife is but a sham.'
'The marriage has been over for a long time.'
'It's a union of handiness – for the sake of our offspring.'
'I only wedded her for her looks, but sadly one cannot live by looks alone. She severely lacks your perfect package of beauty and brains.'
'If I end my marriage now, my sons may be overlooked for a place at the Academy D' Anybody Who Is Anybody. I need to stay with my wife for another three months until our boys have their acceptance interviews – otherwise their future prospects will be compromised.'
'In three months hither, I will be free to end the union. Please wait for me my darling as I cannot live without you.'

With every fibre of her being she wanted to believe what he was saying. Against her better judgement she agreed to continue seeing him as long as he left the union in three months. After all, she could not deny her feelings.

They continued meeting in secret.

When Innocent ran into Countess Confidence on the Right Bank she tried to avoid her. As if by instinct, the Countess made a bee-line for her and tried desperately to talk some sense into the young Princess.

'Ma chère, please end this now. You deserve a prince who is free to love you and who can lavish attention upon you.

'Do not believe his lies. You must face the fact that if he can cheat on his wife, he is quite capable of lying to his concubine,' she cautioned.

'*Concubine* … *Concubine*, you make me sound so cheap!' said Innocent indignantly.

'Wake up, Innocent! That is all you are to him,' Confidence countered.

Innocent could feel her blood boil and she went beet red. Despite her anger over the Countess' words, she kept her cool determined to give Confidence no more cause to call her a child. She turned calmly to the Countess and continued.

'My dear Confidence, although I appreciate your concern, I can assure you that he would never cheat on me. His wife does not comprehend his needs the way I do. She cannot compare to my clever companionship.'

Countess Confidence shook her head.

'Why must one so clever peril her heart in this way? It will all end in floods of tears,' she concluded.

Innocent could feel herself losing her cool. She had quite enough of Confidence's warnings and quickly excused herself before saying something she knew she would later regret. As she walked away from earshot she could no longer contain herself and began ranting against her friend.

'Why … why you … nosy … meddlesome … know-it-all-better-than-you. I didn't ask for your advice – you … cynical … interfering … insensitive … insufferable … clueless … overbearing … wearisome woman,' cried Innocent under her breath.

For the next few months, Innocent continued her relationship, sustaining herself with the lie that her Lord would eventually leave his wife. With his secret out and her determination to still see him, Lie-A-Lot felt reassured that he could maintain the status quo by having his main course at home and dessert in Innocent's bedchamber.

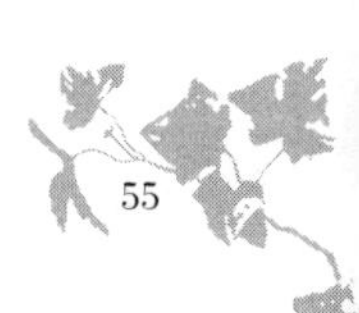

She had never felt so alone within a relationship. She particularly dreaded every holiday and occasion for celebration as Lie-A-Lot would always spend those days with his family.

Things finally came to a head on the occasion of the Lord's fortieth birthday. His wife Lady Denial was planning a birthday bash to end all birthday bashes. It was the talk of the town and Innocent shook with jealousy when she heard.

She demanded that Lie-A-Lot leave his life with his wife immediately. After all, *she* was ruining both their lives.

For the first time in her life, Innocent was experiencing the *jaws of jealousy*. They had taken hold of her and however much she tried she could not shake them loose. She suddenly lost control of her decorum as she raged to herself:

'Why doesn't she let him go?'
'She is a pathetic and desperate woman for hanging on.'
'I bet she is not as good in the boudoir as I am.'
'I bet she is ugly.'

Her ranting lasted for two hours, all the while her face contorted in anger. It was not a pretty sight. After listening to herself rage against the hapless Lady Denial, she felt ashamed and disgusted with herself. The chambermaids overhearing her anger commented, 'This lady protests way too much!'

Even though Innocent had never met Lady Denial, she felt she knew her from all the stories and tales told by Lord Lie-A-Lot:

'We sleep in different quarters.'
'She is a shrew of a lady.'
'She tortures me with her lack of intellect.'
'I can no longer take her boring conversations. I will tell her it's over tonight!'
'She doesn't understand me like you do.'
'She will take all my money and leave me destitute.'
'She will turn the children against me.'

Innocent was determined to save her beloved from this *terrible Lady*, who would eventually destroy him with her drivel. She would confront her. She would go to see her tomorrow. But before she could face her mortal enemy she would go down to the cloth district to her favourite boutique, Chez Chic, the most elegant in town, and pick up a gown.

When she arrived at the boutique, Madam Chic, the proprietress was serving a fashionable lady. When she retired to the back to wrap the lady's gowns, Innocent exchanged pleasantries with the lovely woman beside her.

When Madam Chic returned, she had the lovely lady's gown wrapped in a gold box.

'Thank you Lady Denial for your custom, and do enjoy your dear husband's birthday bash.'

'I will Madam, it will be the birthday bash to end birthday bashes, as my husband and I are retiring to the Northern Region next week. Good day Madam, good day Princess, it was lovely to make your acquaintance.' And with that, Lord Lie-A-Lot's lovely lady left.

Innocent could not believe her ears. In all the boutiques, in all of the towns, Lady Denial had to walk into her boutique and spoil her illusion. To make matters worse she was nothing like Lie-A-Lot had portrayed and was, Innocent had to admit, a delight to be around.

She felt such a foolish fool. She was humiliated and had been deceived in the worst way. She started to question her intelligence quota. At that moment she believed that chivalry was truly dead. Innocent ran out of the boutique in a fit of tears and when she got home, locked herself in her room, no longer able to deny the truth about her relationship.

As she went through lie after lie, she began to think of all the ways she would get back at Lie-A-Lot. She would go and tell Lady Denial all that had transpired. She would go to his birthday bash and spectacularly spill all in front of his guests. He would not only lose her – but also his family. Yes that would be the best revenge. He would also lose his reputation and his business. After all, he deserved this fate.

She stayed awake the whole evening plotting her revenge until she knew exactly what she would do and she would reclaim her pride in the process. She fell asleep as the sun was rising, smiling in satisfaction knowing that she too could be devious.

She woke up to a knock on her door. It was Lord Lie-A-Lot, totally oblivious to the fact he had been knocked off his pedestal.

As Innocent primped herself in front of the mirror, she was shocked at the woman staring back at her. She had a grey pallor to her face and she looked as if she had aged ten years. Her anger the night before had turned her into someone she hardly recognized.

As she opened the door, and Lie-A-Lot walked in, she froze. She had spent the night planning her revenge. She was going to lie and tell him she had found a far worthier suitor who had just proposed to her. She was going to spin a *yawn* about how wonderful and better in bed this imaginary suitor was in comparison to him. She was about to say a lot of personal and hurtful things, until she saw the old and bitter woman staring back at her in the mirror.

If she lied to Lie-A-Lot, she was no better than him. She had been lying to herself for far too long. It was now time for the lies to be laid to rest for all their sakes. All Innocent had now was herself and she yearned to be able to see her true reflection in the mirror once again.

She cleared her throat and looked straight through the lies at the man that she still loved. With composure and compassion for both of them she put an end to the charade once and for all.

'Oh I am so glad you came by my Lord, I have some news. After much deliberation, I will be returning to It Is What it Is. You are a married man and I happened to meet your wife yesterday in a boutique.

It pains me to say that she is indeed a beautiful and lovely lady and I can see why you wish to stay with her. But my dear Lord, I am a beautiful woman too and deserve a man who is free to declare his love and affection for me. I leave tomorrow with the memory of all the lovely times we shared together.'

Lord Lie-A-Lot was stunned. He had stopped listening when Innocent had got to the part in her speech and said 'I happened to meet your wife in a boutique yesterday'.

'My … my … wife … you met my wife … b–but what did you say? Did you tell her about us … Innocent my dear … You wouldn't want my children to suffer … W–What did you say?' stuttered Lie-A-Lot, stunned with the implications of being implicated.

Suddenly sickened, she became conscious that when she told him she was leaving all he was concerned about was being caught out by his wife. She realized at that moment just how futile a fib her whole relationship had really been. She had been nothing more than a supporting player in his mirage of a marriage.

Desperate for air she turned on her heels, heading out the door, leaving Lie-A-Lot alone with his pleas.

'My love … my love … please tell me what you said to my wife … Innocent, Innocent …'

She did not look back, terrified Lie-A-Lot would see the tears welling in her eyes.

He left with his chapeau in his hands, sheepishly returning to his wife, wondering when and if his wife would confront him for his indiscretion. Living with the daily fear of not knowing what she knew was torture. He had lost control of the situation, which had sincerely unsettled him.

With the sentence, 'I happened to meet your wife,' Innocent finished Lord Lie-A-Lot off. And he was never to stray away from home again.

Innocent felt lonelier than ever. She decided that maybe returning to It Is What It Is was not such a bad idea after all.

7
Countess Confidence

Countess Confidence accompanied Innocent to the docks where she would board a ship to ferry her back to It Is What It Is. Confidence gave her a long hug and wished her well.

Innocent looked at the Countess with tears in her eyes.

'My dearest friend, you have stuck by me from Bad Boy to Lie-A-Lot. Despite my refusal to heed your first-class advice, my questionable choices and crass behaviour you never ceased to be my loyal friend – you must think me a fool!'

'Non, non, ma chère. It sometimes takes a young lady a long time to limit her liking for lousy lovers. I don't judge you dear Innocent, as I too have made many dire decisions.

Do you know who I was before I changed my name and married my charming Count? Princess Insecure and *IN* wasn't the only thing I had in common with you. At your age I made my own questionable choices as I courted cads and cowards who made me cry constantly.'

'You?'

Innocent's eyes widened, she couldn't imagine the Countess being anything other than Confidence. The Countess continued.

'It is only from a place of love that I have cautioned you. I wanted to spare you the wear and tear on your heart that I have had to endure. But alas, sure as the sun rises every day, young women and some older ones, will always favour the pull of a jerk!'

And with that Confidence and Innocent laughed out loud, hugging, joking and comparing jerks until it was time to go. As she waved goodbye to the Countess from the barge, Innocent felt blessed to know that she had found love in Joie De Vie after all.

8

Prince I-Only-Mean-What-I-Say-At-The-Time

Innocent had returned to the South of It Is What It Is, full of hope for the future. She had settled into her old apartments. Standing in the courtyard one morning awaiting her carriage, she noticed a man standing over the water barrel. Innocent fluttered at the fine figure of a man bending in front of her. When he stood up, Innocent was pleasantly pleased at how his face matched the exquisiteness of his bottom.

As she stood staring at him, he suddenly turned around and seeing the beauty before him, bowed boldly to her.

'Prince I-Only-Mean-What-I-Say-At-The-Time, at your service dear lady. Do I have the pleasure and the privilege of living in the same dwellings as such a delightful Princess?' he schmoozed, smiling at Innocent.

She smiled back and true to form, without any vetting, rushed heart first into a new romance. The Prince was a kindly young man with gentle blue eyes and jet-black hair. He worked as a sports reporter for the local paper, The Southern Slant, covering all of the fencing, archery, tennis and jousting events in The Kingdom. He had an athletic body which had caused many a princess and a few princes to positively pass out.

It wasn't long before he introduced Innocent to his beloved mother, Queen Panache. She was an elegant lady in her forties who originated from Joie De Vie. As a young girl of eighteen, she had arrived in The Kingdom of It Is What It Is and was soon swept off her feet by Prince I-Only-Mean-What-I-Say-At-The-Time's father. The marriage had been short-lived, lasting only long enough for her son to be born and to discover her husband was a hurtful heel.

After two failed marriages, Panache finally found herself in a happy union and lived life lavishly – lapping up cultural events, soirées, shopping and several grand tours of all the neighbouring kingdoms. Innocent couldn't help but admire Panache's love of life and the Queen couldn't help admiring Innocent's love for her son.

Panache would often spend time with the young couple taking them to art galleries and grand dining rooms. For the first time Innocent felt a part of someone else's family. She was a *daughter-in-law* at long last!

She felt proud to have captured the heart of such a sturdy stud and a super mama. Prince I-Only-Mean-What-I-Say-At-The-Time came to care for Innocent deeply and wanted to please her greatly. On their mid morning sojourn, the Prince would often take her for a stroll and tell her all the things he wanted to do for her. He painted a colourful future of wedded bliss, monetary largess, perfect offspring and travels abroad with his mother. Innocent daydreamed so incessantly about their future together that it began to feel real to her.

Every day, the Prince became more proficient in wooing her with wild promises:

'I will take you away on a long sabbatical to our glorious Chiefly City of Chaos and Congestion Charges.'
'When I buy my own jousting team, I will become rich and then we can marry.'
'I will cook the greatest feast that has ever been served for you, my love.'
'I will throw a glittering ball for you.'

Innocent couldn't help but fall in love with their potential future which the Prince had mapped out. She even fell in love with the future children that they planned to have, whom they decided to name Princess Hope and Prince Chivalrous. They even bought little stuffed bears for both of them at a marketplace one day.

She relished the thought of Panache being *her children's* Grandmama. She often imagined shopping for stylish baby attire with her.

She convinced herself that Panache would give her son a ring from the family jewels for his proposal. Yes she reasoned *this* Prince had greater potential than any of her previous beaus.

However after six months of blissful courtship, it became evident that this Prince's potential had hit a plateau. Innocent became frustrated by the lack of princely progress in all the planning. The promises had yet to materialise, and Innocent became weary of daydreaming and wished to start living the reality he had pledged. She began to wonder if he would ever live up to his pledges.

It wasn't that Prince I-Only-Mean-What-I-Say-At-The-Time was a bad person who meant to let Innocent down. It was just that he would often lose interest in things after initially getting excited about them. This was partly due to a lifelong condition that he had suffered with since childhood called AND (Almost Never Do). As hard as he tried, he could not focus long enough on one thing to ever see it to fruition.

Much of this had its beginnings in his childhood, when as a young lad he would often be last in his class at his jousting school. His father was the top ranked seed in the sport and he was embarrassed by his son's inability to be a chip off the old block. He often would let his son know that he was a great disappointment to him. The result of this berating was an aversion to failure.

Innocent tried to put her doubts aside and be patient for the sake of the charming Panache, who she had grown to love, but after twelve months of dating and waiting, she came to the conclusion that this Prince had peaked.

'Regrettably one cannot live by potential mother-in-law alone,' she sadly told herself.

This was as good as it was going to get with Prince I-Only-Mean-What-I-Say-At-The-Time. Alas it was not the potential future that she had envisioned with him and his marvellous mother. This Princess and Prince needed to part company permanently.

Coming from a place of love, she discovered a new found compassion within herself. While previous princes' shortcomings had made her profoundly angry and hurt, this particular Prince inspired feelings of empathy. She did not want to hurt him or give him another experience of failure and rejection, so she took it upon herself to spare him the truth. She went about making her own future plans for a pain free getaway.

They had always planned to go to the Chiefly City of Chaos and Congestion Charges together. There was no reason that she still could not go, so she white-lied to the Prince that she was taking a sabbatical to spend time with her parents in the Chiefly City.

She knew that the Prince would not have the courage to come with her or try and talk her out of going, so this would be her easy escape route.

They went out for their last supper and he promised he would visit her. Innocent knew that he wouldn't, and with love and good wishes tinged with sadness, they parted company.

She met Panache the next day for high tea to say farewell. Panache had met many potential brides that her son had courted, but Innocent was by far her favourite.

'Alas my dear Innocent, my son does not love himself, so he cannot truly love another. Even though I have loved him lavishly, it seems his inability to capture his father's affection has left him limited in his love-life. I had great hope that you might have been the *One* to change things for my son and that a marriage proposal from him would have been imminent. It is such a great pity that things have not turned out the way I had wished my dear, as you would have made the most sublime daughter-in-law,' said Panache sadly with tears in her eyes.

'And you, dearest lady would have been the most marvellous mother-in-law,' replied Innocent, who felt that her heart had broken twice in two days.

As she packed to leave, she came across the little stuffed bears they had bought together. She placed them on the window ledge and leaving them behind said a sad farewell to little Princess Hope and Prince Chivalrous, and wondered what might have been.

9
Innocent Does the Chiefly City of Chaos and Congestion Charges

As soon as Innocent relocated to the Chiefly City of Chaos and Congestion Charges, she resolved to take a sabbatical from princely pursuits! Tired of dating duds, she focused her energy on setting up her new residence in a magical mews house right in the middle of the city.

She loved the busy buzz of the brilliant city. It had the fastest and most frantic pace of any place she had ever lived in. There was so much to do and so many places to go. The city had a unique transportation system called the Under-the-Ground Carriage System, made up of very long, horse-drawn carriages which transported large amounts of people via large underground tunnels. The carriages could be caught at various stops scattered throughout the city. Each carriage catered for up to fifty people and had velvet covered seats with room for twenty-five on each side.

The first time Innocent travelled underground, she noticed that everyone who rode the carriages did anything to avoid eye contact. They would read The Town Crier newspaper or they would bury their face behind a book. She realized that the books were more for effect than reading, as several people were holding them upside down.

She also observed people looking at their own shoes for the entire duration of their ride. Passengers also spent a great deal of their time looking around at others, inspecting every detail of their person, being particularly careful not to be caught in the process. Innocent had never seen so many darting eyes directed at her.

She couldn't help noticing how serious everyone was. No-one smiled or talked to their fellow passengers. When Innocent said 'hello' to a lady who had sat down beside her, the lady jumped out of her seat screaming in a panic. Everyone followed by rushing to the exit leaving Innocent sitting by herself. Speaking to strangers was obviously not the *done thing* and she would politely refrain from any future familiarities.

For Innocent the most terrifying aspect of travelling on the Under-the-Ground Carriage System were the closing doors. Each carriage had a special door system that opened sideways. Two doormen operated the ropes which opened or closed the passenger doors, much like a curtain. Despite carriages arriving at the station every few minutes, on many occasion from nowhere would leap a crazed commuter catapulting themselves carelessly into the small space between the closing doors. The mad dash would often result with a pile-up of passengers brought down by the impatient and ignorant daredevil. Many injuries resulted for both the mad dashers and bystanders alike.

During one journey, Innocent was in the unfortunate position of standing by the doorway, when a male mad dasher only managed to get halfway through the closing doors. In desperation he grabbed at the nearest thing in the carriage – unfortunately it was her right arm! As the carriages sped down the tunnels at breakneck speed, Innocent received three degree bruising as the impatient, incapacitated imbecile hung on to her for dear life. She vowed to stay well clear of arm's reach and pledged never to be in that much of a hurry.

One day as Innocent was strolling through the Under-the-Ground tunnels, she caught sight of a tall, blond, shapely woman walking in front of her. On her feet, quite unusual for the dower and dark city, she wore bright red leather shoes with a slender heel, that strapped up to her ankle. She noticed that every male passenger who passed the young woman turned to look at her.

Innocent started to get agitated, as *she* was used to being the centre of attention. She didn't like the feeling of being bested by other beauties, particularly since she had just turned twenty-three. She immediately sought to overtake the young woman so she could critique and criticize her features and make herself feel better.

'I bet she is not so pretty at the front as she is from the back, and all the mesmerized men concur with my conclusion,' Innocent said to herself reassuringly.

She rushed passed the young lady and trying not to be an obvious observer, casually dropped a handkerchief in front of her. The young lady was forced to stop, and as Innocent picked up the handkerchief she found herself face to beautiful face with her reverting rival.

She looked into the young lady's blue eyes enviously and scanned her stunning features. The lady stared back with hardness in her eyes. Innocent sighed in relief, she might be beautiful but she had a horribly hard and haughty disposition – pretty perturbing to prime princes. She felt blessed that she had been bestowed with both heart and beauty and suddenly pitied the young woman as she watched her walk away.

In the City, Innocent observed how people always seemed to be in a harassed and harried state as they moved hurriedly along. This was no more apparent by the popularity of the decidedly dangerous and deadly sport of *traffic dodging*. People would attempt to cross the carriageways by running recklessly and speedily across the road as soon as an opening would appear. They dodged and dived their way around the barrage of cruising carriages careful not to get carried away by any of them or caught beneath their wheels.

The carriage drivers were also in a hurry, and did not consider a dashing dodger in front of them a good enough reason to halt. For convenience there was a medical carriage stationed on every other street corner for any unfortunate pedestrian who might get knocked off their feet and require immediate first aid. It was a bountiful blessing that the carriageways were full of mounds of manure which provided a comfortable cushion for any casualties to land on. Many a pedestrian was grateful that *shit happened*.

Innocent had decided that traffic dodging was definitely not for her. She valued her person far too much to make the dash. The one-time she did attempt a crossing she waited for over an hour. When the road was crystal clear, she ran like the wind and wound up wedging her designer wedges in wet manure in the middle of the carriageway. No matter how she tried, she could not free herself or her favourite footwear from the fertilizer.

Suddenly she caught sight of the crowds of carriages now cruising towards her. Her flight or fight instincts frantically kicked in as she unstrapped her stylish shoes and stepped through the manure to safety.

After bathing her feet in a local lake, she swore she would never cross the carriageway again. In future she would pick up a carriage for hire and ride reassuringly across the road.

She later discovered that traffic dodging was licensed for adults only. Children had their own special crossings on the carriageways called Stop, Look and Listen Lines, where they could cross in comfort and safety as carriages careened carefully to a stop. She found this a more dignified and civilised way of crossing and often hitched a walk with the wise children.

Innocent needed a distraction from the difficult demands of living in such a large place. She needed something useful to do with her time. The City was the centre of culture and music. Innocent had heard that music-making was the language of love and that it might be a useful idea to learn all she could for when she resumed her princely pursuits.

She had excelled in music and art as a child, and had taken mandolin lessons for a number of years until she left her home castle. She had not picked up her mandolin since Bad Boy had deserted her. Free from male distractions she now realized just how much she had missed playing.

She enrolled in the Royal School of Much Music, a modern Mecca for musicians of every calibre. She decided to learn to play a new instrument called a Virginal, and felt a born again player as soon as soon as her fingers touched the keys. She rediscovered her love for music and threw herself into her renewed passion until true to form she discovered a new distraction.

10
Sir Us and Them

Innocent had met her new suitor, Sir Us and Them, two weeks after she had registered in school. He was a burly-looking man with blond hair and long legs which gave him a giant gait whenever he walked. He had come to the school in order to study the business of music promotion.

He came from a long line of Toffs from one of the poshest districts of the city. Us and Them was a member of the exclusive Toff Set – consisting of himself and two others of similar social standing. Innocent knew he was not marriage material but she began to feel overwhelmed and lonely in the large city, and thought he would make a competent companion for outings.

One day he took her for a walk in Regal Regent's Park, feeding the ducks in residence, along the way. As Sir Us and Them stopped to get more breadcrumbs from the crummy seller, he spotted a couple with their four children who were also feeding the birds. Us and Them leaned over and whispered quietly to Innocent.

'My dear, let us move to a more suitable spot. We don't want to stand too close to those out-of-towners over there,' he said pointing.

Innocent looked over. All she could see was a sweet-looking man and woman with their four adorable children also having fun in the park. The man and his two sons were wearing small blue hats and blue robes, while the lady and her two daughters were wearing blue capes with matching blue bonnets. Every member of the family had long curly locks which tumbled down their shoulders.

'What do you mean? 'I think they look like a lovely family and how fashionable they look in their blue outfits.'

'Don't be fooled by their demeanour. They come from a strange faraway land and they have funny ways of worshipping and spending their money. I have heard tale that they give away ten percent of their Privy Purse to charity. What could they possibly be up to by such a blatant act of giving? It's best to keep well away from all of *them*.'

'Well I think it is a lovely thing to want to help people. What makes you think that would mean that those people are up to no good? They don't look like they would hurt anyone to me.'

'My dear Innocent, I have it on good authority from my dear old friend, Prince Propaganda. He heard a story from someone who met someone who was married to someone who lived two streets from some of them, that they spent a great deal of time laughing and smiling. That could only mean one thing … They were up to something and were laughing at us for not knowing what they were up to.'

She looked at her companion, totally perplexed by his convoluted conclusions. She wondered how anyone could condemn a child. Wishing to counter his harsh judgements, Innocent smiled lovingly at the children who were blissfully feeding the ducks.

Us and Them shook his head in disapproval.

'It seems you have a lot to learn, it is a good thing I am here to teach you,' and with that he directed her through a narrow clearing in the trees.

Innocent had also made friends with a poor couple who always sat outside the school on a mat, selling old scrolls and manuscripts. They were both rather scruffy and shabby in dress. Innocent loved their sunny disposition. They were always smiling and talking to people who gravitated towards their welcome mat. They served a neighbourly need as no-one left their company without a smile. Innocent couldn't help ponder that in a city of serious, solemn people, these two valuable vagabonds had true wealth.

On one visit to see her two friends, Innocent brought them a loaf of bread and some ale. As they chatted, she suddenly felt an arm reach over and pull her away. Startled, she was about to scream when she turned around – it was Sir Us and Them, scowling at her.

'What on earth are you doing conversing with company so incompatible? My dear Innocent anything could happen – you could get robbed or worst of all painted with the same broken brush. People might think you are their friend.'

'But I *am* their friend,' said Innocent mortified at the moron making such a spectacle of himself.

'Please unhand me,' she demanded glaring at the bigoted buffoon.

'Very well, but don't say I didn't warn you and don't get too close, you might catch something nasty.' Innocent turned away from Us and Them and resumed her conversation with her friends. Frustrated at her failure to heed his warning, he scurried away through a narrow passageway on his way to classes.

The next day, Us and Them invited Innocent to high tea at his Aunt's manor house by the park.

'Innocent, my Aunt Vicountess Victim, has invited you to tea so she can check out your pedigree. Her daughter, my dear cousin Lady Why Me, will also be there to meet you. It will be beneficial for you to be around *better-most* people for a change.'

She had a nagging feeling that accepting his invitation would be erroneous but accepted nevertheless, anxious not to miss an opportunity to make new friends. After all, the Chiefly City was so large she still felt lost in a crowd.

They arrived at 2:05 p.m. and were escorted into Victim's parlour. They were greeted by sobs from a lady in her late fifties with platinum hair and a plump body. She was slumped over her chair rather dramatically. She reminded Innocent of a character from the popular Tragedy Plays.

'Why Aunt Victim, whatever is the matter?'

'Oh my dear Nephew, you are five minutes late and I feared you had let your dear Aunt down. I couldn't believe that you would be so thoughtless to let my tea turn cold.'

'There, there, dear Aunt, I am sorry to have distressed you so. Please dry your eyes so you can get an eyeful of Innocent.'

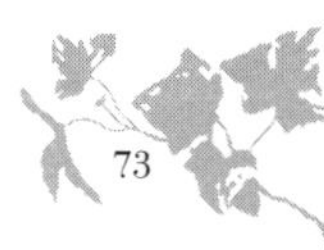

The Vicountess dabbed her eyes as she looked Innocent up and down with the scissor glasses she wore around her neck.

'Did you not want to come today, young Innocent? Is that why you delayed my dear nephew from coming here?' she said accusingly.

'Of course not Vicountess, we were delayed in traffic and tarried longer on the carriageway than expected stuck behind several horses that were relieving themselves,' assured Innocent.

'Oh that terrible troublesome traffic, that is why I refuse to stray too far from home. I blame the politicians for allowing all the riffraff to have horse-drawn carriages. In my day only the *better-most* people would have been able to afford to travel in carriage style. Ever since the peasants' revolt gave them social mobility even their horses are revolting. Manure mounds have mounted up throughout the carriageways causing horrendous humps and hills creating hazards and hardships for decent people like me,' cried Victim shaking her head.

'It is indeed a terrible tragedy dear Aunt. Those poor horses are given free rein to dump in our part of the city causing chaos and discomfort to decent folk,' added Us and Them throwing in his two sentences.

Oh boy, thought Innocent, these two are full of more *shit* than the horses.

'Let us change the conversation dear nephew and turn to your lovely companion.' Victim faced Innocent and looked her over carefully.

'Where do you come from my dear?' she asked putting down her eye glass, replacing it with a larger glass. She scrutinized Innocent from head to toe.

'I come from the Borough of Look At Me,' replied Innocent disconcertedly.

Victim gasped, 'Look At Me that dreadful borough! When I visited there last, I had the most unpleasant experience with a shopkeeper. When I asked to try on a gown, he suggested I take a size eighteen. Well you can imagine my humiliation at the very suggestion. I have always squeezed into a size sixteen. He made me feel so awful at the suggestion that I had to retire to my rooms for two whole days.'

Innocent straightened her back ready to defend her dear borough.' Well I am sure the shopkeeper was only trying to be helpful and meant no harm. We in Look At Me pride ourselves on good customer relations.'

'Well that certainly wasn't evident when I was there my dear. I have never been subjected to such below posh par behaviour,' said the Vicountess, victorious in her victimhood.

Innocent felt her blood boil and was about to fight her corner when a young girl in her early twenties marched into the room. She was extremely skinny with blonde hair and pointed features which contorted into a scowl.

'Hello cousin,' said Us and Them.'Princess Innocent may I introduce you to my delightful cousin, Lady Why Me.'

Why Me pushed passed Innocent almost knocking her over as she headed straight to her mother.

'Huh – talk about below posh par,' Innocent muttered under her breath.

'Mother, why must I have to wait for the dressmaker to come for my fitting?' whined Why Me.

'She had just informed me that she cannot come until tomorrow morning. The Crystal Ball is to be held in less than eight months time. What if she doesn't finish on time? I will have to wear last year's ball gown. I will be humiliated. Why is this happening to me mother, tell me what I have I done to deserve such disservice?'

'There there, my dear child. Those of us in high positions often have to endure the disrespect and disdain of others who do not appreciate the demands of dominating social standing.'

'Where is the dressmaker from?' piped up Us and Them, 'I bet she is from foreign parts.'

By now Innocent had an awful headache and was desperate for a cup of tea. She wondered if she would ever find like-minded people in the great City to lift her from her loneliness.

Tea was absolutely abysmal as she endured the rants and raves of Victim and Why Me for over an hour. If this was the *better-*

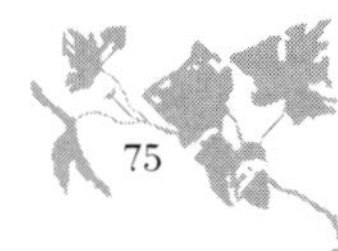

most people the Chiefly City had to offer she would gladly learn to live with her own company.

When it was time to go, Why Me looked up at Innocent as if noticing her for the first time.

'You are not planning on going to the Crystal Ball are you Ignorant?'

'That's Innocent, my name is Innocent,' she corrected. 'And no, I am not going to the Crystal Ball as this is the first I have heard of it. It does sound wonderful though.'

'Yes it does sound wonderful – a pity you won't be going. Dear cousin don't forget that you are escorting me in eight months time, in the place of Prince Blame, who can't attend due to urgent business. You can't let me down like Blame has done. Promise me you will be there. Don't let this Princess distract you from your duty to me.'

'Of course not cousin, family always comes first. I am sorry dear Innocent, but you understand,' said Us and Them stoically.

That was one ball Innocent would be glad to miss. Spending another moment in the company of either Why Me or Victim was a fate she was not prepared to endure ever again. And with that, Innocent bid a blessed adieu to the poisonous pair.

She seriously questioned her sanity when she agreed to go out with Us and Them the following day. Innocent was learning how loneliness could lead to lunacy. He had invited her to the theatre for a music recital of an up and coming trio of toned tenors. They were about to take their seats when an elderly man with a tan sat down beside them. Sir Us and Them looked shocked and told Innocent to get up quickly.

'What on earth is the matter?' she said coolly.

'Look beside you,' whispered Us and Them. Either that man has been in the sun too long, or he comes from foreign lands. As I am not sure which, I think it is best we sit somewhere else.'

Innocent shook her head. She had always been brought up to believe in the equality of everyone. Her parents proclaimed that knowing and being around people from all backgrounds was both a blessing and boon to the Borough. The premier people pleasing

Borough of Look At Me was always happy to welcome people of differing heritage as long as they were willing to adhere to its posh principles. It was therefore an interesting and eclectic place. Innocent's life had been enriched by diversity and she could not understand Us and Them's separatist stance. She began to feel angry and could no longer be silent.

'What a sad and small-minded man you are for failing to see the similarities of folk. All souls come from the same place. We are all brothers and sisters of a kind. It is people like *you* who persist in perpetrating separatist myths which only lead to misery.'

She had not realized how loud she was speaking her soliloquy. Suddenly there was a round of applause from the audience.

'Here! Here!' they shouted in support. Innocent felt rather pleased with herself, she bowed to the audience and smiled at Sir Us and Them, who sensing the crowd's opposition to his opinions made a quick exit, scurrying off through a narrow doorway in disgust.

Innocent separated herself from Sir Us and Them permanently. She was embarrassed at having ever entertained him and realized that her reputation had been sullied by her association with him. Although she had distanced herself from him, she became conscious that as people passed her in the school corridors, they often gave her disapproving looks. She lamented at how stupid she was to have spent any time with him and wished she had ended their entanglement sooner.

She was now lonelier than ever before as people avoided her.

11
Lady Lack and the Library

Innocent threw herself into her studies. She decided to pay a visit to the school library – a large imposing building. Feeling lost she approached the librarian whose desk label read: *Lady Lack, Head Librarian*.

She noticed the librarian was looking her up and down. Lack pursed her lips as if she had just sucked on a lemon. She was a rather plain woman, with mousy, long brown hair, and permanent frown lines etched on her face.

'I was wondering if you would mind explaining how to use the library,' said Innocent shyly.

'Hum,' said Lack. 'You mean to tell me you don't know?' *Everyone* knows how to use the library. You must be a foreigner from far afield.'

Gracious, not another one, thought Innocent, feeling disheartened by the human condition.

Lady Lack proceeded to tell her the ins and outs of the library, with all the enthusiasm of a woman wearing wet shoes. When she had finished, Innocent was more confused than ever.

The next day she returned to the library. As she fumbled to find a scroll on music writing, Lady Lack approached her.

'Will you be quiet for goodness sake? There is no rustling of scrolls allowed. If you continue to make noise you will be asked to leave.'

Innocent was embarrassed. She had never been told off in public before and it was not a pleasant experience. 'I … I … I'm sorry, I didn't realize I was making so much noise.'

Lack glared at her disapprovingly.

A few days later Innocent visited the library again. She found a selection of scrolls which had the most beautiful sonnets and songs written on them. Innocent lost herself in the lamentations of love. For over an hour, she was entranced at how beautifully the words were woven together, and wished that she had the talent to write so poetically and powerfully.

Without warning Lack approached her. 'Madam, you have been here for over an hour. You are monopolizing the chair which is for general use. It is time for you to move along and take out the book you want.' Lack was staring down at Innocent with a smirk on her face. She was starting to get the feeling that this lady did not like her.

Innocent had always prided herself on being well liked by lots of people. Wherever she went she always managed to maintain her popularity. However, amongst the large populous of the Chiefly City, she was just one more pretty face with a title. Here one had to prove themselves in order to stand out – all Innocent had proven was that she had become a social flop.

Innocent's *likeability factor* took another battering from Lack a week later at the Book Borrowers Check-out Desk. She was holding a pile of books on temperamental musicians when they fell from her hands and landed on the ground with a thud, which reverberated around the entire library. Innocent looked up in horror in the direction of Lady Lack, who came charging towards her.

'You stupid girl, what do you think you are doing, disturbing the peace. If you can't behave in a dignified manner, you will be barred from entering.'

By now everyone was staring in Innocent's direction. She had never caused a public scene before and felt utterly humiliated. She swiftly moved to pick up the books only to drop them once again in a state of panic. A book clerk – well versed in Lack's lashings – came to Innocent's assistance and helped her gather the books and took them to the Borrowers Check-out-Desk.

'Stop making so much noise,' Lack yelled. 'You have committed a crime against serenity and you will leave my library *at once*!'

Innocent walked out of the library in shame – acutely aware that all eyes were upon her. As the kindly book clerk attempted to hand her the books, they slipped through her hands once again causing the entire room to break into fits of laughter – Lack laughing the loudest.

Innocent avoided the library until her books were due for return. She waited for the eleventh hour of the due date before returning. Sneaking in, she surveyed the annals from behind a large pillar, desperate to avoid Lack. Feeling her nerves dancing in the pit of her stomach, Innocent ran behind a bookshelf. She was now within five feet of the counter. She took a book from the shelf and peered through the space, on the lookout for Lack. With the coast clear, she tiptoed to the counter and deposited her books. Minutes from a clear getaway, she heard footsteps approaching from behind. Innocent froze in horror as she felt a cold hand on her shoulder.

'You are late!' said Lack loudly, ensuring that the entire library would hear her. 'Your books are now overdue. Lateness is a sign of larceny. I could have you arrested for Grand Theft Autobiography!' Innocent was terrified.

'I–I am not late, Lady Lack. The books are due today. If–if you check the date stamp, you will see I am right,' pleaded Innocent, almost hyperventilating.

'Date stamps can be forged,' said Lack viciously. I knew you were trouble since the first day you stepped in here!'

Innocent could take no more. Defeated by Lack she ran out of the library, her eyes streaming with tears. She stood on the steps trying to regain some composure, but by now she was weeping uncontrollably. Her public showing had convinced her that she was not cut out for life in the big Chiefly City of Chaos and Congestion Charges. Resigned, Innocent decided she would leave at once. She was about to return to her house and pack when she heard a gentle voice behind her.

'Please don't cry, my lady. Lack is a silly, spiteful and surly woman who takes pleasure in humiliating pretty and perfect princesses. You should be flattered – she only picks on the prettiest princesses.'

Innocent looked up to see a pretty and petite girl with long, auburn hair and blue sparkling eyes. The girl looked a similar age and stood almost at the same height. She had the kindliest smile Innocent had ever seen. She took out a silk handkerchief from her small bag and offered it to the weeping Princess.

'I am Princess True. Can I be of any assistance to you?'

Grateful to have found a friendly face at last, Innocent took the silk handkerchief and still sobbing attempted to dry her eyes.

'I –I am Princess In–Innocent. Thank you for your kindness.'

True gently put her arm around Innocent's shoulder.

'I was in the library and saw that most dreadful display. Do not blame yourself for Lack's crass behaviour. When I first arrived, Lack picked on me too. I took it personally until I realized that she is nothing more than a deeply unhappy woman who takes out her dissatisfaction on anyone who has what she does not – happiness. She is only happy when she is making someone else's life a misery. Do not give your power away to her. If you keep smiling when she has a go at you, she will realize she no longer has control over you, and will eventually give up her quest to make you as miserable as she is.'

'Oh I see,' said Innocent relieved that she had not lost her likeability factor after all.

Princess True invited Innocent to tea for two. It would be the beginning of a beautiful friendship.

The next time she went to the library, she was determined to hold her head high when she faced her nemesis. As she sat reading The Town Crier newspaper she heard the familiar footsteps behind her. This time she was prepared and taking a deep breath, greeted Lack with a large grin.

'You again, making noise!' screeched Lack.

'Why Lady Lack how lovely it is to see you. You look radiant today. Have you had your hair newly styled? I must depart and meet my friend True for tea. Do have a wonderful day.' Innocent smiled brightly, blinding Lack with her light.

Completely taken aback by losing her *Intimidation Factor,* Lack retreated in defeat. Innocent had killed Lack's tactics with kindness. Although the librarian attempted to continue her intimidation campaign, two more friendly exchanges with the young Princess, finally forced Lack to close the book on her Innocent chapter.

12
Princess True

The most marvellous Princess True was a mandolin protégé. In her, Innocent had discovered a *soul sister*. They hit it off immediately and with her help she began to feel at home in the Chiefly City – putting to rest any plans to depart.

True was such a loved and genuine person that Innocent's new association with her repaired her damaged reputation. People surmised if True could be friends with *that woman* – who once courted Sir Us and Them – then she can't be as bad as everyone thinks! Innocent gained social acceptance and standing in the school, and gradually started to make new friends.

They became inseparable – best friends. Innocent had not bestowed the title of *Best Friend* on anyone since her schooldays and took the label extremely seriously. The two Princesses liked the same things, the same fashions, the same foods and both adored the Pink Palace performing group. They would spend hours talking of their hopes and desires and laughing at all their failed romances and similar bad taste in men – joking that if only one of them was of the opposite gender they would be perfect partners!

Innocent loved her companion dearly and so enjoyed her friendship that the frantic worry over finding her *One True Prince* subsided. Friendship she surmised was far more fulfilling than courting.

Together they decided it would be wonderful to do a school project. They had both enrolled in *Project Managing Your Prince* and were keen to show off their skills. Once they found the perfect project they would proceed in their plans.

The next day, they were walking down the school corridor when a young, skinny lad with an overgrown fringe, spectacles and spots, bumped into them and dropped his pile of books at their feet.

'Oh forgive me my dear ladies, I am so sorry to have caused you so much distress, please forgive me,' he nervously repeated over and over. Innocent and True took pity on the nervous, nerdish figure before them. They looked at each other and smiled. As if by telepathy they both nodded: here stood their perfect school project!

The remorseful Sir Sorry, had spent his entire life under the sad illusion that everything was his fault. He was in a perpetual state of saying 'I'm sorry'. He had even told his parents that he was sorry for inconveniencing them by being born. He had decided that the only way to make up for his sorry existence was to become a well-respected and well-paid composer. Only then could his mother feel proud that the pain she endured in childbirth had been well worth the extreme effort.

He had a gentleness about him that touched the friends, dearly. They could see that beyond the spectacles, spots and apologies, was a handsome gentleman waiting to wow the world. Before Sir Sorry had even gathered his books, they had perfected a plan to makeover the unsuspecting apologist.

Sir Sorry was flattered and flabbergasted that two such beautiful princesses were flapping around him – shocked that such a sorry schlock would be in such demand. He kept apologizing for not being more like Prince Charming.

The first thing that the princesses performed on Sorry was a facial. They gathered the finest remedies for red pimples and pasted it all over his face. He sat frozen for two hours apologizing profusely for his pimply protrusions.

Next they took him shopping to Thread Needle Street and stripped him from his outdated attire and into the most fashionable garments. They finished him off with a new hairdo, which gave him the fringe benefit of being able to see clearly for the first time. Sorry apologized for being so much trouble.

As Sir Sorry stepped into the light they were dazzled at the remarkable transformation. He stared at his new self in the mirror, apologizing profusely to himself for not making the change sooner.

Innocent and True then coached Sorry on the finer points of impressing a lady. They taught him the Chivalrous Arts, which included bowing, Balcony Courting and laying down one's cloak over a puddle for the protection of a lady's footwear. They even taught him the dying art of listening to a woman's conversation.

Finally they took him window-shopping down Diamond Lane.

'Diamonds can definitely be a man's best friend when it comes to impressing a lady,' counselled Innocent.

Sir Sorry apologized for not having the funds to purchase large diamonds for his two best friends.

Innocent and True felt confident that in Sir Sorry, they had *created* the perfect suitor. They patted themselves on the back, joking that they should open a finishing school for lacklustre princes with potential.

Soon students in the music school started taking notice of Sir Sorry. Men marvelled at his magnetism for monopolizing such magnificent princesses. Women were impressed by his impeccable manners. Suddenly men wanted to be like him and women wanted to be with him. Everywhere he wandered, he attracted a curious crowd of people.

As the best friends received kudos for their remarkable reinvention, Sir Sorry became alarmed by the swelling crowds surrounding him. While Innocent and True had remodelled his face and facade, they had forgotten to remodel his opinion of himself. To the outside world he was a man to command attention, but inside he was still the scared and insecure apologist he had always been. Everyone now wanted a piece of him, and the pressure caused Sorry to break down in the middle of the school corridor one day.

Surrounded by crowds of admirers Sorry got himself into a state and began to yell.

'This sorry soul has deceived you. I am not the man you think I am. I am but a dreary soul trying to make his mark in the world. Beneath these fashionable clothes is a clod that has done nothing to earn your admiration. If you do not see your folly at following such a flop around, you will be just as sorry as I am.'

And with that, Sorry took his leave far from the *flattering crowd*, who were even more impressed by his expressions of humility and honesty – making him even more in-vogue. Innocent and True congratulated themselves on a job well done and threw themselves back into their studies leaving Sir Sorry to don a daily disguise to escape his fans.

When the musical term was complete, Princess True made a shock announcement to Innocent.

'I have decided to forego my music studies in favour of taking a seat at the University of Useless, Unemployable Degrees. I have decided to obtain a Degree in Bead-Works.'

'But True you excel at music and have such a promising career ahead of you. Why would you exchange all that for bead-works?'

'My dearest friend, I like music greatly, but I love beads more. It has been a passion of mine for many years. I studied music to please my parents and they promised that once the term concluded, if I still felt a pull to beads, I could give it a go.'

Innocent wanted her friend to be happy, so she wished her well in her new pursuit. Princess True commenced her studies at the University of Useless, Unemployable Degrees, which was located in the opposite side of the Chiefly City from the Royal School of Much Music.

She took her place at the university and promised Innocent they would meet up soon. For the first couple of weeks Innocent and True were able to take their weekly dinner and stroll together. Innocent felt relieved to see things between them had not changed.

However, as True immersed herself in her bead studies, she gradually had less and less time to spend with her dear friend. Innocent became frustrated as True's *RSVP*'s to her parties and dinner invitations diminished.

The situation came to a head when several weeks later, True declined Innocent's invitation to a Pink Palace performance. Innocent had gone to great lengths to procure entry permits to their concert and became livid at True's refusal to go.

'But how could you turn down a Pink Palace performance when you know how much I love them. What could possibly take precedence over Pink Palace and me? What have I done to deserve such dire treatment from a usually devoted friend?'

'My dearest Innocent, please do not take this *RSVP* personally, but presently I am preparing my thesis postulating the healing benefits of beading. It is my utmost priority. Could we not take a rain check and do dinner instead next week?'

Innocent could not believe her ears. 'You're putting a piece of paper before me, your dearest friend. How could you be so insensitive? You need to get your priorities straight and decide whether it be this Princess or the paper!'

'Please do not place me in this predicament,' pleaded Princess True. 'You are my greatest friend and I love you dearly, but if I neglect my paper my academic standing will be put in peril.'

Despite True's protestations Innocent would not be moved from her position.

'It has become apparent by your unwillingness to budge that your paper means more to you than I do. I can no longer settle for second best and feel that we must go our separate ways,' Innocent concluded.

'B–but, you can't mean that?'

'I am afraid I do. Our friendship is *over*!'

Princess True was devastated by Innocent's shock announcement and her eyes started to well-up.

'I am deeply saddened by your position and have no choice but to respect your wishes. I will miss you terribly. I–I wish you well,' and barely able to contain her tears, turned and walked away.

As Innocent watched her friend depart, she suddenly felt a wrench in her heart. She was about to call out to True when her princess pride stopped her.

'Changing positions would be a sign of weakness,' said the chatter in her head. In agreement, Innocent committed to her *crime against friendship,* turning her back on True. As she

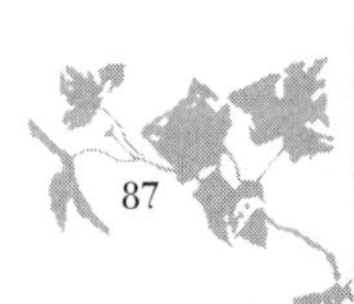

marched away from the scene of the crime, she tripped and fell, landing unceremoniously on her derrière.

When Sir Sorry heard the news of the broken friendship, he of course blamed himself and apologized for not being there for his two best friends in their time of need. He was so sorry in fact, that he took the rest of the school term off to recover from the guilt. With her two closest friends gone, Innocent needed another distraction to fill the empty space.

13
Innocent Gets A Job

The loss of her friendship with Princess True left a gaping hole in Innocent's heart. She missed True more than any of her former lovers. Suddenly she lost interest in her studies, and instead of resolving the situation with True, she would distract herself by leaving school and obtaining paid employment.

Innocent had never had a job before. After all, being a Princess of her calibre was a full-time career in itself. She decided to give it a go. It was the latest craze, as more and more royals had seen their royalties reduced by the recent *Bloody Labour Revolution*. Parliament had gone into the red and raided everyone's Privy Purse, forcing folk everywhere to labour harder than ever.

Visiting a Royal Placement Agency to see what was on offer, she dressed in the most conservative looking attire she could find. She was greeted by Sir Show Me the Money.

'Tell me dear Princess, what particular position are you pursuing?'

Innocent looked perplexed, she didn't expect him to ask her *that* question. She assumed he would tell her what position would suit her.

'Uh–I am not really sure as I have never worked for money before,' she replied.

'Oh you are a privileged Princess,' he replied. 'Can you take dictation?

'No!'

'Can you dispatch multiple messengers?'

'No!'

'Can you file scrolls?'

'No!'

'Can you look perfectly pretty every day?'

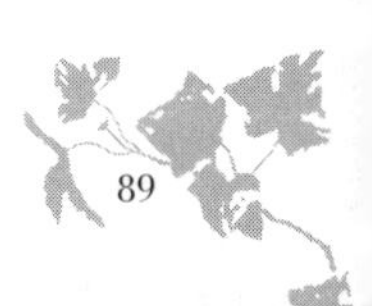

'Oh yes, I can do that really well,' gushed Innocent overjoyed he had found something she could excel at.
'Perfect, I will not have any problems finding a suitable position for you.' And he went about examining his client list.

After reviewing Innocent's life experience with her, Show Me the Money found the perfect position for her. He explained the job entailed working as a junior writer for a daily newspaper called The Town Crier. The readership had been decreasing of late and the management had decided that it was the direct result of the news being too depressing.

As most people didn't put in the work required to claim their own happiness, they needed to live vicariously through the stories and victories of others. The Managing Editor of The Town Crier decided that in order to generate a broader readership for her own depressing bi-lines, the paper needed to entice people with a new bias towards happy endings.

They were looking for a fresh and pretty face to put a positive spin on how worldly events ended up. Who better than a perfect privileged Princess, who had never worked a day in her life, to be able to create fanciful endings? Innocent was dispatched and was immediately offered the position.

Innocent loved working in an office and relished the thought of filling her own Privy Purse with the fruits of her labour. Best of all, she was able to share her talent for lying to herself about others. She emulated the writers of the Fairy Tale Land Press, by perpetuating pipe dreams of happily-ever-after.

Innocent's bi-lines presented people in the best possible light reflecting her own bias towards seeing people the way she wanted them to be and not who they *actually* were. She perpetually put people high upon a pedestal, sugar coating their behaviour. She reported on political disagreements being solved by a simple handshake and hugs between good men and women, eliminating all the hysterics and name calling that had really gone before. She focused on the good works people were doing rather than the bad. When people slipped up in the public eye, she came up with a multitude of excuses explaining their erroneous behaviour:

They weren't feeling well that day.
Their parents didn't give them enough hugs.
Deep down they were very nice people.
Their schools were not in the 'right' borough.
They didn't have the right friends to play with.
Responsibility was not a subject on their school curriculum.
They didn't get to throw their toys out of the pram when they were younger.

Innocent's childlike view of the world proved very popular for people looking to escape from the challenges and harsh realities of their own lives. Her column was a triumph and circulation of The Town Crier increased dramatically.

Innocent began to make new friends at work – filling the gap left by True. Her co-workers consisted of a circle of career journalists. Their reporting styles were markedly different and provided the newspaper with a balanced view of life.

There was Queen Rumour, the Managing Editor; she was responsible for reporting on faults, failings and flaws of people in the public arena. She also had a patronage position as a judge on a crown court and inspired fear and loathing by her high rate of convictions.

There was Baroness Bitter, a seasoned reporter of all that was wrong in the world. She had been credited with helping the *Blame Culture* take hold of The Kingdom. She had a particular following amongst failed businessmen who loved to blame parliamentarians for their financial fiascos.

Baron Bombastic wrote the daily opinion column. His caustic calling crushed many promising careers in politics, playwriting and private venture.

Lady Haughty was the expert on Haute Couture. She was a style-setter, who shaped seasonal wardrobes. Her snobbery was renowned in reporter circles. Every season Haughty would clear out her closet and her personal assistant. One of them penned a bestselling-unauthorized biography of her entitled *Dogsbody for a Bitch*.

Sir Short-Comings reviewed the performances of people in the public realm, condemning those who rose to any occasion. He felt it was his duty to keep egos at a low-level playing field.

Finally there was the overseer of them all, Baron Press. He had owned the paper for the past twenty years. At fifty he was an imposing figure with shimmering silver hair. Dapper and debonair he was a man of few words but nevertheless a keen observer. He kept very much to himself and did not mingle with his hired help.

Innocent was welcomed into the fold and struck up friendships with her colleagues. Throughout the day, the banter was always lively as Innocent was introduced to the world of *office gossip*. It was an entirely new experience for her and like her colleagues she developed a talent for tattle tales. Tittle-tattle raged morning, noon and night throughout the office.

Bombastic, Bitter, Haughty, Shortcomings, Rumour and Innocent formed a clique of clicking tongues. No-one outside their circle was off limits. From the well-known celebrity to the well-intentioned concierge working in the building, everyone and anyone could become fodder for focus. Rumours and remarks roamed the halls.

'Did you see what she was wearing?'
'Did you hear whose bedchamber she hopped into?'
'She is looking positively awful these days!'
'He is a crook.'
'Her husband has a roving eye.'
'Have you seen his receding hairline?'
'Her bum looks huge in that!'

Innocent never knew that putting others down could make her feel so good inside. She wondered if she had finally found the secret of happiness!

Immersed and integrated into the life of an office gossip, Innocent found it harder to do her work. With her purity poisoned, it took more of an effort to produce pedestal peddling copy and her pen ceased to flow fluidly. She had lost what she'd once had, and worried about whether it would return.

One morning, Innocent left the office for an assignment, she was just about to get into her carriage when she realized that she had left one of her gloves behind. She was about to re-enter the office when she heard Bombastic mention her name.

'I hear that Innocent has been around the block and been a blockhead when it comes to choosing a companion.'

Haughty interjected. 'I guess it follows that anyone with her dubious taste in clothes would also have poor taste in accessories – how I hear, she refers to her princes!'

Innocent heard all her colleagues break out in laughter.

Sir Short-Comings jumped into the character assassination fray. 'Did you read her latest column? What dreadful drivel! Somebody told her she was a writer once, and she believed them.'

'I am sure she is sleeping with Baron Press to be able to retain her tenable position,' speculated Bombastic.

As she stood outside the office door, Innocent was dumfounded. How could her friends turn on her in this way? She believed that as a member of the clique she was immune to being salacious subject matter. Now she was fodder just like everyone else. Oh the shame of it all, thought Innocent.

She was about to run outside when she spotted Baron Press. He had also overheard the poisonous prattle. Innocent blushed with embarrassment.

'Let the one who throws stones, not get hit by one,' he smiled gently to her. 'Why does one of your disposition, dirty yourself by dishing dirt and associating socially with those assassins?'

'But I work with them and have to fit in somehow. They are my friends,' said Innocent sounding like she was desperately trying to convince herself.

'Appearances can be deceiving. Whilst they are good enough to bring in readers to my newspaper, as friends they are not fit for purpose! Peers who do not like themselves cannot like anyone else. They are all jealous of you. Deep down they wish to be like you and liked as you are. As they are unable to go up to your level they have brought you down to theirs,' observed the Baron.

'Mudslinging is dirty business! Walk away now my little one and redeem yourself or you are destined to live a dirty, disparaging life.'

Innocent nodded at her kindly mentor and made an agreement with both herself and Press to muddy the waters no more. Every day Innocent came into the office and did her job and apart from simple pleasantries, stopped socializing with the clique. Although she knew she would become even more favourable fodder for the group, she realized it was better being out than in.

14
Innocent and Sir Shake and Peer

Innocent found life after office gossip positively exhilarating. Free from the constraints of gossip, she had an abundance of energy, which she decided to channel into her work. Her writing became less of a job and more of a passion. For the first time in her life she felt she had more than just her looks and charm to offer.

Taking on her new role as *Serious Writer*, Innocent decided she needed a mentor to perfect her craft and decided to ask the top journalist at The Town Crier – Sir Shake and Peer.

Shake and Peer loved shaking up the world of the rich, royal and famous, by peering into their lives and reporting his findings to the public. He had a global perspective on the world of words, believing people everywhere would relish reading of royal tragedies and intrigue. His penmanship produced prolific sighs of relief from people the world over, positively overjoyed for proof that there were families out there even more dysfunctional than their own.

He was so popular that his words had great influence in everyday life. He was instrumental in popularizing techniques for silencing a shrewish spouse. He also started the trend of Balcony Courting much to the chagrin of physicians who saw their caseloads double as they had to tend to young unbalanced suitors. He also became influential in both horse trading and spot removal.

He influenced an entire school of artists who developed the peepshow experience – a box painted on the inside with two peep-holes on either side, which when peered into provided a three-dimensional experience. It seemed everyone was jumping on the Shake and Peer wagon.

Innocent adored the sophisticated and sharp, Shake and Peer, and loved learning all she could. For the first time ever, Innocent had a purely platonic friendship with a man. Shake and Peer was married to an older woman, and as much as Innocent was attracted to him, she dare not cross the lust line. One married suitor in her lifetime was quite enough.

Mind you, Shake and Peer was so devoted to his craft that the only thing he was interested in caressing was his quill pen. The office assassins often commented how his wife had grown weary of his work.

Shake and Peer was a master craftsman who loved writing. He was happy to share his time with someone who shared the same love. Innocent often accompanied him to interviews and to eavesdropping sessions. Shake and Peer taught Innocent that all the people of the world were performers on their own life stage, and therefore, anyone was prime pickings for peering into.

'I report just the facts, my dear Innocent, just the facts,' he would tutor her.

Innocent felt that Shake and Peer was a man who truly understood her and saw beyond her physical beauty. When Innocent wrote, she felt more content than she had ever done, and for a while stopped worrying about being a *Solo Princess*.

Shake and Peer critiqued her work and helped her sharpen up her writing. Whenever he praised her work, she felt exhilarated. She felt confident that with his guidance she would one day become an eminent writer – not just a gossip columnist.

Sadly things came to an abrupt end when Sir Shake and Peer unexpectedly told Innocent he was leaving The Town Crier to pursue a career as a playwright. He had pushed the boundaries as far as he could at the newspaper, and although many in the office thought he was away with the fairies, Shake and Peer was determined to give up his career as an influential journalist for the stage.

'My dearest Innocent, it has been a pleasure pursuing our pen passion together. You have the potential to be a great writer if you focus on your craft. Don't get distracted by the frivolities of life, only write about them!' And with that, Shake and Peer kissed Innocent's hand and walked out of her life and into history.

15
Baron Press

Shake and Peer had been such an influence on Innocent's daily life that his departure left a huge gap. He had been her mentor, and without him and his validation, the sparkle went out of her stories. She convinced herself that she could not write without his guidance and inspiration, and this proved increasingly frustrating. Her copy became littered with mistakes and on more than one occasion, the printer came to personally see her and direct her to make the necessary corrections. She began to lose confidence in her ability as a writer, resulting in a loss of interest of her craft. Now she desperately needed to find someone to fill the gap which her mentor, Shake and Peer had left behind.

She did not have to go further than the boss's office, and decided to keep company with Baron Press. Although he was no Shake and Peer, the Baron was an extremely cultured and worldly man. He was extremely ambitious and committed to expanding his newspaper empire.

Innocent knew that Baron Press did not mingle with his staff and so she began to make frequent visits to his office in the guise of seeking his advice on her column. Using her charms, she gradually engaged the Baron in conversation.

Well-versed in the art of communication, Press captivated Innocent with his lively and insightful discussions. Before she knew it, she was spending hours in his office talking about all manner of subjects from political intrigue to poetry. Her writing began to take second priority over socializing with the Baron. It didn't take long for Innocent's new found love for writing to be replaced by her new found love for Baron Press.

The Baron, in turn, adored Innocent's childlike view of the world. Along with expanding his newspaper empire, he took great pleasure in expanding Innocent's horizons. He took her to the best musical recitals, the best operatic performances, and the best plays by new playwrights such as Plagiarism. They travelled to monasteries in the mountains to master the art of meditation. He took her to watch performances of the travelling belly dancers from the Eastern Kingdoms. She loved the Baron's world: inside it she felt safe and appreciated.

Innocent and the Baron became the tattle talk of the office. However, he was always nothing short of a gentleman toward his protégée. Their relationship remained platonic for months as they both enjoyed having a non-physical relationship.

Eventually, Innocent began to feel Press pulling on her heartstrings, and decided to take the *non* out of the *physical* and pursue a new relationship with the Baron. She hatched a plan to give her office colleagues something to really talk about.

As he walked her home after dinner, she parted her lips and planted a kiss on her platonic partner. Locked at the lips they lingered and lingered … until Press pushed away.

'Innocent I am twice your age and married to my newspaper. I am a confirmed bachelor and cannot give you what you need and want.'

She heard but didn't listen and locked lips again with the Baron. This time he didn't pull away.

As much as the Baron adored Innocent, his position remained unchanged.

'I am a confirmed bachelor and that will never change,' he reiterated before each lovemaking session. Innocent would just smile at him. He will change his mind, she thought, ever the optimist.

Much to the Baron's chagrin, Innocent resigned so she could focus entirely on her new relationship. Although her writing was not as fresh as it was, Press had hopes that Innocent's columns would go global, along with his plans to expand his newspaper empire. He firmly believed that she had a real gift for writing, and with a return to focus, she could become just as renowned as Sir Shake and Peer.

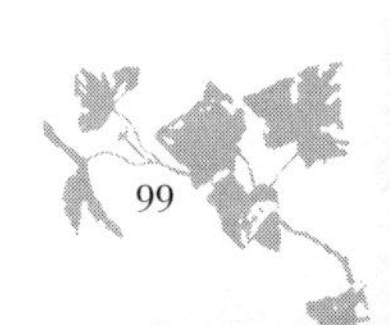

Alas Innocent was not yet ready to take herself seriously and gave up the opportunity of a lifetime to revert to the familiar. She excitedly wrote to Countess Confidence about her new suitor, suggesting a surprise proposal was imminent and that the ring would probably come from the Eastern Kingdoms.

The constant Countess corresponded by cautioning Innocent to curb her expectations –

Ma petite, I have heard that the great Baron Press is a confirmed bachelor after his disastrous first marriage. Are you sure you have not confused your work of producing happy endings with your personal life? Be cautious ma petite, do not put undue pressure on Press, or you will prevent a proposal from ever happening.

As had become the routine, Innocent ignored her friend's advice. She had waited long enough, and would promptly propose to Press herself.

'Darling Press, don't you think it is time that we wed.'

The Baron smiled at Innocent and shook his head. 'My love you know I am not the marrying kind. Let us not spoil what we have and leave our wonderful courtship unfettered.

I have another proposal of sorts for you, my love. I am going to the Eastern Kingdoms, to set up a new daily publication. Won't you accompany me and help me in my work?'

'I will gladly accompany you, as soon as we are bonded in wedded bliss,' she replied, still not listening to what he was telling her.

'Innocent my love, as great as my affection is for you I am a confirmed bachelor and my position will not be moved.'

Becoming angry she screamed at him, 'I have not endured six years of lousy lovers to end up in a marriage-less union. I want to be a *MRS* not a *MISTRESS!*'

Baron Press started to feel pressed and responded angrily.

'Why do you give such credence to a marriage decree? It is only a piece of parchment my Princess. From my own excruciating experience, it eliminates all the enjoyment. I had warned you of my weariness for weddings and yet as you ignored my words, I assumed we had a mutual agreement.'

Innocent finally heard Baron Press for the first time. As much as she loved him, she loved the idea of marriage more. She told herself it was her prize at the end of her long fought out battle. Her tone softened as she relented.

'You will not change your position and neither will I. Two lovers going in separate directions cannot walk on the same path.' And with those words they agreed to go their separate ways.

The Baron held his petite protégée against his person for five minutes, before he spoke. 'A word of caution Innocent – listen with discernment before you decide to take another foray into the world of relationships. It seems I have taught you everything but how to listen. Forgive me for being such a fool.'

And with that they kissed and with tears in their eyes parted company. A veteran of broken affairs, Innocent did what she did best and picked herself up in preparation for the next possibility, as her Baron sailed solo off into the sunset.

16
Innocent and the Super Soul Mate

Deciding to make a swift sojourn to recharge her ego's engine, Innocent boarded a boat. She sailed off to the island known as The Kingdom of the Long White Clouds – so named for the phenomenon of creative cloud clusters that cascaded over the land. The people were a down-to-earth group of plain talking, plain-named friendly folk, whose ancestors had come to the scenic country seeking a simple, soulful life.

The journey took over two weeks and Innocent spent much of her time staring out to the endless sea, wondering what Baron Press was doing.

The boat docked in the bountiful beach area, which always attracted a large crowd of transient travellers looking to find themselves amongst the boundless beauty.

Innocent spent time taking long walks on the promenade and the surrounding rain forests. While her days were full, she had to admit that her nights were lonely without company. A cloak of melancholy formed a shield between her and the other visitors to the island. For the first time in her life, she felt invisible, as no-one seemed to notice her.

After two weeks as the invisible woman, Innocent started to feel better. It had been six weeks since she said goodbye to the Baron and with each day passing she felt a little lighter. As she watched the sun set one night, she finally felt free of any forlorn feelings.

She headed back to a local eating establishment near where she was staying, with the old spring in her step. It was a serene setting, sitting under the open star-filled sky – utterly breathtaking she contemplated.

As she ordered her meal, a rather masculine man in his early thirties passed her with two drinks in his hand. She could not help but notice his tall and muscular build. He wore a beautiful, long, black leather coat with matching buccaneer boots. As he passed he smiled at her and said, 'hello'. Innocent scanned the suitor from foot to face observing that he was heaving with masculinity. She smiled back but was rather disappointed when he swiftly walked by.

Minutes later as she was sipping her wine, she was surprised when the masculine man appeared by the side of her table.

'May I join you, my dear lady?' And before she could answer, he had sat down beside her.

'I would have been here sooner, but I just had to drop off the drinks for my two colleagues. I'm Plain Shane from the north side of this great country.'

He explained to Innocent that he was a native of The Kingdom of the Long White Clouds and he was visiting the region for a big business bash hosted by his work union.

'I am a member of the Union of United, Undervalued and Under-Paid Underwater Urchin Merchants. We lads dive, duck and dreg the seabed for desirable and delectable commodities – such as fish, cockleshells, corals, seaweeds and anemones. Our booty is sold both locally and imported to faraway kingdoms.'

'Oh you are a physical man,' squealed Innocent. 'We don't get many of your breed where I come from. Most of our men folk use armour, weapons and lances to demonstrate their physical prowess.'

'And where do you come from, dear lady? Why would someone so boldly beautiful be sitting all alone?' Innocent blushed feeling slightly embarrassed by his words, *sitting all alone*. He probably thinks me a sad, lonely figure of a woman, she thought to herself.

However, nothing could have been further from the truth as his question began the conversation of a lifetime. The two strangers became intoxicated with one another as they talked for hours about family, friends, home, history and insights.

As he talked, Innocent thought that this man is as far from plain as one could get. He was different from the men she had encountered. This citizen of the Long White Clouds had no airs, graces, titles or pretentions. He was simply a man – comfortable in his own skin and conversation.

'How blessed for you to be born without the burden of performance,' Innocent declared.

'There's no need for that here, that's why the ancestors sailed to this cloud covered kingdom in the first place, looking for a laid back life. The cloud clusters do all the creativity and us folk just enjoy the scenery,' Plain Shane exclaimed with pride.

'I envy your birthright. Life appears so easy and breezy for you – so different from the folk in It Is What It Is.'

'It is,' said Plain Shane shrugging his shoulders and beaming his broad smile at a now besotted Innocent.

As they laughed and cried recalling more past life events, Innocent felt as if she had hitched a ride on one of the roving, rolling clouds that passed over them.

She felt her heart soar as Plain Shane said that one day he wished to show her where he lived and all the wonders of the sea. Their conversation was only stopped by long interludes of staring intently into each other's eyes.

They both had the sense that they somehow knew each other before. There was a feeling of familiarity and safeness as they sat together. Could this be my *soul mate* she wondered …

They were in their own beautiful world, oblivious to the other guests at the dining establishment, when to their annoyance the waiter interrupted their magical space.

'We are closing in fifteen minutes. Please would you settle your account?'

As if awoken from a trance, the two looked up at the waiter. Plain Shane drew his eyes back to Innocent, who noticed a sudden sadness in his eyes. He gently smiled at her.

'My dear Innocent, what an amazing evening I have had with you. You looked so alone sitting at this table that I thought I could be of service and of company for you. Yet it is *you* who has provided me with the service of your inspiring and wonderful company. I wish it could go on forever. But tomorrow I depart for home.'

Innocent felt herself wishing that his next words were an invitation to come with him. It was madness, but she knew that if this man, who was but a stranger a few hours before had asked her to spend the rest of his life with her, she would gladly and madly go.

She fell off her cloud with a mighty crash as Plain Shane continued.

'My wife is waiting at home for me. That is such a funny word for me to say out loud, my wife! Up until six months ago, I swore I would never settle down – I was an affirmed bachelor. I had never been the family man type. But then I met my wife, who like me, does not wish to have children and who loves to dive in the sea as much as I do. It is a rare gift to meet someone who you have so much in common with,' he continued.

'She recently was very sick – so sick that we feared her days may be short. When she recovered I realized how much she meant to me and I asked her to marry me. She said yes and we married one month ago.'

Innocent felt a surge of jealously at the first mention of the word wife. It was as if someone had taken away a great gift only moments after giving it. She felt her heart sink. As if sensing her disappointment he stared intently into her eyes – hoping it would somehow take away her pain. She stared back and almost simultaneously they both started to tear up. Plain Shane took her hand.

'I guess timing is everything,' he said sheepishly. 'If we had met six months earlier who knows what might have been.'

'But I would like to have children one day,' Innocent responded and they both stared at each other somehow feeling in their soul that they had been together before – perhaps even for a lifetime.

Plain Shane held on to Innocent's hand even tighter, grabbing onto the last few moments with this fantastic, magical, beautiful lady, before him.

'There is an ancient lore from the indigenous population of the Long White Clouds. They believe that each of us has a soul which when the body dies, comes back into many lifetime incarnations. The soul is playful and joyful and seeks to gain as much knowledge and experience as can be absorbed. Like any pupil attending school, the soul chooses the subjects he or she will study in each lifetime. They will seek out those experiences and those people who can teach those life lessons.

Some souls choose to divide into two pieces to learn about love, longing and separation, and spend lifetimes trying to reunite. Some souls will reunite for almost an entire lifetime, others for a few years and others simply for a few hours.'

'That's beautiful,' Innocent whispered, wishing the conversation could go on forever.

Their hearts full of love, Innocent and Plain Shane silently stood up. He kissed her hand.

'I will walk you back to your room he smiled reassuringly.' She took his arm and they began the short walk towards goodbye.

Innocent savoured every last minute she spent with him. They walked slowly, wishing their last moments to linger. She hung on tightly to his arm, feeling the energy between them. They walked silently to her room almost blindsided by their brief encounter. As they arrived at her door, Plain Shane again took her hand and kissed it. They stared silently into each other's eyes. He began walking away slowly, still holding onto Innocent's hand. They held on for as long as the distance permitted and finally let go as he moved further and further away. Staring back at Innocent, he blew her a kiss and she responded in kind as she took her key out to open the door to her room.

Once inside, she stood against the door for what seemed like an hour going over the wonderful evening that had magically transpired. What surprised her more than anything was she felt more inspired and invigorated than sad about saying goodbye to this *soul mate*. It had been one special moment and now it was time to let go. Innocent hardly recognized her former hurt self.

She realized that she had travelled a long way to receive this precious gift. It was an evening that would last forever, as the treasured memory often surfaced throughout her lifetime, warming her heart and bringing a smile to her face.

As Innocent's ship pulled out into the open sea, under the blanket of the star-filled sky, so too did Plain Shane's vessel. As the two ships navigated their way out of the harbour they turned around and passed each other and sailed off into the night.

17
Innocent Goes Speed Princing

It did not take long for Innocent's holiday glow to wear off. Within four weeks the old doubts and fears began to resurface. Innocent started to panic. She was almost twenty-four years of age and no closer to a betrothal ring than when she had first left her home castle. She started to feel a desperate sense that time was running out.

She figured that since she had met her soul mate already, maybe she should stop being so fussy and settle for a nice prince with a decent Privy Purse. On further reflection, if even her soul mate had not been perfect – with his wife and lack of interest in having children – she could at least give other men the benefit of her doubt. Maybe her soul was tired of the search and needed an endgame.

She decided to speed things up and take up the sport of *Speed Princing*. It was the latest courting craze in The Kingdom for impatient singletons. Like a glass slipper – each hopeful young maiden would be given six potential matches to try on for size.

For an exorbitant fee of fifty gold coins, Innocent received her list of six potential suitors, courting one at a time. If she liked one particular prospect and thought he was her *One True Prince*, she would forego the others on the list, choosing a refund or credit. If she was not entirely satisfied with a match, she could move effortlessly onto the next one.

Innocent was excited and was sure that from this list of six eligible princes, she would surely find her *One True Prince*.

The first prince she tried was an attractive, tall man, named Prince Apron Strings. Although he was kindly and fun, he couldn't seem to make a decision without first running to his mother.

For their first courtly outing Innocent suggested they attend the Royal Tennis Tournament, a one hour carriage ride away. Prince Apron Strings decided to defer to his mother, Queen Umbilical Cord – a member of the Mummy Knows Best Movement – to determine if the outing was indeed suitable. She was not supportive of the endeavour and recommended he give tennis a miss.

'My dear boy, you know how terribly carriage-sick you get on long journeys,' she cautioned. He agreed and they went to the local theatre troupe instead.

Often when he invited Innocent for supper, Queen Umbilical Cord accompanied them.

Sometimes when they were out having a pleasant stroll, his mother would dispatch the royal messenger and request his presence at her castle to help her with some household duty.

Innocent began to resent his mother and wished Apron Strings had more backbone when it came to standing up to the Queen.

On the evening of their one month courting anniversary, the Prince took Innocent to the most scrumptious eating establishment in town. They were about to order some fine wine, when Queen Umbilical Cord's messenger appeared. He handed the scroll to the Prince.

'It's a message from Mummy. Apparently the new royal stoves are not working and she is expecting important guests for a royal feast. She is in a right royal tizzy and needs my help immediately. I will go to Mummy's aid, and return to you, my love, as soon as is princely possible.'

Innocent could feel her blood boil. 'If you leave now we are over! I am tired of playing second violetta to your mother. You decide if it's me – or your mother – who comes first!'

Apron Strings, smiled a sheepish grin. 'My darling Princess you are the light of my life, but Mummy will always be the sun.'

Innocent could not believe her royal ears or the wimp of a man who sat across from her. 'Could this Prince be *real?'* she asked herself.

'Well then, you have made your choice – it's over!' And with that she stormed out, to the accompaniment of claps and cheers from the other dining guests, never looking back.

Prince Tight was the next prince on her hit list. He was a very successful carriage designer. But despite being royally flushed, he did not like to part with his gold coinage. He wore old, outdated outfits and always had muddy manure on his shoes. He was so careful with his coinage that it was common for him to save money on shoeshines by hitching a ride on the Under-the-Ground carriages and wiping off the muck on to the seats.

Innocent's first date with Prince Tight, was lunch at the local alehouse. When they finished eating and the cheque arrived, he only put enough gold coinage to pay for his portion of lunch.

She didn't mind at first, after all, she was an independent Princess who had independent means. She even surmised that such a fact would make her more attractive to him.

However, as she got to know Tight she discovered it was not only his gold coinage that he did not like to part with. He didn't seem to like sharing anything that belonged to him, whether it was his time, his affection, his kisses, his friends or even his conversation. He didn't like letting go of anything that belonged to him, fearing that he would somehow be taken advantage of and lose everything he had. Innocent found life with Tight positively restrictive.

After five weeks of dating him, she decided that it wasn't so much fun paying her own way all the time. For the first time in her life, she didn't feel much like a Princess. She decided that Tight was definitely not for her and moved on to prince number three.

Prince Possessive was a stock farm trader in the financial district of the town. He was debonair and very intelligent. He was an avid collector of fine objects.

From the first time he laid eyes on Innocent he lavished attention on her. He kissed her hands repeatedly and laid his cloak down whenever she walked over a puddle. Possessive arranged for his carriage driver to take her wherever she wanted to go. He wined and dined her every night. He offered her advice on the best places to invest her gold coinage. Possessive seemed like the perfect gentlemen and after two months of dating, Innocent believed she had finally found her *One True Prince*.

While out shopping with her maid, Innocent spotted Prince Possessive's carriage driver watching her, which she thought was rather odd.

As she moved on and sat down to have a cup of tea at the teashop, she saw the carriage driver again.

'Oh my goodness, I think Prince Possessive's carriage driver is following us.'

'Why would he do that?' inquired the maid.

'I don't know, but I am going straight to his office to find out.'

As she arrived at Prince Possessive's lavishly furnished office, he was overjoyed to see her and showered her with hand kisses.

'What do I owe this wonderful surprise my love?'

'My dear Prince, I was alarmed today to see your carriage driver follow me around the town and hope you could find out why.'

'Oh my silly, wonderful Princess, it is I your love, who sent him to follow you. I wanted him to report all your great movements. If we are to be married soon, I want to know all that you do my love.'

She gasped. 'You sent him to follow me? You wanted him to report my movements to you? You want me to marry you?'

Innocent often imagined how she would feel the first time anyone proposed to her. She never imagined that it would give her the creeps!

The Prince pranced around the room.

'So my love, we will get married as soon as possible. Soon there will be no need for you to venture outside of my castle. You will have everything your heart desires and my servants will go shopping for you.

You will be a sparkling addition to my grand collection of fine paintings, antiques and tapestries that adorn my castle. You will top them all and become my greatest trophy.

How does next Monday sound for our wedding?'

By the time the Prince looked around, Innocent was gone and running as fast as she could to her carriage. As desperate as she was to walk down the aisle, life as another object of affection in Possessive's collection was not quite what she had in mind.

He followed her home where her maid was waiting with a hastily written note saying she was sorry but she had left for Joie De Vie – permanently. With no forwarding address, Possessive was forced to return to his office.

Innocent watched him leave from behind her curtains, thankful that he had believed her fanciful story. She was now free to try out prince number four.

18
All The Best Princes

All The Best Princes was by far the most perfectly primed prince Innocent had ever seen. His tresses were tended in the most meticulous of manner and his garments were supremely stylish. Innocent had never seen so many ruffles in her life. He always greeted Innocent with both a kiss and a flower arrangement resulting in her rooms overflowing with the sweet floral scents.

A Master of the Chivalrous Arts, he was a recipient of several Orders of the Garter, the highest award for chivalry in the land. He was particularly proud of his collection of garters that came in a variety of shades, which could be matched to any outfit he was wearing.

He was a patron of the arts and took Innocent to many a great performance, including the great Opera – *The Brasic Bohemians* at The Gilded Cage of Music and *Harmonious Harpsichords* – playing for one night only at Herbert's Hall.

He also took Innocent to see his favourite actor – King Cool – perform his new play on stage. Cool was famous for playing a particularly popular police constable, keeping law and order in the land by catching shady suspects with the aid of his sunspecs.

All The Best Princes had purchased front row tickets for the performance that night. He perched excitedly in his chair clapping and cheering with every Cool soliloquy and pregnant pause. At the end of the performance, the Prince fought diligently for the sunspecs that Cool had thrown into the audience. He put up the good fight with a rather plump-looking lady who was desperate to get a piece of Cool. The sunspecs came in handy, as a wayward hand had hit him in the eye as he claimed possession of the glasses.

To Innocent's delight, he knew all the finest tailors and designers on Thread Needle Street. He revamped her entire wardrobe and employed face painters to give her a new look. He found the best shoemakers to fashion fabulous footwear, the likes of which Innocent had never seen before. She could not believe that she had encountered a man who was even more stylish than the women of Joie De Vie!

Innocent spent hours talking to the Prince about fashion, music and courtly manners. It was as if she had a new best friend. She speculated on what a cultured life she could have with the Prince if they married and what a supremely fashionable ring he would buy for her.

He was always a perfect gentleman and after three months of courting, Innocent started to question why he had not progressed passed hand kissing.

One evening they were attending a lecture on courtly manners when the Prince bumped into an old friend – Prince Buff. He was accompanied by another handsome prince called Prince Dandy. Innocent was in her element as she suddenly found herself surrounded by three stunning and stylish princes.

'So … how have you been my … my *dear* Prince,' said Prince Buff awkwardly.

'Fine … And how have you been?' replied All The Best Princes hesitantly.

As they exchanged pleasantries, Innocent saw the soulful looks in both of their eyes. When they parted she noticed how melancholy her Prince had suddenly become. He did not talk to her for the entire carriage ride home. When they got to her apartment door, the Prince grabbed Innocent's hand and got down on one knee.

Innocent began to get excited – this was it, she thought. By tomorrow she would be betrothed.

'*Yes–yes–yes*! I *will* accept your proposal,' she blurted out excitedly, before the Prince even had a chance to speak.

But he was too distracted to notice her outburst.

'It's no use,' the Prince piped up, 'I cannot go on living this lie without my true love any longer, this lie is over,' and he began to sob uncontrollably.

'My Prince, I don't understand your anguish. I will accept your proposal. You will *never* have to live without me!'

All The Best Princes still had his head in his hand and was oblivious to anything Innocent was saying.

'Prince Buff and I used to be betrothed but sadly eight months ago, we parted ways as he felt he was not yet ready to settle down with one prince. I had never experienced such heartache in my entire life and I swore off men from that moment on.'

That is when I signed up for Speed Princing and met you. I thought courting princesses would be easier, but tonight after seeing Buff in all his glory, I realize I can no longer go on living without him. Can you forgive me for my dastardly deceit?'

Innocent could not believe her ears and her mouth dropped lower than she believed humanly possible. Hers must be the shortest engagement in the history of courting, she surmised! She recalled her romance over the last couple of months with the Prince – the concerts, conversation, the shopping.

The shopping – a torch suddenly went off in her head.

How could I have not seen that this courtly Prince was too good to be true? Her heart sank. In the past she had to compete with other princesses, the sea, a wife, a newspaper, a mother, and now another prince. Innocent wondered if she would ever find a suitor free to love her.

'Say you will forgive me – dear Innocent – you are the most wonderful of princesses with the greatest taste. If I did not prefer princes, you would be my premier pick. Won't you do me the honour of being my best friend?'

Innocent looked straight into the Prince's soulful eyes and she remembered how much she enjoyed his company. Every girl needed a best male friend, particularly one with such divine tastes.

'I will agree to become your best friend if you promise to continue our shopping sprees.'

'That is a deal my darling Innocent. Now you must excuse me, I have a prince to pursue and with that he kissed her hand and ran to his beloved Prince Buff.

Innocent had lost a prince but gained two style consultants.

19
Prince Fear

Innocent had been invited to the nuptials of her new best friends Prince All The Best Princes and Prince Buff. She was delighted to have been asked to be the Chief Bridegroom Maid and even more delighted to wear the luxuriously lavish gown that they had created for her. She marvelled at what a handsome bridegroom All The Best Princes made and hoped she could do similar justice to her own future intended one day.

She was full of the joys of wedding planning when she was approached by one of the other guests – the dashing and dapper, Prince Fear. He had made a fortune as a founding father of the Insurance Industry. It had been a novel notion that had taken off and now Fear headed the largest company in the industry. He bowed sweepingly.

'Madam, may I be permitted to say what a marvellous-looking Bridegroom Maid you make!'

Innocent smiled at the man standing before her. She noticed how well put together he was, at six-feet tall he was the perfect height for her proportions and had clear blue eyes and dark hair. He had high cheekbones and a small black goatee.

I quite enjoyed a beard in the past, thought Innocent, recalling her rendezvous with Baron Booty.

Prince Fear asked her to do him the honour of dancing with him. She was more than happy to oblige. He impressed her with his careful ballroom manoeuvres as he attempted to avoid swerving into the other swingers.

What a considerate man, she thought, and how fortuitous to meet at such an occasion. It must be a sign she decided.

They spoke all night until he excused himself at 11:30 p.m.

'I must depart before the stroke of midnight,' he explained. 'As you must have read in the Fairy Tale Land Press, one never knows what may occur upon the stroke of midnight.' He kissed Innocent's hand and arranged to meet her the following day for a walk in the park.

When she arrived at the park, she was surprised at Fear's attire. He was dressed from head to toe in a suit of armour. She would have missed him entirely if he had not opened his mouthplate and called to her.

'Ah my dear Innocent, how lovely to see you again, shall we go for a walk?'

As he stiffly and loudly walked in his full metal jacket he began to explain, 'I never leave home without my suit of armour. One never knows if a runaway carriage might inadvertently bump into one's person, or an archer's arrow might accidentally miss his target and hit the unfortunate sod who was walking by. One must always be prepared for these occurrences.'

Innocent had never met anyone who thought along those lines and was most impressed at this Prince's forward thinking. As they walked in the park, she was struck by how many archers' arrows actually ended up shooting in Fear's direction. After the fifth one flew by, Innocent flew into a panic wondering if it was wise for her to get her own metal suit.

The following day Fear extended an invitation to the seaside. He arranged to pick her up in his carriage for the two hour journey. When he arrived there was barely enough space in his vehicle for Innocent. Prince Fear had filled the carriage up with hampers of food and a large barrel of water. He explained that if the carriage broke down unexpectedly, at least they would have enough provisions to keep them going.

Throughout the journey, Fear talked incessantly about all the insurance policies he created and possessed, and how it was important to be prepared for any situation. Fear based decisions on protection for any number of situations that might unexpectedly occur to him. He told Innocent he had insurance for broken bones and broken carriages. There was insurance for protection against staff who may steal from him and gold-digging women who might marry him. He even had a range of policies to provide care for any illness, which may befall him in thirty years time. His personal favourite was insurance for one struck by lightning or any violent person he may come across. But the most popular policy, he told Innocent, was insurance to pay for people to get out of being drafted for either the army or parliament.

He boasted that not only had he invented most of the insurance policies out there, but he was the industry's biggest customer. He explained that he had even help spread the industry by taking out policies, offered up by rival companies in case his own firm flopped.

As they got halfway to the seaside, the carriage hit a rock, and the wheel needed to be changed.

How fortuitous Innocent thought, that Fear had insurance to pay for a new replacement wheel.

By the end of the two hour journey, Innocent started worrying about her own lack of insurance and asked Fear if he could advise.

When they arrived at the seaside the Prince had his driver unload the delicious hamper that his well-vetted cooks had prepared for lunch. Fear suggested they picnic on the beach. He instructed his driver to get the fly net that was stored in the back of the carriage. The Prince explained that the net was protection against flies that were attracted to picnic lunches.

'Flies are dirty. They entertain on excrement and therefore carry germs. We must ensure they cannot get to our food,' he reassured her.

Innocent sat under the net eating with Fear, feeling secure and safe as flies swarmed outside. As she peered through the net she noticed that none of the other picnickers seemed to be disturbed by the flies. This Prince seemed to be a regular *lord of the flies*, she told herself.

After a couple of hours under the net, the Prince noticed there were dark clouds looming in the sky.

'Oh dear, It looks like rain and that means the possibility of thunder. It will not be safe for us to ride back in the carriage in the middle of a thunder and lightning storm. So I think it wise that we stay here for the night at a suitable seaside coaching inn.'

While Innocent had enjoyed dirty weekends in the past, she felt it was a little premature for her to engage in one with this new Prince. She may have been a racy royal, but all decent Princesses waited *at least* a week before entering into the realm of physicality. After all she had her reputation to consider.

'Why sir, it is far too presumptuous of you to assume that I would be ready to stay overnight with you at this early stage of our courtship,' protested Innocent indignantly.

'Madam, please be assured I was not suggesting anything improper. I would need to get you checked over carefully by my physician before I would get to know you carnally,' he shot back at her. 'After all I do not know where you have been!'

'I beg your pardon, sir. How dare you make such a crass comment! I'll have you know that I am a very clean Princess. I have *never* been with a man without wearing *the best* leather sheaves,' Innocent screamed angrily at him.

'Well my dear, one must always be careful in the transference of germs.' May I suggest when we get to the inn, that we have our own separate bathrooms and bedrooms – just to be on the safe side?'

Innocent was livid and beginning to tire of Fear. What she had first admired in him was now becoming irritating. 'I would be most happy to concur with your suggestion sir, she said sarcastically.'

They checked into the local coaching inn and were given two rooms on the upper floors. By now there was an impressive thunder and lightning display outside and Fear clung tightly to Innocent's arm as they climbed the stairs.

'Oh I do hope the lightening does not strike the inn,' he screamed in Innocent's ear, making her jump.

She had definitely decided that Fear was not for her and she couldn't wait to head home. After she escorted Fear to his room and checked under his bed as he requested, she decided to have an early night and settled into bed. She was in the middle of a deep sleep when she was suddenly awoken by a violent scream. Fear came knocking frantically on her door.

'Let me in Princess Innocent – oh please let me in – help me, help me, help me!' he yelled, pounding his fists on her door.

Innocent shot up out of bed terrified upon hearing his screams. Her heart was now pounding and her entire body shaking. She was terrified of what she might find. As she slowly opened the door, she was almost knocked over as Fear sped past her.

'What is it Fear? What on earth has happened?'

Fear's eyes were wide open in horror. 'Oh my dear Innocent, it was simply horrible … horrible. There was a giant spider crawling in my room. I think it is a venomous spider out to poison me. Won't you please let me take shelter in your room, oh please save me, save me – ' Fear screeched as he covered his face with his hands and curled up in a ball on the bed, quivering and quaking.

Innocent couldn't believe her ears. Her heart was pounding so loud that she thought it was going to leap from her chest. She wanted to hit Fear right in the face!

'You scared me half to death and my heart is now beating so fast, I can hardly catch my breath – and what for? A stupid spider!' she screamed at him.

'Y–you spineless jellyfish! You are welcome to my room, for I am leaving it and you immediately. I will find my own way home.'

And turning on her heels, leaving the ball of Fear, she grabbed her clothes and ran down the stairs, deciding that living with Fear even for one night was too horrible a prospect to bear.

20
Prince Teach-Me-All-You-Know

After her journey with Fear, Innocent decided she needed a little fun. She decided to return to Speed Princing and match number five. It was always her lucky number and she felt overly optimistic. Anything would be better than Fear she thought.

Number Five – Prince Teach-Me-All-You-Know – was twenty years of age and five years younger than Innocent. He was part of a new breed of young men called BOBCATS, which stood for *Bedding Older Babes Confidently Asserting Their Sexuality*. Innocent had never been courted by anyone younger in years and was curious. She joked with her maid as to how it might feel to corrupt a younger man.

Innocent was wildly attracted to the young Prince. He was charming, confident and cocky. He had a boyish face and a beefy body. His strapping shape made Innocent swoon. He was full of fun and made her feel eighteen again. She affectionately called him Teach-Me-All and he in return called her Boss of the Bedchamber.

He was tickled by her talents and felt on top of the world. She was equally in her element as she excitedly despoiled the dashing, younger Prince.

Life became one big party as they took pleasure in playful pursuits such as the travelling carnivals and the beer bashes. They travelled to the best beaches where they bathed all day in the sun. They camped at all the muddy music festivals they could find. For Innocent, life became light and fluffy for the first time ever.

One day, Prince Teach-Me-All-You-Know suggested they go to the pleasure island of Get High With Me where prolific partying was the preferred pastime. They set sail immediately and upon arrival settled into a small beach lodge steps away from the sea.

Teach-Me-All was true to his nickname. Innocent had never partaken in such hedonistic, hardy party-going, in her entire life. He was a good tutor and for weeks they frolicked fearlessly, feasting on fine wine and fattening food. They sniffed the new snuff being passed around and swayed all night in song and dance. Hazy Herbal Weed flowed freely and there were clouds of smoke everywhere.

To Innocent's delight they ran into her old idols Pink Palace who were also partying on the pleasure island. The group consisted of the percussion player Prince Nameless, the string players Princes Unknown and Unnamed and the lead singer, Prince Anonymous. They had become even more popular in the ensuing years since Innocent had first attended a performance with Prince Bad Boy.

Prince Anonymous took a shine to Innocent and they went for walks alone together, whenever Prince Teach-Me-All-You-Know passed out – which was now occurring on a daily basis. Innocent told Anonymous of her life, and he penned the tune *Another Prick in the Wall* for her, which would prove rather popular. As he performed his composition, she squealed in delight at being part of his catalogue of songs and he was equally delighted to be added to her catalogue of conquests.

Innocent was free to rollick and roll with Prince Anonymous, until he parted for a world performance jaunt. She was exhausted from her week of making sweet music and passed out beside a sleeping Teach-Me All-You-Know as soon as her head hit the pillow.

It was two days hence till she rose from her bed to find her young lover sitting on the bed waiting for her to resume their revelry.

'Hey Innocent, you have been snoring for two days. I thought you would never wake up.'

'Snoring, what are you talking about? I don't snore. I am a Princess with both breeding and good breathing,' replied Innocent, thoroughly mortified at the suggestion.

'Hey all prolific party-goers snore, welcome to the club Princess, now let us go to the tavern.'

After her flirtation with her famous friend, she felt rather guilty and continuing on a course of celebration seemed the least she could do for her clueless Prince.

By the end of four weeks Innocent was spent.

'I am positively pooped. I cannot continue carrying on in this fashion. Let us depart and detoxify before permanent damage sets in.'

'Princess, you worry too much, just relax and enjoy living lightly.'

Innocent, feeling frustrated began to take a second look at her lover. She had to admit that she could no longer keep up with him and wondered where they would go from there.

'Tell me, Teach-Me-All, what makes you tick?'

'What do you mean love,' said the Prince hoping Innocent was not about to get serious.

She continued, 'What matters to you? Where do you wish to go from here?'

'Right to the long bar,' countered the Prince cheekily.

'I fancy a drink and a snuff, what do you say? Are you coming?' said the Prince sniffing after developing a full-blown case of the *foreign import flu*.

'Don't you think you are drinking delinquently and snorting senselessly? Do you ever tire of the party? Do you not wish to one day return home? After all you have to settle down eventually.'

'Settle down,' said the party-loving Prince indignantly. 'I am only twenty-one. I am all about taking pleasure wherever and whenever I can find it. I thought mutual pleasure seeking was what we both wanted? There is still a lot I can learn from you. Now enough of this serious side, the bar awaits us.'

Innocent took a long hard look at her Prince. They had spent a wild and wonderful year together but as powerful as the partying pull could be, she now balked at blatant thrill seeking for the sake of seeking thrills. It seemed to Innocent that the line was now blurred and what used to bring her pure abandoned pleasure now seemed more like bloody hard work. Besides, she did not feel comfortable with the dark circles that had developed under her eyes and the dearth that had developed around her derrière.

She made a quick decision to desert her Prince.

'Darling Prince we have reached a juncture and as adorable as you are, I don't think we are well suited for one another. My partying prime is over and yours has just begun. It's been fun, but now we are done.' And with a racy smile Innocent suggested, 'Let us go out with a big bed-banging finale.'

The Prince needed no persuading and after the lingering, loud, lust-making session, the BOBCAT and the Princess parted company. Innocent caught the next boat home, leaving the young BOBCAT sniffing to his own destructive devices.

When Innocent arrived home she decided to give the remaining prince number six on her list, a complete miss!

21
Innocent Goes Sparring

When Innocent arrived home she felt positively sluggish. Although she was only twenty-six years old she felt so much older. She could no longer fit into any of her clothes and when a market-seller tried to give her a senior discount for people over thirty-five, Innocent decided that the wear on her body had to be repaired. She decided to visit the great Spa of Tub, where people could not only get cleansed but also trim down to a tub-fitting size. The spa was located in the Borough of The New Forest.

Baroness Booby Trap, a connoisseur in the Body Beautiful Arts, ran the exclusive spa. The Baroness had a blossoming bosom, which was of legendary proportions. The spa did a booming business as women from all over aspired to look like her and men aspired to look at her.

The Baroness was not just a pretty pair of boobs as she had diligently devoted her life to the pursuit of beautiful and bountiful health. She had been at the forefront of a movement propagating the positive properties of plants for the body. The radical idea of eating freshly grown fruits and vegetables for health was a far stretch for many who found taking health potions far easier.

She had also been involved in a campaign to eradicate the scourge of scurvy from the navy. Lemon Aid as the campaign had been called became a call to arms for people to sponsor a sailor by buying enough lemons for them to sail to optimal health with. As a result of her efforts millions of seafarers were saved from scurvy, proving that something bitter could end up being something sweet.

Baroness Booby Trap had recognized that most people were completely unaware that they even had a body beyond what they saw on the surface. People lacked an understanding on how to oil their well-run machine and keep it from going rusty.

The Baroness decided that she would use all her assets to bring people to her spa to spread the message of hearty health.

Innocent checked herself in for a much-needed three months of rest, relaxation and re-education. She had always taken her looks and health for granted, but as she now entered her late twenties, she realized she needed to pay more attention to it.

At the spa there were several planned lessons to participate in and to promote new health habits. Many of the Baroness's ideas were considered radical and controversial. Nevertheless, Innocent found them fascinating and easy to follow.

The first lesson she attended was the *Art of Breakfast Eating*. The Baroness advocated the importance of a hearty morning meal to break the fast of the evening. She explained that eating breakfast not only silenced hunger pangs, but also engaged the engine of the body in energy producing endeavours, which allowed one to be awake for the entire day. Innocent had not eaten breakfast since living in Joie De Vie, and realized that she had quite literally been hungry for years.

Baroness Booby Trap revealed her secret to maintaining her booty beautiful in the *Art of Drinking Water.* Here Innocent learned how drinking jugs of water could effortlessly and efficiently eliminate thirst and hunger pangs.

Making Fruit Your Friend a how-to guide for learning to pick only ripened fruit that had fully flowered to fruition. The Baroness took the position that picking fruit before it was ripe was a rip-off.

Purging with Prunes – particularly popular with people who had busy daily schedules.

Learning to Live with Legs – a radical idea of walking for weight loss – an idea that had carriage drivers up in arms.

Sleeping for Sanity – an idiots guide to waking up to life, by sleeping seven to eights hours per night.

Proportionate Plate Placement – advice on how to limit portly producing portions by the use of small plates.

How to Turn Trampoline Training into Toned Thighs – Innocent noticed that this was the most popular course with the male guests, who gaped garishly as Booby Trap demonstrated the benefits of bouncing.

The Baroness also believed in cultivating a healthy mind for having a healthy body. Just as the bodily functions needed to purge regularly so did the heart of holding any past anger and pains. Booby Trap had come up with an exercise technique called *Anger Resistance Training* where a routine of rigorous moves to music was accompanied by protestations of profanities.

'Give me an F … give me a U … give me a C … give me a K … give me a Y … O … U,' called out the bold Baroness in rhythm as she rigorously moved her arms up, down and to the sides, over and over.

Booby Trap also employed the use of heavy, hanging, sacks of hay with a face painted on them. She demonstrated techniques of sparring with sacks, while imagining it was a particular person who had caused past pains.

With every jab at the slab, the Baroness encouraged the release of swear words. Innocent threw out vulgarities and violent punches at the sack that she imagined to be her past sullied suitors. She screamed at the top of her lungs.

'HI–YAAH, Lie-A-Lot, you W @%*!, wasting my time with words. HI–YAAH, Bad Boy, you B@%*!, wasting my virginity. HI–YAAH, Booty, you frightened F@%*!, throwing away what we had. HI–YAAH Captain Unavailable, you cut throat C@%*! Who do *you* think *you are* rejecting me?'

Innocent had to admit that she thoroughly enjoyed swearing. Although she knew it was unladylike behaviour and her mother would be appalled, it felt bloody good and was a great way to temporarily release tension.

The Baroness also believed in cultivating cleanliness to ward off diseases. It was an idea ahead of its time as most people believed in bathing only on birthdays. Booby Trap had a particular aversion to public water closets. She believed in avoiding any physical contact at all costs.

She tutored on *Touch Free Toileting Arts*. She coached her clients on how to relieve themselves without having to make physical contact with the toilet seat.

Innocent learned how to squat solidly over the seat while maintaining her balance and posture. She learned how to balance on one foot like a ballerina when a lack of a handbag hook required a leg up. She learned how to open a cubical door using her foot, knee and hip. Innocent was surprised at how supple she was as she learned how to turn on a tap using her feet. Finally, how to kick open the front lavatory door to avoid touching the dirty handle. She noticed gleefully that these techniques gave her the added benefits of a tight derrière and toned thighs.

And finally Innocent signed up for *Snorers Anonymous*, a support group to help princesses come to terms with the indignation of nighttime grunting. She had never quite gotten over the shock of being told by Teach-Me-All-You-Know that she snored and found the group support comforting.

22
Magical Musical Troubadours

One day Innocent decided to explore the forest which surrounded the spa. She put on her walking shoes, grabbed a walking stick and headed out into the wilderness. She walked for miles as the majesty of the tall thin trees that encompassed the forest, mesmerized her. The sweet serenity of the surroundings captivated her so much, that she got lost.

Innocent was starting to feel panicky when she heard some music coming from a clearing. She walked towards the sound of music and upon coming to the clearing saw the most charming caravan she had ever seen. It was painted bright red with gold stars and suns dotted throughout. It had blue trim all round. The caravan had a sloped roof and four windows with flowerpots attached. It looked like a small house on wheels. Even the four Clydesdale Horses that pulled the carriages had matching red saddles and blankets decorated with the same sun and stars.

Not far from the caravan were four men with long hair, wearing long blue velvet capes, sitting by a fire playing string instruments. Innocent had never heard such magical music in her entire existence. Their music beat all the other songs Innocent had ever heard in quality and harmony.

Mesmerized, she moved closer and startled the horses. The four men suddenly stopped playing and looked at Innocent.

'Hello my dear lady, what are you doing out here in the forest on your own?' asked one of the musicians.

'I beg your pardons sirs, but I seem to be lost. I took a stroll from the Spa of Tub and seem to have lost my way,' replied Innocent rather demurely, clearly taken by the amazing quartet.

'Well you are just in luck,' piped up the smallest of the quartet, as we have been invited to perform a concert there tonight. We will give you a ride back in our caravan.'

'I would be most grateful sirs, and thank you for your kindness.'

The man wearing rounded spectacles and a cheeky grin approached Innocent and took off his hat and bowed to her. 'It is our pleasure. Let us introduce ourselves, we are the Magical Musical Troubadours, we come from The City of Love. We are on a tour of the world spreading the music and message of love. We travel the long and winding roads in the hope of spreading our message that love is really all you need to succeed.'

'Wow,' said Innocent totally in awe of the sagely figure before her.

He continued, 'Let me introduce you to the gang. My name is King Lyric and I am responsible for making music with a deep message. This is my brother, King Melody.'

A handsome man with a boyish face stepped forward.

'I am responsible for creating unforgettable magical melodies which move people to tears. This is my brother, King Strummer.'

A tall, thin, serious-looking man with soulful eyes stepped forward.

'I am responsible for creating soulful sounds which reverberate within one's spirit. This is my brother, King Drummer.'

The smallest of the four stepped forward. Innocent couldn't help but notice that he had rings all over his body. He was wearing ten rings on his fingers, two through his ears, one through his nose and numerous large rings around his wrists and hanging from a large chain around his neck. Innocent couldn't help thinking how well prepared this musician would be for a marriage proposal if the need ever arose.

'I am responsible for bashing out beats which cause people to break out in dance.'

Innocent stepped forward and curtsied. 'My name is Princess Innocent. I am on my life's journey. I am responsible for creating chaos for myself by picking inappropriate, irresponsible and irritating suitors.'

'Pleased to meet you Innocent,' said the quartet in perfect harmony.'

'There might be a message in your life story, dear Innocent,' said King Lyric.

'Oh really,' gushed Innocent. 'Do you think so?'

'Could be,' nodded King Melody.

'Let us prepare the horses and while we are riding to the spa, let's see what we can come up with.'

Innocent stepped inside the caravan and into the sphere of love. The inside was full of light emanating from the windows. There were hearts painted on all of the walls of the caravans. There were plush red seats with heart-shaped pillows. There were even four heart-shaped beds tucked into the corner with beautiful quilts decorated with white doves, draped over them. The walls were adorned with masks decorated with musical notes. On a small desk were four incense candles that filled the air with sweet jasmine smells. Outside the windows were wind chimes blowing in the breeze.

As they made their way to the spa, the boys went to work creating a song for Innocent. She marvelled at how the four brothers worked in perfect harmony and sheer synchronicity to create a composition. After much nodding and note writing they played Innocent her song.

'We call it *In Innocent's Life* smiled King Strummer, who began plucking his string instrument, accompanied by Strummer and Drummer.

King Lyric cleared his throat and began singing –

'There are princes Innocent has courted,
In her life, though some are strange.
Some are weird and totally inappropriate, some are really bad and some insane.
All these princes had their moments, of fun, laughter, joy and pain.
Some she wished she had sent packing and some she wished had remained.

Though she knows she will have an unexplained affection, for all the peculiar princes she has bedded before.
She will often stop and shake her head in disbelief that she ever dated them at all.
In Innocent's life journey she will love even more.
In Innocent's life journey she will love even mmmmmmm mmmmmmmore.'

'You *a mused* me …' Innocent squealed. 'You *a mused* me …' she fluttered as she fainted onto the floor. When she came to, the four brothers were fanning her.

'Princess Innocent we have arrived,' shouted King Drummer, into her face.

She flapped her eyelashes furiously, flirting as fast as she could, never thinking it was possible to fall in love with four men at the same time. They helped her up and ensured she got to her room safely.

'See you tonight Princess,' said King Lyric, 'we will be playing your song.' Each one of them kissed her hand and bowed as they took their leave. Innocent was left star struck and speechless as she walked around her room lost in *La-La Love Land*.

Innocent made sure she had front row seats to the spa show. She gained her fifteen minutes of fame as the Magical Musical Troubadours played her song. Everyone was most impressed at the impression she had left on the musicians. The audience mellowed out to the magical sounds as love filled the air. It was an evening Innocent would never forget.

23
Chief Eagle

'My dear Innocent, as you will be leaving us in two days I would like to invite you to come on a visit with me to see my magical friend, Chief Eagle,' said Baroness Booby Trap one morning.

'It is not every day that I invite a guest to meet the Chief, but I have grown rather fond of you my dear and feel that you would appreciate the experience.

He is descended from an ancient group who were the first nation to live in the New Forest. His ancestors sailed from a faraway kingdom, called Canada, which in their language means large landmass of lovely bilingual people.

They speak their own language that is harmonious with nature, and expressed through wise words, grand gestures and decisive deeds.

You must not be shocked by their wardrobe – their style is *au natural* – skimpy animal skin suites derived from the fruits of the forests and designed to reflect oneness with nature, not naughtiness. They came almost a century ago to share their natural knowledge with the people of It Is What It Is but sadly retreated in haste to the New Forest when they were asked to put some clothes on.

My good friend Eagle is the Chief of his people. He is a Master of the Natural Arts. There is a lot I feel you can learn from him and his people before you depart.'

Innocent was positively excited. She had heard tale of the First Forest Nation, but they were so secretive and selective about whom they let into their territory that very few people had ever seen them. In fact, many folk of The Kingdom believed they were nothing more than a myth.

Booby Trap readied her carriage and together with Innocent made the hour-long journey into the forest alone. They stopped at a large clearing. Innocent had never seen such large majestic and magnificent trees in all of her life. They were even grander than the trees she had seen during her recent extended walk in the forest. Innocent felt as if through the stillness of the trees, they were somehow communicating with her. She was at once struck by the sound of silence that was present around her.

As they stepped out of the carriage a solidly built man, with long dark hair wearing an animal skin, greeted them. He was covered in muscle and moved majestically. Innocent's mouth dropped wide open at the magnificent man standing before her.

'Innocent may I introduce my good friend Chief Eagle. Eagle this is my new friend, Princess Innocent.'

He was a man of few words and he motioned for Innocent and Booby Trap to follow him to his tremendous tepee for tea. Innocent had never seen a tepee before and was struck by its structure. It stood ten feet high and was triangular in shape, covered with what looked like a smooth and shiny animal skin. Emanating from the top were four, large white feathers.

Eagle opened the entrance flap for them and Innocent stepped into a world of wonder. The gentle smoke filling the tepee immediately struck her. The floor was covered with soft animal pelts used for seating. There were at least twelve men and women sitting down, sipping sweet tea, smoking and smudging Sweet Grass.

Innocent was struck by how silent the sitters were. Whenever she had attended a gathering in the past it had always been a noisy affair with people shouting over each other trying to be heard. People talked but barely listened as they impatiently waited for their turn to get their point across. But with these ancient travellers she noticed by the simple smiles and sharing of the pipe that there was a special dialogue being created between these people. She was suddenly overcome with serenity.

Innocent noticed they were passing around a beautifully carved, thick wooden stick, with animal faces carved on them. Booby

Trap explained that this was a council meeting to discuss the current needs of the community. The wooden object was called a Talking Stick. It was passed around the group and whoever wanted to share their words of wisdom would take it, indicating they had something to say. The stick was carved with the figures of the Raven and the Eagle who were ancient symbols of strength and wisdom. They were to remind people to speak their words wisely and sparingly.

'Talking tongues take away from tasks to be done,' said Eagle seriously. 'Once a man's word was worth more than his signature – it was his bond. Now your words are like the *empty jesters* at court – meaningless.

We are a proud nation of *doers* not talkers as are your own people. Innocent must tell her people to stop talking and start doing. The meaning behind words is the *power* of the voice within. Be still and listen and you will become powerful,' he said imploringly, hoping that somehow she could be the channel to pass on his knowledge to her people.

Although she was fascinated by his beautiful words, she did not yet have the capacity to take in all he was saying. She nevertheless nodded and smiled sweetly, wondering if the rather splendid Chief was single. He motioned for her to sit and join the circle.

Innocent's long dress and tight bodice made it a struggle for her to sit. It took her five minutes to join Booby Trap on the floor. As she sat she was handed a pipe. Before she had a chance to smoke it, Eagle showed her how to smudge, by using her hands to direct the smoke over her head.

'Eagle's people believe in the power of smoke to take away all worries, anxieties and illnesses,' the Baroness explained. Innocent had to admit that the smoke made her feel noticeably calmer in her demeanour.

As she mellowed out she was approached by two women with a blanket forming a wall around her. They motioned for her to take off her robes and replace them with a skimpy skin suit that they had brought for her. It consisted of a strip to cover both her boobs and her bum. Innocent was so marvellously mellow that modesty went out the tepee as she put on the skimpy outfit. She looked for her friend but Booby Trap and Eagle had both disappeared.

She had never worn such *barely there* gear in all of her life and felt positively relieved that she had spent the last few months in a spa. She couldn't help notice how liberated she felt not constricted by the constraints of her corset and costume – she could breath! Here she could let it all hang out, without having any hang-ups. As the women took the blanket away, they disappeared along with the twelve other people. Suddenly a supremely studly man in a skin suit walked in carrying a big bowl of what looked like berries and other plants.

He motioned for Innocent to sit down on the animal skins. Having been use to loads of layers of clothing as a cover, Innocent madly manoeuvred her body to ensure she didn't flash the man anything that may cause both of them to blush when she sat down.

After strategically placing her hands over her body, she managed to sit down decently. He proceeded to take his bowl of precious booty and present it to Innocent. 'Medicine for insides and outsides,' he proclaimed as he handed her an aloe vera plant. He showed her how to both drink it and drip it over her skin.

He handed her a long cucumber.

'What I am supposed to do with that?' Innocent asked with a cheeky grin on her face.

'It has many uses,' said the man. He took his knife and chopped the cucumber into two circles and showed her where to place them.

'It's good for producing perfect eyes,' he said proudly.

He then got out some berries and buried them in boiling water and presented Innocent with a tea.

'To calm the tummy,' he said.

Then he produced a vial of oil.

'For me,' he smiled, and drank half. He rubbed the rest on his hands and he motioned for Innocent to lie down, and to her delight proceeded to rub the oil all over her exposed back.

'A marvellous massage,' he said and gave innocent an experience of pleasure she had never known before. As he rubbed and kneaded her body she felt as if she was in heaven and he didn't feel so bad himself. She loved being laidback and felt that within the fruits of the forest she had found her own sanctuary.

After an hour of blatant bliss, Booby Trap returned to the tent. Innocent was slightly perturbed by her interruption. She didn't want these marvellous hands to stop moving. Her magical masseuse stood up and packed up his things and Innocent thanked him for her hour of pleasure.

'Alas my dear it is time for us to go,' said the Baroness, noticing Innocent now had a positively pink glow about her. Booby Trap picked up the blanket so Innocent could get dressed. When Eagle joined them Innocent asked if she could keep the skimpy skin suit. What a kinky carnal costume it will make for my future frolics, she thought to herself.

Chief Eagle escorted Innocent and the Baroness to their carriage. He pulled out a large white Eagle Feather and presented it to the Princess.

'The eagle flies closest to the sun. He shares his feathers as a gift – a reminder that Mother Earth's bounty brings the exhilaration of the reaching the mountain top to us all when we appreciate that all we need to be happy and healthy surrounds us. When you are feeling melancholy in body or spirit, sit still among the nurturing nuances of nature and let her heal you.'

Innocent took the delicate feather and examined it and was deeply moved. She had never acknowledged or appreciated Mother Nature before and felt positively humbled to be in her presence through the eloquence of Eagle. She thought of all the trees that had been felled in the Borough of Look At Me to make room for wider roads, posh palaces, palatial gardens and commemorative statues, and felt a sudden sense of shame. As their carriage pulled away, both Innocent and Booby Trap rode in silence and serenity.

The three months Innocent had spent in the spa were some of the best moments she had ever experienced in her entire life. She had been in her element and for the first time in a long time felt like the truly beautiful Princess that she really was. She felt royally renewed. Her skin was glowing, her extra weight had shifted and her thighs and buttocks were rock hard. She was happier than she had ever been. She was a picture of health. As Baroness Booby Trap waved her off, Innocent assured her she would continue to follow the healthy path.

When Innocent returned home, she resolved to maintain her focus on healthy living. She stocked her apartments with healthy food and went for long walks. However, by the third week without the support of the Baroness, she returned to her old ways of skipping breakfast, sleep, sound nutrition and solitary walks. Within five weeks her solid thighs and buttocks were soft and she lost her resolve. She was relieved when she was able to find focus in a new project – Prince Rescue Me.

Best Supporting Actress in a Starring Role

24
Prince Rescue Me

'Dar– darling, you must allow me to take you for a café tomorrow to repay your k–kindness,' said a rather woozy Prince Rescue Me, thus beginning Innocent's penultimate dysfunctional relationship.

Although he was a year younger than Innocent, in terms of pain and suffering he was at least ten years older. He was quite frankly a mess – spending most of his time *making misery* in the taverns of the Boulevard of Broken Promises.

He had also developed an unfortunate *Crummy Cracker* addiction. A concoction of chemical laden coco leaves, in a toasted cracker. The morish morsel gave whoever consumed it an instant rush of invincibility and merriment. The concoction sent the consumer racing around at breakneck speed losing all sense of reason. The rush was so heady that for whoever crunched the Crummy Cracker – one was too many, and a thousand was never enough.

Within the taverns, Rescue Me could always find a Cracker Tout and spent most of his paltry Privy Purse on them.

When he had no more money to buy the Crackers, he pawned anything of value that he owned including his saddle – which made riding a house rather uncomfortable, his ceremonial crown and family silver. He often associated himself with dubious characters in exchange for the means to feed his Crummy Cracker cravings.

Innocent met Prince Rescue Me when she was volunteering at the first aid station of the Royal Jousting Tournament. It had been recommended as a good place to meet princes, so she happily offered up her services. When Rescue Me had fallen over a barrel and grazed his leg, she administered first aid to him. Despite his rather dishevelled appearance and dozy demeanour, she found him rather cute. He had chiselled cheekbones and a strong chin. He had sad, soulful, brown eyes.

When he suggested they meet for café the next day, she jumped at the chance. She offered to pick him up in her carriage and when she arrived for their date, he was asleep. When his footman aroused him and told him a beautiful Princess was awaiting him – he couldn't remember ever meeting her. However after being assured that she was definitely worth the effort, Rescue Me got ready for their date.

When he was sober, Rescue Me could be very charming and Innocent became enamoured with the handsome Prince, who made her laugh. Could this be my *One True Prince*, she pondered.

A few missed engagements and two very glazed pupils later, Innocent discovered that all was not well in *paradise* as she uncovered his unfortunate Crummy Cracker addiction. Sensing his vulnerability, she felt sorry for him and decided that he was a perfect match for her immense desire to care for a man, and resolved to straighten him out. After all, he came from one of the best and oldest royal families in The Kingdom and he lived in one of the most historic castles ever built. She believed he had the pedigree to be a truly great man given half a chance. Besides that, any suitor that could make her laugh the way he did was worth the work.

In a moment of clarity, Prince Rescue Me alerted Innocent to the perils of courting him.

'I warn you dearest, I am hard work as many beautiful ladies before you will attest. I shall break your heart and it will all end in tears.' But despite his warnings Innocent convinced herself that this Prince was a fix-a-upper, whom *only she* could remodel.

When it became obvious that he had a paltry Privy Purse she decided to subsidize his income to ensure he maintained the standard of living that she thought he deserved. She bought him a new saddle and when he started crying because he could not get his favourite crown back from the Ye Local Trade-In Shoppe, she gave him the money to get it back, which he preceded to spend on more Crummy Crackers.

Innocent resolved that it would be best if Prince Rescue Me refrained from eating Crackers. So she went through all his castle cupboards and emptied all the Crummy Cracker boxes she could find, throwing them into the castle moat where they unfortunately ended up in the jaws of the small crocodiles inhabiting the water. Bouncing off the moat rockery, the crocodiles went on a Crummy induced frenzy through the Chiefly City as Rescue Me jumped into the water desperately looking for even a soggy Cracker to consume.

With not even a soggy Cracker in sight, Rescue Me boiled over with rage.

'How *dare* you touch my Crackers!' he screamed at her. 'Get out of my castle now!'

'You don't mean that,' said Innocent with tears in her eyes.

'Oh yes I do, get out I *never* want to see you again.'

She ran home in floods of tears, convinced it was the end of their relationship. However, realizing that she had become a vital link in his Crummy Cracker supply chain and that she was the only means to pay off his Dodgy Dope Dealer debts, Rescue Me sent a note to her apologizing for his outburst.

Never had she taken care of anyone before and became immensely proud of how well she performed. For the first time ever, she understood how a mother must feel!

Prince Rescue Me had a regular routine. He was fine for a little while, becoming the gallant Prince that Innocent always knew he could be, but eventually slipped back to his old weary ways.

Once in a moment of clarity, he let Innocent take him on a romantic visit to The City of Love in The Kingdom of Beautiful by Design. It was a city like no other with a thousand canals meandering meticulously and magically. Anyone who visited the city could not help but fall in love. The Master Craftsmen of Love had built it 200 years previously. They had come to create a city that communicated the emotion of love through architecture, design and artistry. The energy of love was so strong in the city that camaraderie and community calibrated at the highest level of any city in the world. Both Innocent and Rescue Me could not but help feel the love.

In such a place of love, Rescue Me blossomed. He chartered a gondola and they cruised around the great city, cuddling and chatting about all their future plans. He gave Innocent the gift of laughter as they giggled their way around the city. Innocent felt as if she had found paradise.

One day she went out shopping alone and discovered the most beautiful diamond ring, dotted with an array of small gems – rubies, emeralds and sapphires. She retrieved her Privy Purse and purchased it, certain that she would soon be wearing it on her left hand. When she returned to the villa where they were staying she showed Rescue Me her find.

It made her feel profusely proud that she had persisted with her Prince and this was her reward. When he proclaimed himself a fool for her, Innocent bought him a fanciful Fool's Mask.

'When we move in together this mask will adorn our bedroom wall to remind us of this magical moment,' the Prince proclaimed. But as soon as they returned, Rescue Me put the mask up on *his* wall and the promise vanished forever as he vaulted into the vortex of his Crummy Cracker addiction. It wasn't long before Rescue Me retrieved Innocent's ring from her drawers and behind her back sold it to feed his Crummy Cracker cravings.

Knowing Innocent's dire disapproval, he attempted to hide his return to true mucked-up form. One night, in the guise of a night of playful fun he blindfolded the playful Princess. As she waited in anticipation and arousal, the Prince went to work on his Crackers.

'I am coming shortly my darling,' he reassured her as he stood by the open window satisfying his Cracker cravings and not Innocent. After waiting patiently for half an hour, Innocent fell asleep and the Prince went on a search and rescue cracker mission.

When Innocent awoke she had forgotten she was wearing a blindfold and thought something terrible had befallen her eyesight in the night. As she felt her way through both the bedding and Cracker crumbs, she fumbled and fell off the bed. She lay terrified on the floor both blinded and blindsided by Rescue Me's deception. Luckily for Innocent, the castle cleaning lady found her on the floor and removed her blindfold, shedding light on the situation.

Things would take a decidedly dire direction when depleted of capital for Crackers, Rescue Me would rummage through Innocent's belongings, taking things of value that he could use to barter for his precious booty. The Prince was a talented taker and Innocent lost a diamond tiara, several gold coins, a pair of silver candlesticks, a crystal chandelier, a gold-plated mantle clock and a charm bracelet. She resorted to barring Rescue Me from her rooms, and when she stayed over at his castle, was careful to sleep with her door keys under her pillow so he could not gain access to her home.

Rescue Me now owed debts to the Dodgy Dope Dealers on a regular basis, and having no patience for postponed payments, they often held him for a royal ransom. He would be held in a dark dungeon and a directive would be dispatched demanding repayment from Innocent. As she was decidedly attached to the Prince, she repaid his debts from her Privy Purse in full.

This Crummy Cracker consumption continued for over a year causing Innocent to eventually crumble. She could no longer compete with his morish mistress. She went into the local library and took out a scroll on crushing Cracker compulsion. It recommended that the only known cure was an extended stay in the Royal Rehab Retreat.

She dispatched a messenger to the governor of the Royal Rehab Retreat requesting an urgent intervention for Prince Rescue Me. She was ecstatic when she received a reply that they had an immediate opening for her Prince.

Innocent went to work making all the arrangements. She packed Rescue Me's robes, put money in his pocket and arranged for a wagon to take him to the Royal Rehab Retreat. After spending the whole day organizing, she had the feeling she was forgetting something.

It wasn't until Prince Rescue Me's bags were loaded onto the carriage that she realized she had forgotten to tell Rescue Me that he was going to Royal Rehab. She asked the carriage driver to wait and went on a search and rescue mission to recover her Prince. She hadn't seen him all day, which meant only one thing – he was making merry in the Boulevard of Broken Promises. She headed down there and found him in the Get Hammered Public House, passed out over a tankard of rye and a pile of Crummy Crackers.

She sent for his trusty footman who carried him to the carriage awaiting him. Prince Rescue Me opened his eyes briefly.

'Dearest, dar—,' he hiccupped as he slumped back in the carriage.

Innocent launched into her goodbye speech.

'I have booked you into the Royal Rehab Retreat. Your Cracker crunching and ale drinking have got to stop. It is wearing me out and is bringing chaos to your castle. Your Privy Purse is spent. All your horses have no saddles. Your cooks have no ingredients and have gone on strike. Your royal flush is no longer working and there is no money for the royal plungers to provide relief. To put it quite bluntly, your castle is now full of shit. It's a mess and if you don't sort yourself out there will be no castle to come back to.

Do you understand what I am telling you?' she yelled into his ear.

'Yes my darrrrr … ' mumbled Rescue Me, barely able to open one eye.

Innocent shook her head and sent the Prince on his way.

25
Master Tao

The Royal Rehab Retreat Programme lasted for fifty-nine days. Panicking that it would not be enough time to restore order to his castle, from the moment Rescue Me departed, Innocent ran herself ragged repairing the mess he had left behind. Convincing herself that upon his release a proposal would be imminent, she went about fixing up the castle that she regarded as her future marital home.

She opened her Privy Purse strings and sent for the royal plungers to relieve the royal flush. She paid for all the castle saddles to be replaced and replenished the castle larders. It took the striking cooks seven days in total to return to the kitchen, during which time, in a bid to keep the household staff from departing, Innocent mastered the art of plate spinning as she substituted herself for the kitchen staff – after all she could not let her beloved return to a castle without household staff to help care for him.

Innocent proudly produced poultry, meat, dairy, dessert, vegetable and fish dishes which were so delicious that the household staff sent the striking cooks on a wild goose chase so they would stay away from the kitchen a few days longer. Soon Innocent's own Privy Purse was considerably lighter than when she began her courtship.

A few months before she had packed Rescue Me off to rehab – during one of his rare moments of clarity – she had invited his mother, Queen Compensation for a visit. Anxious to impress her *future mama-in-law*, she had worn herself out trying to make everything *appear* perfect. Unbeknownst to Innocent she had not needed to try so hard, as Compensation was simply impressed that she was willing to take on her son. The Queen would have been happy with *just* a cup of tea!

Deciding that his mother would make a wonderful ally in her quest for marriage, Innocent decided to prove herself worthy to the Queen by taking care of Rescue Me's castle all by herself. Even when she began to crumble under the strain, she refused to ask his mother for help, deciding it better to be a *marriageable martyr* than risk her future mother-in-law thinking her not capable of taking care of a husband and home.

By day twenty-five, her hands were full of calluses and she had dark circles under her eyes. When she gazed in the mirror she hardly recognized herself. Worst of all she had suddenly developed a shooting, searing pain in her shoulder and back and could barely move. The pain was so intense that she chewed her nails to stop her from crying out in despair.

She sent for the physician immediately who prescribed morphemic medicine for her malady. Innocent popped the potion to ease the pain, but after two weeks all it had managed to produce was a stoned and sick feeling in her head and stomach. For the first time, she felt as if she was in Rescue Me's soiled shoes. In fact Innocent felt so rotten from the nasty narcotic that she wondered what Rescue Me ever saw in getting stoned in the first place.

By day thirty-nine, she was feeling so bad that she dispatched a message to her dear friend Baroness Booby Trap. If anyone would know what to do to make her feel better, her *healthful* friend would!

By day forty-three, Innocent had received a reply –

My dearest Innocent
I am so sorry to hear of your sore and searing back. I have dispatched a messenger to my good friend Master Tao. He comes from the Eastern Kingdoms where they have been practicing magical medicine for millenniums. If anyone can cure what ails you, this maestro of medicine can. I have asked for him to visit you tomorrow.

Wishing you renewed health
Baroness Booby Trap.

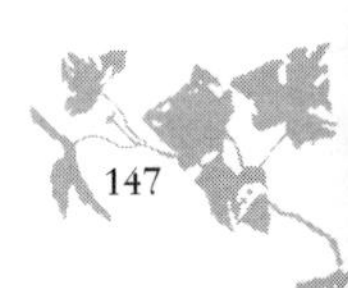

Relieved that she would finally get some relief, Innocent slept soundly for the first time in days. The next day Innocent's page showed Master Tao into her boudoir. She had never met anyone from the Eastern Kingdoms before.

She remembered Baron Booty telling her of his wondrous adventures when he had dropped anchor there. He had told tale of how the number 8 was revered in the Eastern Kingdoms and people organized their lives around the lucky number. He spoke of grand garrisons of soldiers carrying 8 swords of all shapes and sizes. Pagoda palaces piled 8 levels high, 8 tea varieties, and colourful costumes with 8 colours. They used wooden cutlery that came in box sets of 8 sticks. He had explained that everyone engaged in mindful meditations repeated 8 times daily accompanied by slow motion, morning manoeuvres, and consisting of 8 sprightly steps.

Master Tao walked over to Innocent and nodded gently to her. 'The Baroness has told me of your difficulty. I am confident that within one week I can help you achieve good health once more.'

The Master fascinated her. He had a peaceful and calming energy that she had not experienced since her visit to Chief Eagle's people. These ancient peoples must know something that we don't, she thought to herself.

He asked Innocent to lie on her stomach. He gently put his hands on her back. The horizontal Princess almost jumped off the bed as he prodded the point of pain.

'We must learn to listen to our bodies as they communicate with us through the signal of pain. Your body is telling you that you need to relax. Your back is so stiff that your energy flow has been restricted. That is why you feel discomfort and pain. Tell me what has troubled your body enough to tell you to back off?'

Innocent spun her sorry tale of Rescue Me's woes and her attempt to fix him. As she unburdened herself she felt her back pain ease slightly.

'My dear Princess, I see that you have been carrying a great burden on your back which has now broken you. It is time that you learned to separate Rescue Me's load from your own. A rescuer often absorbs the pain they attempt to remove from a loved one. Rescue Me's emotional pain has become your physical pain! You must learn to refrain from being Rescue Me's *busybody* and be Innocent's instead.'

Innocent nodded to the wise Master, willing to follow any advice that would relieve her from her suffering. Tao continued:

'You must learn to talk to your body. Focus on your point of pain and tell it to relax. Tell your body to go from tension to relaxation.'

'Hello dear *back* – this is Innocent speaking. You have nothing to worry about. Prince Rescue Me is safely tucked away at the Royal Rehab Retreat. You can now take a deep breath. He can't take your things, lie to you or disappear for days on end. He is safe and so are you. You have nothing to worry yourself over. Just relax.'

'Very good Innocent, I can feel your back relaxing already. Tomorrow I will come to visit you again. After 8 treatments in 8 days your back with be in working order again.' And with that he bid her and her back adieu.

For 8 days Innocent mastered the art of talking to her body. She became so good at talking to herself that by day fifty-two of Rescue Me's programme she had talked her pain into leaving her body.

'Master Tao you are indeed a miracle of modern medicine. How can I ever thank you for releasing me from the clutches of pain? I am forever in your debt and will remember your words of wisdom always.'

'You have done well, my dear Princess, remember to tell your body to relax 8 times daily for maintenance. Don't just wait for pain to occur. May you learn to carry a lesser load and may your life be a little lighter.' And with that the blessed Master Tao bowed his head and departed to help another.

Innocent spent the next three days in bed sleeping. Her sleep had been severely interrupted and she was desperate to catch up.

By day fifty-six Innocent finally got out of bed and looked at herself in the mirror. She was shocked by her appearance. Her

hair was matted, her skin pale and pimply and she had packed on the pounds. Her nails were broken and chewed up.

She had only three days to prepare for Rescue Me's return and she panicked at her pimply predicament. She told both herself and her back, that her appearance would not matter to her new and improved Prince. He would understand the sacrifices and sufferings she had made in order to help him.

She made final preparations at the castle to ensure it was in perfect order for the Prince's arrival. As she was preparing herself, she heard a horse canter up outside. She rushed down expecting to greet her Prince, but instead it was a messenger sent from the Director of the Royal Rehab Retreat.

Innocent opened the scroll which was addressed to *Loved Ones and Significant Others of Rescue Me*.

Here are a handful of helpful hints to assist your loved ones in continued sobriety:

1. *If your Prince falls off the wagon, please return to the above address.*
2. *Please allow your Prince to launder his own garments.*
3. *Please return the responsibility of your Prince's Privy Purse to his possession.*
4. *Please ensure your Prince attends the local chapter of SIN (safety in numbers) for group support, as soon as possible.*
5. *Please ensure you attend your local chapter of EE (Exhausted Enablers) as soon as possible.*
6. *Please look into why you have attracted and added a Cracker addict to your repertoire of royal romances.*
7. *Please ensure your Prince avoids any of the following stressful situations for the next year – tournaments and jousting competitions, royal balls, card games, walking past ale houses, walking down the aisle …*

Innocent paused from reading. Surely they can't mean that she has to wait another whole year to marry the Prince? Hadn't she waited long enough already?

Just then Rescue Me pulled up in his carriage and upon seeing her, sprang sprightly from his seat. 'Innocent darling, how delightful it is to see you on this auspicious day

As he looked her up and down he was shocked by her appearance. 'How tired you look, and your beautiful hair is so unkempt. What has happened to you?' Mortified, she pulled her hand away.

'If you must know I have been run ragged, ensuring your castle was in perfect order for your return. As a result, I have been flat out on my bed with a bad back. I have barely had a moments rest in the fifty-nine days you were retreating.

'Oh you silly darling Princess we have staff for that kind of thing. Come to think of it you look like one of the staff at the moment,' and he broke out in fits of giggles.

She had hoped that rehab would make him a more giving person but alas here he was fifty-nine days later and he couldn't even give a compliment, she thought – feeling discomfort in her back once again.

'Come my darling let us go inside and I will tell you all about my plans to sail solo on an expedition for the next year.'

Innocent could not believe what she was hearing. 'What do you mean sail solo?'

'My darling only by solitude and serenity can true soul-searching be discovered. A year is not long to wait and upon my return we can meet up for a café and perhaps even resume our royal romancing.'

She was fuming. 'Me – m – meet for a café! Wh – What about my marriage proposal? You need to stay here and honour your commitment to me! I have been a patient Princess for long enough, it's time you made your move,' she screamed, indignant.

Prince Rescue Me seemed surprised. 'My dear Innocent I never thought you could be so selfish, you should be supporting me in my sobriety, not pressuring me to propose to you. After all, I never made you such a promise.'

Innocent was livid and his particular use of the word *selfish* rang in her ears like a giant bell. 'Selfish … selfish … selfish you say.'

'Well yes, quite frankly my dear Innocent and if you cannot understand then I feel it is best that we not meet for a café. Besides, I have been advised to walk away from any female fraternization.'

'Advised to walk away! Well I should have been the one to do that month's ago!' she screamed incredulously.

With that she turned on her heels humiliated and hurt, royally regretting that she had not heeded his earlier warnings about how much work he actually was. She suddenly became depressed realizing that her listening skills hadn't improved much since being with Baron Press.

As she berated herself she did not hear Rescue Me calling out to her. 'We will always have The City of Love. You have been a good friend and I won't forget you!'

'Don't worry my dear back, we don't want him back, everything will be okay,' she repeated over and over to herself all the way home.

26
Prince Good

After the demise of her relationship with Rescue Me, Innocent felt angrier than she had ever known herself to be. She had never worked so hard on a *project* in her entire life and could not believe that all the effort and gold she had put into Rescue Me could no longer be recouped. Innocent felt duped by her own duplicity. She swore off men deciding distrust of any future dates would now become *order of the day*. For the first time in her life Innocent developed a hard shell as her bitterness began to set in.

Three months after she had parted ways with Rescue Me she was sitting having a farmer's lunch at the local tavern – seeing how the other half lived – when a handsome prince approached her.

'Madam, may I present myself? I am Prince Good. Would you allow me the honour to sit in your company for lunch? It does not seem right that such a beautiful lady as yourself should be sitting solo in this public house.' He gave Innocent a sweeping bow.

Innocent looked up from her plate of food rather disinterested. I bet he says that to all of the princesses he meets, Innocent cynically thought to herself.

'Please yourself, sir.'

And with that Prince Good sat down. 'Pray tell me your name?'

What is he after? She thought

'My name is Princess Innocent,' she replied, staring coldly into the handsome Prince's face.'

'What a perfect name for such a perfect Princess.'

'Oh *Please*, I wonder how many times he has used that line,' Innocent muttered under her breath. The Prince was so enamoured he did not hear her display of cynicism.

'My dear lady, won't you do me the honour of letting me call upon you tomorrow and take you to the theatre?'

'If you insist,' said Innocent, smiling falsely. All the while thinking that she would say anything for a quiet lunch!

When Prince Good called on Innocent the next day, she was indeed surprised. So much so, that she had not even bothered to get ready, convincing herself that he was just another insincere suitor.

Determined not to become attached to Good, she kept him at arm's length throughout the date. In fact she insisted that they sit several seats from each other in the theatre. This constrained conversation considerably as Prince Good had to commandeer his messenger to communicate to Innocent.

Prince Good put Innocent's behaviour down to a demure demeanour and was more captivated than ever. He asked her out again, this time taking her for a long carriage drive around the park. He bought her blankets to keep her warm and cushions to keep her comfortable. He was, Innocent had to admit, one of the nicest Princes she had ever met and she began to warm to him.

Innocent enjoyed several more outings with Prince Good and her hard shell began to crumble. After four weeks of steady courtship, he made arrangements to take Innocent to one of the finest eating establishments in the city. He told her he would arrange for a carriage to pick her up and he would meet her at the establishment. Innocent had just finished getting ready when Prince Good's messenger came knocking on her door. He handed her a note.

Innocent could feel her back become stiff and her blood begin to boil. Before she even opened the note she convinced herself that whatever was written in the message was a lie, covering up for a mistress or a wife. She began to be angry with herself for trusting yet another prince as she read the letter –

My darling Innocent, I am running an hour late as I am attending to urgent business. I will send my carriage to pick you up in one hour. I fear an extra hour is like a lifetime away from you. I cannot bear to wait to see my lovely lady.

Yours always
Prince Good
XXXXXXXX

'Urgent business indeed, said Innocent loudly, as she stomped around her room.

'He is a *fool* if he thinks he can fool me. I can tell he is insincere by his inadequate amount of kisses.'

She decided that he had stood her up and she started to get undressed and readied herself for bed. Even when the carriage driver came knocking on her door, she was so angry at Good that she decided not even to answer.

An hour later the worried Prince came knocking frantically upon her door. 'My darling Innocent please let me in so I know that you are not ill.'

Innocent put a robe on her and answered the door. 'Oh I didn't expect to see you here.'

'What do you mean my love? Did you not get my message?'

'Yes, but I came to the conclusion that as you had already broken your word to me about the time of our meeting, you would break your word again to me and not show up.'

'My dear Innocent I am grieved that I have led you to doubt my sincerity. Please let me make it up to you, by taking you out for dinner tomorrow?'

Innocent half-heartedly agreed, but the damage was done. She no longer trusted the Prince. Sensing her disappointment and feeling dejected Good decided that he was not yet worthy of Innocent's hand and put the ring away that he had just purchased – now the cause of the distance between them.

For the next month the Prince arranged more outings. Despite the fact that Good was true to his word, Innocent found herself mistrusting him even more. She told herself that if something was too good to be true it usually was – and continued to keep him at arm's length.

Prince Good could sense the distance between them and did everything in his power to close the gap between them. He wined, dined and timed her, always ensuring he arrived when he said he would. He wrote beautiful sonnets to her expressing his undying love and commitment. He even bought her chocolates daily. But alas, when even chocolates could not penetrate her heart, he knew their relationship was doomed. Heartbroken he concluded that Innocent's shell was impregnable.

With tears in his eyes he came to Innocent's apartments one day.

'My darling Innocent, these past three months I have truly grown to love you. Alas, instead of rejoicing at our rendezvous, I lament at the low level of esteem you hold for me. You constantly look for the bad in me, when I wish nothing more for you to see the real Prince Good that I am. I feel a failure in your eyes and fear your lack of faith will flatten me. I therefore must bid you a sad farewell so you can find a more worthy Prince.'

He kissed Innocent's hand and walked away leaving Innocent crushed. At that moment she realized that she had found the Prince she had always been searching for only to push him away – led by her assumptions. In her folly, she had brought her fears into being which had brought her relationship to breaking point. She collapsed in a fit of tears, swearing off princes forever.

27
Innocent Eats Cake

The next relationship Innocent had was with cake. After Prince Good – coming on the heels of Prince Rescue Me – she was emotionally exhausted. The pooped Princess had run out of steam and turned to cake for comfort.

Innocent loved the instant high found in the first bite of a piece of cake. It provided a euphoric feeling, a momentary munch of pleasure, a royal rush to the head. As long as Innocent indulged in cake she had no need for princely pleasures.

In many kingdoms cake had historically been used for therapeutic purposes. An empress who suggested that peasants eat cake to calm their nerves in times of trouble had established the practice.

Cake became Innocent's only comfort for her woes and her cake fetish developed into a full scale feeding frenzy. Morning, noon and night Innocent crammed her cakehole with as much cake as she could have delivered from the local bakery. It didn't matter what cake was on offer – Fairy, Angel, Marble, Black Forest, Chocolate or Cheese – Innocent wasn't fussy, as long as it tarted up the taste buds with sweetness and succulence.

Unfortunately, it didn't take long for her thighs to resemble an unbaked, lumpy cake batter. Gazing in her mirror one day, Innocent had never known such plumpness. Her princely partings had always caused her to shed pounds, now she was shedding dresses. Her curves now had curves and to her dismay she had to purchase a new plus-size wardrobe, at Ye Size Six Shoppe.

'Oh the shame the shame,' she cried. 'What will mother say?'

Reluctantly Innocent gave up her cake and started filling herself up with her new compulsion – *The Help Yourself Movement*.

28
Innocent Seeks Self-help

Without her cake fix to fulfil her, Innocent became fixated on all her fallings and flaws. She was worriedly wondering if there was something seriously wrong with her. Why had she had such awful woes in her pursuit of princely pleasures? What was she doing wrong? She began to dangerously doubt herself. She started to scrutinize herself from head to foot. She critiqued the way she looked, the way she walked, the way she styled her locks, the way she danced, the way she wore her garments and even the way she spoke her words. She was beside herself, believing she was badly below par.

She visited her royal physician and pleaded with him to cure her of her ills. He gave her a Confidence Potion, which she was to take daily. While it did manage to perk her up, it had the unfortunate side effect of rendering her so sleepy that she spent most of her time in slumber.

After two weeks of serious sleepiness, Innocent could take no more. The cure was worse than the ailment she thought, and threw the potion down the royal flush.

A friend suggested that she seek solace from the burgeoning *Help Yourself Movement*. It was run by a professional guild of practitioners who were Masters of the Persuasive Arts. They provided sagely advice and wisdom to those in need. Their marketing motto was: *depend on us to be independently happy.*

The Help Yourself Movement provided many paths and possibilities for people to partake in. There were many learning centres where the populace could go to participate in a number of programmes and therapies. These places were a perfect respite for people like Innocent who had lost their own centre. She went through a list of courses, confident that one of them could help her chart a new course in her life.

The first lessons she purchased were based on a new therapy called *Speed Spending*. It consisted of power shopping, whereby one would purchase prolifically over a period of time as a perfect distraction from the pain of life.

Innocent leaned how to become a powerful Ye Shopper. She got out her Privy Purse and parted with her money at breakneck speed, spending seriously on new apparel, jewels, sweet smelling scents, shiny shoes, spa treatments, colourful face paints, chocolates and cakes. Her mews house became so packed with her shopping spoils that she had to charter a room from her neighbours for storage.

At first she experienced exhilaration with each purchase, but the joy was fleeting as Innocent became aware that no item or accessory could permanently fill her heart. Looking around her heaving rooms she realized that she had more baggage than ever before. The only thing not heaving was her Privy Purse!

Next Innocent decided to visit a new progressive type of therapy centre called a Hair Salon. It had been started by a renowned barber called Count Cut and Paste, who recognized the benefits of providing a sanctuary where broken people could get both a new haircut and advice which got to the root of their problems.

Feeling perhaps a new hairdo was just what she needed, she wrote to Count Cut and Paste explaining her situation. When she arrived for her appointment she was greeted by the fabulously flamboyant Count who had flaming red hair and a flowing cape. He greeted Innocent with enthusiasm.

'Princess Innocent, please let me look at you.' He stood silently scanning her from head to toe. He spent five minutes surveying his subject. She began to feel extremely self-conscious. He held up both his hands and facing Innocent, framed her face with them.

'Hmm … I see … hmm … yes … yes … that is it … aha … yes, yes that's it,' he said ominously as Innocent waited anxiously for his verdict.

She tried to speak but he quickly cut her off.

'Please my dear Princess, an artist must not be interrupted while surveying the situation,' he said seriously.

He held his arm out to Innocent and led her to a special throne with wheels and helped her sit down. Innocent was forced to face a large mirror the size of which she had never seen. It seemed to magnify every pore and blemish. Staring at herself, Innocent felt she was definitely not the fairest of them all. She could now sympathize with the Queen from the Fairy Tale Land Press, whose disagreeable mirror turned her into a homicidal maniac.

'My dear Princess as you can see you are indeed a beauty, but there is always room for improvement. I would suggest that a new cut and colour will be just the trick to make you stand out amongst the crowd and get noticed by your *One True Prince*.'

Before Innocent had time to answer, he had wrapped a large black cape around her neck and wheeled her away from the mirror. He went to work with his scissors leaving Innocent to nervously look at her lovely brown locks falling onto the floor.

After he finished cutting he brought out some hair dye, a new product from the Eastern Kingdoms.

'It is *henna* and it will give your hair a shiny hue – just the thing to turn princely heads.'

He spent over two hours covering her head with the dye. Innocent was so relaxed she went into a deep sleep. She woke up after three hours.

'Ah Princess, you awake just in time to see my finished product.' He wheeled her chair to the giant mirror. Innocent looked up and let out a scream. There staring back at her in abject horror was a Princess with pink puffy hair!

'Now you are a Princess who will attract real attention. You will stand out from the crowd.' Count Cut and Paste gushed oblivious to Innocent's horror.'

'My hair–my hair!' she screamed. 'What have you done to my hair? You have ruined my lovely hair. Oh the horror, the horror of it all, my life is over. What am I to do? I will become a laughing stock and I will never be courted again. I will be solo forever. I can never show my face again. Oh my hair, my hair my kingdom for my hair. Out, out damn pink! I demand you do something. Do something NOW, NOW, NOW,' yelled Innocent, hysterically.

'What a *Drama Queen*,' said the Count, clearly not amused by Innocent's behaviour.

'Do you mean to say that you do not like my creation?' he said coldly to her.

Innocent glared at him. 'What do you think? This is positively the worst style I have ever had. I absolutely hate it and demand you reverse this disaster!'

The Count threw down his scissors. 'Madam you have insulted me. I am Count Cut and Paste, the most renowned barber in the land. You have mocked my creation and broken my heart. I must retire to my boudoir and put my ego back together.' And with his hand clutched over his heart, he made a hasty retreat.

'Where are you going? You stupid man, I demand that you come back and fix me,' screamed Innocent, her face now as pink as her hair. Innocent had never been so angry. Her hair had always been her crowning glory and this moron had sullied it.

'Did you call me … st … st … stupid? Oh my, I have never been so insulted, I … I feel faint … I must sit down … oh … oh … somebody … catch me, catch me … ' and with that the Count collapsed in a heap on the floor.

What a bloody Drama Queen, thought Innocent, and with that she stepped over the Count and screamed at him.

'I demand you get up and fix my hair or you will be sorry!' Innocent picked up the scissors and started to wave them at the semi-conscious Cut and Paste.

He opened his eyes and stared in horror at the mad woman standing over him armed with a pair of scissors.

'Help! Help!' he screamed and started crawling away from Innocent on his hands and knees. 'Don't hurt me, don't hurt me,' he pleaded.

'Get up, get up!' she screamed at him, only to have the Count faint again.

Innocent shook her head and dropped the scissors.

'You will be hearing from my legal counsel!' she screamed at the unconscious Count. And with that she grabbed his cape and put it over her hair and ran to her carriage.

She got home and immediately dispatched a message to her good friend All The Best Princes. If anyone could help her with this dodgy do, he could.

By the time All The Best Princes arrived with Prince Buff Innocent was hysterical. This was by far the worst thing to befall her. How would a man ever look at her again without laughing?

'Darling Innocent, in a few months the pink hair will have grown out and you will be back to your beautiful self,' reassured All The Best Princes trying desperately not to keep staring at her frazzled pink hair.

'A few *months* you say! But what am I supposed to do in the meantime – hide myself away?' she cried, tears streaming down her face.

'No my precious, we have an alternative solution. We have bought a wig for you to wear while you are waiting,' and he pulled out a long blonde wig, which he placed on Innocent's head.

'Darling you look divine. You will now be able to let us know if blondes indeed have more fun.'

Innocent looked at her blonde self in the mirror and decided that she looked rather good. Maybe things were not so bad after all. This could even be a blessing in disguise, giving her the boost she had been looking for.

She noticed that as a blonde she did indeed get more attention. She had more requests for courting than ever before, usually by men more interested in talking to her chest than to her. She also noticed that in general people communicated differently with her. They often spoke very loud and slow, often using grand hand gestures to explain themselves. She also noticed how often women would glare at her, especially if she was in the vicinity of their husbands. After a couple of weeks Innocent decided that life as a blonde was not for her and she purchased a brunette wig which she wore until her own brown locks grew back.

After realizing a new do was not the answer, she resumed her quest for the perfect *Help Yourself Path*. She registered excessively and compulsively for every therapy, class or lecture that was available, determined that one would give her the answers she was looking for.

There was:

✓ *teach me, I can't do it myself.*
✓ *take my money.*
✓ *preach what I don't practice.*
✓ *how to feel even worse about your life: bringing on guilt fear and depression.*
✓ *it's your parents fault!!!*
✓ *it's a miserable life!*
✓ *I'm ok and you are definitely not.*
✓ *it's our way or no way.*
✓ *we are right and everyone else is completely wrong.*
✓ *forget reality, come live in the clouds.*
✓ *are you completely stupid?*
✓ *how to spend the rest of your life analysing yourself and getting nowhere in the process!*
✓ *learn how to make money by lecturing people about what is wrong with them.*

And her personal favourite: ✔ *WE ARE NOT A CULT!*

Although each class had a different name, Innocent found that each of them had the same elements of charging excessively for constant self-analysis and self-criticism led by self-important people.

There were several techniques using smoke and mirrors that the Help Yourself Movement engaged people in to help them feel better about themselves. Innocent tried several of these including:

1. Self-flagellation techniques, where she learned to use a horse whip to hit her back and shoulders as she recited all the mistakes she had ever made in her personal life while standing in front of a mirror. She found this to be a rather painful experience and decided it was not quite what she was looking for.

2. Walking on hot ashes as a preventative measure to mirror the pain one would feel if they continued to pursue the wrong path. Innocent learned that she had a high tolerance level to pain and was immensely proud.

3. Gazing at oneself in a giant mirror demonstrating protestations of self-love for hours upon end. Many people used this technique as a great tool to help them form a career on the stage. Innocent found she had a real talent for mirror performing and thought perhaps she should pursue a career as an actress.

4. Spending seven days visiting divorce courts and seeing the end results of looking for love in all the wrong places. These were particularly popular with people who were pleased to see there were others more miserable than they were. Innocent breathed a sigh of relief knowing that could have easily have been her if she had ended up with any of her unsuitable suitors.

5. The tug-of-war for people who were unable to come to satisfactory conclusions in major disputes. Here people could gain back their dignity by engaging in a tug-of-war, where the loser would end up in the mud and the winner claimed the right to be right. Innocent found these competitions highly amusing watching people lose their self-respect as they were pulled into the mud.

6. Planting roses in one's garden and window box so one can stop and smell the roses every day. This became one of Innocent's favourite techniques as she became rather attached to her beautiful red rose that she had grown and nurtured. As she cared for her rose daily, she couldn't help but think of what a good mother she would be one day.

7. Standing up in front of a large crowd of people declaring one's demons, in the hopes of embarrassing oneself enough to do something about it. Innocent took centre stage for almost two hours describing her dismal dating faux pas with the duds she had dallied with. The audience roared with laughter believing she was *really* a court jester – a plant – hired to entertain them. After all, this woman couldn't be for real!

8. Standing up in front of a large crowd of people declaring over and over again what one wished for. The hope being that if one talked about something enough times they may actually start to believe in the possibility.

Innocent declared, 'I want to find my *One True Prince* and live happily-ever-after, as a wife and mother,' over 200 times while taking to the stage. By the time she was finished most of the audience were asleep and she now believed that she had more of a chance of growing wings to fly with than ever meeting her longed for prince.

Although Innocent met loads of lovely lost people and felt invigorated after the indoctrination, within a few days away from the group support she found herself sinking back into her old melancholy. Although she learned a lot from her studies, none of it was particularly practical and could not be applied to her everyday life. There seemed to be plenty of tedious talk but no tutorledge on how to take action.

After six months of stupendous spending on study, all she had managed to achieve was serious mood swings. She felt no better about herself and was certainly no closer to finding her *One True Prince* than when she started.

29
Innocent and the Friends' Frenzy

Innocent remembered how much her friendship with Princess True and Sir Sorry had filled her heart and decided that a friends' frenzy would facilitate a formal distraction from her cares and woes. To forget her melancholy she would fill the hole in her heart with friendship and fun.

The Friends' Frenzy Fraternity was set up by an opportunist who realized the earning potential of filling a lack by providing a list of potential pals. For a fee one could forage the Friends' Frenzy Fraternity files, finding profiles that took ones fancy.

Innocent found several profiles of friends who would fill her social calendar five days a week. If she could keep herself busy she would not have time to be sad.

The first friend she found was Baroness Bolshie, a big, busty, booming broad, broadcasting bulletins on, t*he right way for everyone to live their life*. With her big mouth, Bolshie began every sentence with '*you should, I believe and I know*'. She was an expert in making people wrong and was a self-righteous, right-hand finger pointer.

Bolshie had been born into a self-righteous household of chaos and commands, where her parents had passed on their own lousy legacy of poor parenting. Oblivious to their obligation to offer their offspring unconditional love, they viewed procreation as a mere exercise in procedure and protocol. Passing on their passion for control, they proceeded to produce a daughter lacking in the fineries of love and self-acceptance.

Never feeling in control of her own life, she deflected her need onto others. As long as she could *right* other people she had a distraction from her own melancholy.

Innocent's doomed romances were like a dream come true for Bolshie. After one awful, energy exhausting evening of Bolshie *righting* roughshod over her romances, Innocent decided the bully was definitely not her cup of tea.

The second friendship she frequented was the lovely Lady Fairweather, a renowned designer of feather-felt hats. After her divorce, she had spent years putting all of her talent energy into cultivating her designs. In Fairweather, Innocent had found a fellow fashionista, who loved finery as much as she did.

For their first outing her new fine-feathered friend invited her to her felt and feather hat studio. Innocent thought she had entered heaven as soon as she stepped into the studio. The room was full of thousands of white feathers of every size and shape. Feathers floated around the room as a gentle breeze blew in from the open windows.

Innocent smiled as she recalled her beloved Grandfather giving her a gift of a white feather, when she was a young girl.

'Always remember my dear child, whenever you see a white feather, angels have come to watch over you,' he told her.

Fairweather showed Innocent how to colour feathers with a rainbow of dyes that she had scattered around her worktables. She had a magical day with the lovely lady and her fantastic feathers.

A few days later they were due to meet up again. Just as Innocent was about to leave to meet Fairweather, she received a message apologizing that the lady had urgent business and would have to postpone. Innocent attempted to rearrange the meeting but after five deferrals, decided that as lovely as Fairweather was, she was not friendship material.

Many a potential pal had flirted with Fairweather's friendship only to be blown away like one of her feathers. In fact one had even penned an exposé entitled, *Frankly Fairweather is Just Not That Into You*. She had put her life and soul into her hats, missing out on the fineries of friendship. While she created fabulous feather hats for the fops, as a friend she was a failure and a flop.

Friend number three was Princess Needy. She was a mirror image of Innocent with the same colour hair, height and facial features. Whenever Innocent looked into Needy's eyes it was as if she was looking at herself.

Princess Needy was a connoisseur of neurosis, requiring constant reassurance that she was worthwhile. She was addicted to approval and well exceeded Innocent's people pleasing prowess.

Needy had the largest collection of glass slippers filling her closet and her empty heart. Innocent initially enjoyed her new friend's company, enthusiastically talking about Needy's glass slipper collection, but after a couple of weeks she began to find her irritating and extremely hard work. When Innocent tried to reschedule a dinner date due to a headache, Needy sent her a note via her messenger, moaning how she had been let down. Feeling guilty, Innocent got out of her sick bed to please her friend.

Innocent sat through three hours of Needy whining and whinging about some person she perceived as slighting her. She was convinced that everyone's goal in life was to let her down.

'You will leave me too one day,' she proclaimed to Innocent.

After two weeks of Needy's nonsense, Innocent was tired of looking at herself in the mirror, and fulfilling Needy's self-fulfilling prophecy, she dumped her neurotic friend.

Duke Do came in at number four. He was a stocky, bright-eyed fellow, thirty-years of age, although his wide-eyed innocence and awkward movements made him appear younger than his years. He was a likeable lad from the town of World's End, which bordered the Borough of Look At Me. World's End was created as a demarcation of the demographics of abundance. Income and status symbols decreased the closer one came to World's End.

His family property overlooked the bountiful borough, beckoning the broke boy. Many families who had lost or never had a fortune resided there. Duke Do came from a long line of underachievers, whose only legacy was an old title and a run-down manor.

He longed to belong to the Look At Me Set. He dabbled in dreams and drivel, vaulting from one venture to the next, hoping one would bring his ship of gold to him.

Instead of sticking to one thing he could be good at, the Duke dabbled in dexterous doing, dashing from one scheme to another, not really giving his all or focus to anything.

He had joined the Friendship Fraternity in the hope of negotiating a new network of potential business partners.

Anxious to impress the *Premier Princess* of Look At Me, the bright-eyed lad spent his entire evening talking about all the things he would be doing to make his fortune.

'In one more month, I will be financially sorted and solvent,' he said over and over again, as if to convince himself. Innocent often despaired that Do was more gullible than even she was.

Duke Do was a Master of the Deceive Yourself Arts, desperately believing in the publicity he was proclaiming. After three months of listening to his *one more month mantra,* Innocent started to tire of the dewy dreamer. *He* brought back sad memories of another Prince with inertia – Prince I-Only-Mean-What-I-Say-At-The-Time. She decided she had enough of her own problems to sort out and ditched him.

Friend number five was the fabulous, famous and fabled Queen BBB. Innocent was surprised when she came face to face with the legendary BBB on a luncheon date. Queen BBB took the name in her youth when she was viewed as one of the most extraordinary beauties of all time.

She had red lips that pouted so prominently that it looked as if they had been stung by bees. She had long and lean limbs and beautiful blonde hair that cascaded down her back like a golden waterfall. Her wide, blue eyes beamed with playfulness. She stood up straight and had a confidence very rare for such a young girl.

Quite simply she was a gorgeous goddess, a glittering, gamine who gentleman were gaga for. Her fantastic features often prompted an array of babbling 'b' adjectives from bedazzled and blown-away blokes beholding her. Men called her *beautiful, buxom, blonde, bodacious, brilliant, bedazzling, bohemian, busty, bella, bonita, babe, baby, brazen, bravissimo, bravo, belle, blimey, bit of alright!*

Jealous women who feared her beauty called her *brazen, brash, brassy and bitch*. 'B's were flying everywhere, until eventually she simply became known as Queen BBB.

Innocent had first heard of the legendary BBB from her friend and mentor Sir Shake and Peer. As a young reporter he had travelled to the south coast of Joie De Vie to the pretty town of Seins, to interview its most famous resident – Queen BBB. Seeing that Shake and Peer had a wonderful way with words, she commissioned him to pen her autobiography *Life Is Tit*.

As a young woman of eighteen, BBB had shot to fame and acclaim after being painted by the premier painter of the time, Sir Big Picture. Always one to make a big splash of paint, Big Picture had created the first live exhibitionist, when he used BBB's body as a canvas. The nude BBB was painted in an array of exquisite colours and designs, carefully covering up her ample assets.

The exhibition proved so popular with the people that Big Picture and BBB, travelled around the globe exhibiting both their talents. BBB became the first worldwide celebrity to have made an explosion felt all around the world. The supreme, sexy blonde became a muse for musicians and playwrights alike.

Such was her power to beguile and distract men that the Grand Duke Diabolical sought to capture her for a wife and use her for his long-standing evil plans and propaganda purposes. Diabolical deduced that if he couldn't conquer It Is What It Is with his bombs, the BBB bombshell would eventually bring The Kingdom's defences down. After all, he deduced, if he could possess BBB, the war weary men of It Is What It Is would realize that he was obviously dynamic and really not that bad.

The soldiers of It Is What It Is would surely prefer the cracking crumpet, BBB as *First Lady* of The Kingdom over a cup of tea and a talk from Sir Orator. In the shadow of Diabolical's prowess, Sir Oracle's influence over his troops would be seriously undermined allowing Capitulation's forces to walk right in.

Fortunately for It Is What It Is, a bedazzled billionaire spirited BBB away on one of his brilliant boats. The billionaire had a fleet of ships scattered throughout the seas of the world, and Diabolical spent the last year of the war unsuccessfully trying to track her down.

By the time she ended up at Innocent's luncheon table she was sixty-two years of age and had settled in It Is What It Is, distancing herself from the pert and pretty residents of Seins. Although still an attractive woman the unforgiving and undiscriminating reaches of time had cruelly caught up with her.

No longer the centre of attention Queen BBB had found that as the years faded so did her friendships. She often frequented the Friend's Fraternity for companionship, when she was not busy campaigning for her causes. As the adulation faded from her life, Queen BBB directed her energy to caring for old horses that had been put to pasture when they became past their racing and jousting primes. With the horses she found a kinship.

Queen BBB was struck by Innocent's doe eyes and beauty and she could feel the pangs of jealousy jaunting from her jilted and jaded heart. However BBB was also struck by Innocent's sweetness and felt compelled to offer her woeful words of wisdom.

'Beauty is a curse. Do not assume it is your ticket to happiness. Enjoy it while you can, my dear, it will not last forever. La beauté est passagère! When you get old, you will be discarded – disgracefully. They have *never* forgiven me for my fading beauty and that will also be true of you. So live and love life to the fullest. But be warned, downplay your lovely looks, do not rely on them.

People may be beguiled and bewitched by your beauty, but bored if there is not a beautiful personality below the visage. Only the most secure of men will ever take you on as their wife. Once they have had you the *Goddess Illusion* will start to crumble as they realize you are really human with the same worldly worries as any other woman. This will send them on a quest for the next great goddess and into another's arms.'

Innocent's mind had started to wander as soon as BBB mentioned that her looks would not last forever. She had been brought up by her mother to always be overly conscious of her appearance. In fact, deep down Innocent believed it was her trump card. She had received so many compliments throughout her lifetime for her lovely looks that she had always taken her beauty for granted and although she was not yet twenty-eight, for the first time ever, she started to feel old. She had been so busy distracting herself since she had left her home castle that she had become oblivious to the passage of time.

In fact, she came to think that she didn't feel any different now than when she was eighteen – except now she was nearly ten years older. Where did the time go? Innocent asked herself picturing the sands of an hourglass pouring rapidly to the bottom. Staring at this once great and admired beauty Innocent felt a sudden ache in the pit of her stomach.

As BBB barked out her bitter experiences, Innocent began to worry. What if I never meet anyone … I will grow old alone and in another ten years, men will no longer find me attractive and like BBB's horses I will be put out to pasture. That will then be me – a bitter and broken beauty, said the voice in her head.

'I never realized my beauty would not last forever.' Innocent blurted out, unaware that she was now nervously verbalizing her thoughts.

'That's what I thought, but it will my dear,' responded BBB, blowing Innocent's beauty bliss out the window.

Innocent suddenly felt even more depressed and desperate to make a matrimonial match. Suddenly she could no longer catch her breath and needed to break free of both BBB and her girdle.

'Dear Queen I must depart, please forgive me,' she declared and dashed away, leaving BBB even more broken-hearted.

Friend number six took the form of Queen Mothering, the most marvellous multi-tasking mother. Since her days as a young Princess, Queen Mothering knew that all she wanted to be was a *Mummy*. In fact, she was so good at it that by age forty, she was a mother of eight. Convinced that eight really was not enough, she decided to add to her brood and began her ninth pregnancy.

As all her children were away doing various summer activities and her dutiful, donor husband was rigorously resting, Mothering decided to feather her empty nest with a friendship fling. She was delighted to take Innocent under her wing and offered her advice.

'My dear, you must settle down shortly – after all you are not getting any younger. A woman is not complete unless she has created her own family.'

Innocent found a mother's shoulder to cry on as she recounted all her missed marriage opportunities.

'My dear Innocent, you must come for tea and sympathy with my *Yummy Mummy Set*. I am holding High Tea Court tomorrow for seven other mothers. You will be the guest of honour.'

As soon as Innocent sat down for tea and fine finger sandwiches the table talk turned to tales of twins, tweens, terrible twos and toys. Innocent nodded and sat silently having nothing to say on the subject. She had never felt so self-conscious and such a failure in her entire life. Compared to these wise, worldly and weary women she felt like a childless child. After all, what real responsibility had she ever had? She surmised that if she could barely take care of herself how on earth would she ever be able to bear the burden for another?

She suddenly felt like a female flop. Mortified she wanted to run away from the faces of responsibility and motherhood. Luckily there was a pregnant pause in the conversation and Innocent sneaked away from the sympathetic sighs of the set. Mothering was definitely not for her, at least not quite yet.

Filling up with friends was another disaster. After three months of bookings Innocent could no longer face the friendly fire of the Friend's Fraternity, which had inadvertently illuminated issues she didn't even know that she had. Her issues now had issues, dealing with others' issues.

'Was there no-one in this kooky kingdom who could bring her any happiness?' she decried exasperated.

Fantastically as soon as Innocent gave up the need for friends, she finally got a real one …

30
Queen Resolute

A forlorn Innocent was sitting on a park bench contemplating her lonely and unfulfilled life, when an elegant lady in her sixties, came and sat down beside her. Despite her advancing years she was still beautiful and had swept up platinum hair that glistened in the sun. She looked rather frail and was pushing a baby carriage with a young toddler. The lady smiled at Innocent as she took out a piece of fruit to give to her young cheery charge.

'Lovely weather we are having,' said the lady.

'Why yes,' Innocent replied, rather startled at being interrupted from her silent melancholy.

'I come here every day,' continued the lady. Little Lady Everything here enjoys the fresh air. I am her nanny, Queen Resolute. We live opposite the park.

'You a nanny, oh,' said Innocent rather surprised that such an elegant-looking lady would be working for a living.

'I had a job once, as a writer,' said Innocent, trying to come back from her rather embarrassing initial response.

'Working is a wonderful experience, one I never expected to enjoy at this time in my life. You see my dear I was once married to my soul mate, King Dreamer. We were wed for over thirty glorious years. We met when he was a struggling artisan. When we married he became an apprentice carpenter. We often struggled, as our Privy Purse was paltry. Nevertheless our hearts were full of love and laughter. Eventually my beloved decided to pursue his primary pleasure of shipbuilding – a business that burgeoned. We lived the high life with wealth and the world at our feet.

Alas, my dear husband was determined to build the most supreme cargo ship to ever sail the seas. He dreamt of trading traditional things with the Eastern Kingdoms to encourage an exchange of cultural understanding.

It became an overwhelming obsession and he put every last penny from our Privy Purse into the process. Finally after three years of busy building his magnificent machine was made. It set sail to the Eastern Kingdoms with a cargo and cabin crew of hundreds.

Before they could reach the shores, a storm swept the ship into the rocks, sinking it, and all of my husband's dreams.

We became destitute as our debtors came callously calling. My dear husband became sick with worry and I was left to replenish our Privy Purse by means of a job. I obtained employment as a nanny with a dear friend.

We moved into their house across the park. As I started employment my dear husband departed, leaving me alone with my job and my most cherished memories.'

As Queen Resolute recalled her life, Innocent was struck by how strong and positive the lady had remained. Innocent felt inspired by the intelligent and articulate Queen and suddenly her own problems started to seem insignificant in comparison.

Innocent could have spent the whole day listening to the eloquent Queen. She had never given much time to older people – the dismissive arrogance of youth – or perhaps the fear of losing youth that age symbolized. But as she took in the Queen's breadth of wisdom Innocent realized the treasure chest she had been missing.

'Oh my goodness, is that the time. I need to get Lady Everything home for tea. I will be here tomorrow if you would like to continue our conversation.' And with that she smiled and bid Innocent a fond farewell.

Returning the next day, Innocent continued her colourful conversations with the Queen. Resolute listened as the Princess wove her tale of woe. She nodded and smiled and reassured Innocent that the long road travelled is often paved with challenges.

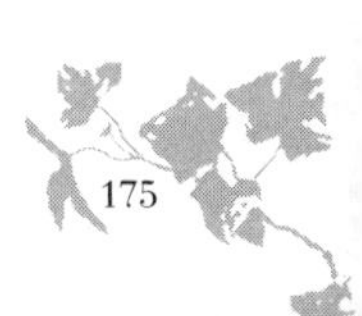

'We must go around the potholes and mud and continue on our jagged journey my dear. No-one's journey is ever just a straight line, it is the bumps along the way that make it fun and interesting.'

Innocent and the Queen developed a fondness for one another. The Queen was happy to impart her knowledge and experience on her much younger friend. Innocent loved listening to the Queen's life stories, particularly of the struggles she and her husband Dreamer endured in the early lean years of their marriage. Listening to the love story of Resolute, Innocent got to live life vicariously as part of a doting and devoted duo. She had to admit that Resolute's relationship reflected a love far superior than she had ever known. In comparison she wondered if she had ever really experienced love from any of her ridiculous relationships.

Innocent felt as if she had known Queen Resolute her entire life. She gained more out of her conversations with the older and wiser Queen than she had ever received from the Help Yourself Movement. Best of all it did not cost anything. The Queen gave her wisdom and words freely and with love. Innocent never imagined that she would find such great love while simply sitting on a park bench. She realized that the best things in life were truly free.

She continued meeting the Queen for two months at their favourite park bench. One day Resolute brought Innocent a gift.

'My dear I want to give you a gift.' She carefully took out a small box and handed it to the Princess.

'Please open it my dear.'

Innocent opened the small box and inside was a delicate bracelet made of small, simple colourful beads. She picked up the delicate band.

'It was given to me by my darling Dreamer. He made it by hand and gave it to me when he first came courting. I would like you to have it as a symbol of our flowering friendship and a reminder of the sweet simplicity of love. '

She was touched by the Queen's generous graceful gesture. 'My Queen I am deeply moved by your kindness, however I cannot take ownership of such a sentimental significant object from your Dreamer.'

'My dear it would give me great pleasure knowing it was now in your safe possession. Please put it on your wrist for me.'

Placing the bracelet on her right wrist she admired its simple beauty. It was a perfect fit.

'I will wear it always,' she gushed gratefully. As she looked up at the Queen she noticed tears were welling in her eyes. The Queen hugged Innocent in a motherly embrace.

'I will hopefully see you tomorrow she smiled,' and took her leave.

The next day, Innocent waited on the park bench, for the Queen to arrive. But she did not appear.

She returned the next day, but Resolute was nowhere to be seen. By day five of no shows, Innocent began to worry. She was about to wander over to her house when an elegant lady pushing Lady Everything in her pram approached.

'Are you Princess Innocent?'

'Yes … I am,' nodded Innocent suddenly struck with a strange, sick feeling, in the pit of her stomach.

'I am Lady Everything's mother, Princess Harried. Queen Resolute our dear, dear friend talked of you often. She told me of your park bench talks, which gave her great pleasure. I have some terribly sad news to share with you. Our dear Queen passed on two days ago. She had been diagnosed with a weak heart. Just before she met you, the doctor told her she had only days to live, but your conversations struck such a chord with her heart strings that it decided to beat for a few weeks longer.

With her last few breaths she dictated this note to me, so that I could pass on her precious words to you.' Princess Harried gave Innocent the note and took her leave.

It would be the last time her friend would ever talk to her –

My dearest Innocent

I shall miss our cheerful colourful chats. I am so sorry that I will not be around to hear all about your future happenings. I suspect that the world will one day see wonderful things from you. Stay strong and remember to embrace all the challenges that life brings, they are gifts given to help you gain greatness. It is a good path you are on.
Whenever you wear the beaded bracelet think of me and may it bring you the same luck in love that I happily had.
Till we meet again

Your friend always Queen Resolute
xxx

Tears filled Innocent's eyes. Queen Resolute had filled the gaping void in her heart and now she was gone. She ran home and cried desperately, the delicate beaded bracelet becoming wet with her tears.

31
Innocent Checks Out the Help Yourself Library

Without the Queen's words of wisdom to guide her, Innocent turned to the words of the Help Yourself Library where she read relentlessly between the lines for answers. She often bought books to the park bench, where she felt Queen Resolute's positive presence.

She found a book called, *Men are Men and Women are from a Town Called Hope*. It was a popular book, which proved that '*ess*' was not the only difference dividing a prince and a princess.

She also picked up a book called *Gentleman Prefer Anyone BUT You*, a useful guide in mastering the Art of Rejection. Finally she tried *Lassoing Lover Boy by Loosing Lard* that provided helpful hints for capturing the heart of insecure, superficial suitors.

If You Are Reading This Book You Are Not Even Close To Being There – a helpful book to point out just how off-track one really was.

Although she found books like the Help Yourself lectures informative, Innocent found integrating the information into her life impossible for more than a few days. Her idea of herself as a failure and a flop was now so unshakable that she felt even more trapped by circumstances. If others could not help her she thought, then she was surely lost, and she sank even further into her melancholy, madly missing Resolute's positivity.

She was about to lose all hope when she received a correspondence from her dear friend Countess Confidence. Innocent had written to the Countess about Queen Resolute and of her monstrous melancholy and as the ray of light she always was, Confidence responded immediately –

Ma petite

I send my condolences for the loss of your dear friend, who I know has passed on to a better place.
I am sorry for your melancholy but have no fear, this too shall pass. I have heard tale of a wonderful master from The City of Love. He travels from kingdom to kingdom helping many people find their happiness. He works alone and has no affiliation. He charges only a nominal fee to cover sundries and living expenses. He is a pure master of his craft. Some say he has magical powers and talks directly with a person's soul. He has temporarily settled in a hamlet, close to your Chiefly City. I am enclosing his address. I am sure he can help you. His name is Master Love.

Always,
Countess Confidence
xoxox

Innocent was intrigued and she immediately dispatched her messenger to Master Love. She received a reply back immediately with an appointment for the next day.

Truth and Love

32
Master Love

Master Love was waiting outside to greet her. He had a huge grin on his face, which Innocent found rather cheeky. He was dressed in plain clothes, had black hair and the most sparkling blue eyes she had ever seen. She was surprised at how humble his appearance was.

She thought about the other masters of the Help Yourself programmes she had attended. They were all were flamboyant in both dress and title.

There was the head of the Institution for Indoctrination: His Royal Reverence of the Most Highest Order, the Honourable Holder of All the Answers. Whenever he lectured he wore the most dazzling crown Innocent had ever seen.

There was the most dutiful Duchess Do-As-I-Say-Not-As-I-Do. She was a bestselling author and renowned expert on finding your *One True Prince* having been married six times. She was always covered with diamonds, emeralds and rubies and furs, the spoils from her six husbands.

Innocent had attended several lectures with the Marchioness Martyrdom who taught people how to effectively place blame on others. She was credited with increasing sales of *Feel Good and Confidence Potions*, so much so that she was sponsored by the medicinal makers. She always gesticulated dramatically whenever she was speaking.

However, here was a humble man who didn't need a royal title. He stood out from the rest and Innocent was hopeful he could help her.

Won't you come in my child, he warmly welcomed. Innocent stepped inside the small cottage to the main living room. It was sparsely furnished except for a long, high bench, scattered with red pillows in the middle of the room. It had huge bay windows facing south, which the sun brightly shone through. Hanging outside the windows were silver and gold wind chimes that made gentle, soothing sounds as the summer breeze hit them.

'Please take a seat on the bench and tell me what ails you.'

Innocent climbed up and recanted her tales of woe, sparing no detail of dastardly deeds and disappointments that had befallen her. As she spoke Master Love listened intently and nodded occasionally. Innocent took an hour to complete telling her tale and finally finished with a heavy sigh.

There was a momentary silence as Master Love contemplated her words.

'So my dear, you are seeking help to reclaim your happiness. Won't you lie down on the bench so I can examine you further?'

Master Love must have caught Innocent's rather mistrustful glance as he sought to reassure her.

'Have no fear, for no funny business is afoot. A fully-clothed examination will diagnose your problem.'

Innocent blushed. She was impressed by how insightful he was. She lay across the pillows and Master Love got out a long, thin instrument. It was made of bronze, no bigger than a large wooden spoon. Its long, thin handle, had a bronze circle attached to the end, affixed with a bendable metallic spring, which bounced as it was moved.

Master Love moved the instrument across the length of Innocent's body, holding it two inches above her. He worked in silence, concentrating on his craft. She could feel her palms perspiring, in nervous anticipation about what he would conclude about her.

After five minutes he put the instrument down carefully and closing his eyes began to make his diagnoses.

'My dear I can see you are severely short of energy. You have spent the last few years servicing, saving or sorting out your many lovers, severely short-changing yourself in the process. You have an *immense need* to care for others and you have sacrificed yourself in the process of pursuing this goal.'

Innocent stared at him trying to take it all in. He continued speaking, his eyes still closed.

'You lack focus as you flit around, flirting and frolicking and thus never accomplish anything. Once you determine what it is that you truly desire, you will claim it as your own.'

'But Master Love I have known for years that what I truly seek is my *One True Prince* and yet my princely quest has come to nothing. Why has this eluded me?'

'Another cannot complete you. You must first determine who Princess Innocent is and have a relationship with her first. When you discover Innocent, only then will your own special prince claim you.'

'What do you mean Master Love?'

He did not open his eyes and continued.

'You need to see the truth about who you have turned out to be. Despite your beauty you have become a brilliant performer, always playing a role depending on whose company you are keeping. You have played siren, saviour, scholar, socialite, student, sweetness and sourpuss all for the sake of security and self-esteem.'

Innocent became dizzy with the dazzling array of words disseminated to her by the Master.

He kept talking. 'Once you learn to be yourself instead of being a perfect, pleasing, performer your life will no longer be a parody and you will find the peace that has eluded you.

You must detach yourself from the idea that true love and joy only comes from princes, places, and platitudes. This line of thought will imprison you forever as you seek something that is only a myth. Joy is not *out there*, attached to some future acquisition it is always alive *inside*, waiting for you to access it. When you learn to give yourself love and put that love into everything you do then you will be free and joyful.'

He still did not open his eyes and Innocent noticed his intense expression.

'If you are going to go through pain don't waste it, learn from it. Life brings you many fleeting circumstances in which to grow. Use them wisely. You must not hold onto those experiences, reliving them over and over, rather treat them as shooting stars, sent your way to shine a light on a lesson you needed to learn. Release the circumstance and hold only onto the lesson. Ask for only new experiences that enhance this life's journey.

Open your eyes wide and seek the truth in every situation. Do not lie to yourself by living in a dream world and putting others on pedestals they have not earned. See yourself for who you really are and you will be able to see others for who they really are. Remember everything you do in your life must be in truth and love. Only then can you find peaceful living in It Is What It Is.'

Innocent looked at Master Love attentively, trying to take in all he was saying. He suddenly opened his eyes and staring directly into Innocent's eyes, concluded his diagnoses.

'Remember *You* are all powerful – a *divine* being who can manifest anything that matters to you. But be warned, if chaos and drama *is what matters* to you – if that is your focus – then that is what you will manifest. Remember thoughts can become forms!'

He paused for a few moments, giving her a chance to take in all the information that was coming through him.

'If you are always giving your power to others or you let them have power over you, you weaken yourself and lose your ability to create. Retain your energy and instead of creating chaos, use it to create calm in your life. Once you learn to be a master of yourself then joy and happiness will seep into your life and all that you desire will reveal itself. You will finally see that what has eluded you has been there all along – waiting.'

And with that, he had Innocent on her feet again.

'A word of caution – you have had much to digest today and I suggest that you take time for quiet reflection. I have returned your energy to you and you will feel positively potent, but do not flitter it away rushing impulsively into any new relationships or ventures. Give yourself six months of quiet time and you will then see results.'

Innocent was not sure that she understood everything in her head, but in her heart she felt so light and happy, she was convinced her soul was singing.

She paid the Master one silver coin for his service. She felt rather guilty giving such a great man so modest an amount. She thought about the Help Yourself Masters, who had helped themselves to hundreds of her gold coins. She had given them permission to take her power away as they helped her develop into even more of a dependent doormat than she had already become.

Yet here was a powerful master who was returning her power to her, for the smallest of fees. Innocent felt humbled to be in the company of such a superb sage. As they exchanged pleasantries, Master Love flashed her one of his cheeky grins –

'One day, when you are ready, all I have told you will take specific shape in your life and you will be ready to put your old *Love Scarf* on with pride.'

Innocent was dumbfounded. She had entirely forgotten about the *Love Scarf* Sir Steady had given her all those years ago.

'B–bu–but how did you know about the scarf, Master Love?' she said shaking her head and now more in awe and wonderment of this magical, mystical master than ever before.

Master Love just smiled and escorted Innocent to her carriage.

As her carriage pulled away from the cottage she heard him call to her.

'Remember Innocent everything you do must be in truth and love. Live life joyfully and remember *you* are your life's creator!'

They kept waving to each other as if they were two old friends, until her carriage disappeared into the distance.

33
Innocent Loses Her Coin

Innocent felt positively invigorated after her appointment with Master Love. She had never been in the presence of someone so perfectly at peace with himself and the world, and she felt inspired just by being in his presence. She convinced herself that armed with Master Love's words of wisdom life could only get better.

For the next few weeks she remained in a positively euphoric state. She believed that after such sagely wisdom, she was unstoppable.

She even hired background musicians to reflect her jubilant state. Every morning they would bring their guitars, mandolins and harps and perform outside Innocent's windows, waking her up to the sweet sounds of music. As soon as Innocent heard the music she would leap out of bed and dance and sing. Her heart and soul soared so high that her feet barely touched the ground.

Innocent believed that now she was a better and more positive person, success could not but help enter her life. Instead of taking heed of Master Love's advice for quiet reflection, the perpetually in motion Princess got incredibly itchy feet for a new focus.

When she read about a fabulous new investment scheme, she believed it was fate. She had never dabbled in financial risk-taking before and found the thought thoroughly thrilling. Besides she needed to recoup the losses she had sustained from her Prince Rescue Me investment. Her Privy Purse had never recovered from that experience, and since that relationship, she seemed to go through money faster than ever.

She had read about the scheme in the Speculative Financial Press, which had all of It Is What It Is in a buzz. With her new found fortitude Innocent felt that by investing, she could make a fortune and preserve her grand lifestyle.

The Isle of Illusion was a small picturesque island 150 miles from the southern-most tip The Kingdom. It had the most pristine beaches and the warmest climate. It had a relatively small population and a few large manor houses.

A new construction company called the Politicians Pocket Fund had decided to develop the island further by creating the concept of the *holiday home*, where people could get away from it all. The place was built as an exact replica of small town It Is What It Is. To accommodate the ensuing holiday crowd, a great fleet of new frigates were also to be commissioned.

The Politicians Pocket Fund was pursuing people with large Privy Purses to help finance the project. For the price of 100,000 gold pieces each investor would get a *piece of the pie*. Demand for the new dwellings on the island would swell the initial investment ten-fold, within a four month period.

Everyone wanted to ride the waves of the tunnel. Both banking institutions and individual investors rushed to buy a piece of the project. Innocent collected 100,000 gold pieces from her Privy Purse, leaving only 100 remaining. She calculated that she could live off the remaining 100 for the next four months until her ship of gold came in, tripling her investment.

After the money was collected and calculated, the culminated coinage was loaded onto four huge carriages to be transferred as payment for the construction workers on both the fleet of frigates and the holiday homes. Upon receipt the banks on the south coast would distribute the coinage to pay for the workmanship.

Everything went to perfect plan until the *Great Crash*. Over the years many a legend surrounded the event. No-one was quite sure of all the details but what was known for certain was that the driver of a large gravy wagon fell asleep at the reins. His horses ran off course and right into the carriages carrying the precious gold cargo – just as they were coming around a steep cliff. It was a messy affair as gravy scattered everywhere and the impact of the crash sent the gold coinage careening down into the deep ravine below.

Fortunately both drivers walked away with minor injuries. The Rescue and Recovery Royal Mountain Constabulary was immediately dispatched to retrieve the precious cargo. Unfortunately the ravine was so deep, dark and dangerous that it was estimated that it would take an entire year to reclaim all the riches.

The crash sent shock waves around It Is What It Is, as thousands of investors saw their gold coins disappear into a deep black hole. They would have to wait for more than a year to recoup their investments as each coin was picked up by hand and sorted into individual piles.

With coin circulation cut in half, disarray developed as diversification dried up. Confident consumers turned into cautious caretakers of their remaining gold coins. With Privy Purses particularly paltry, paying in deposits diminished. Credit eventually dried up as banks no longer wanted to part with their remaining piles of precious gold pieces. Shopping came to a standstill as purchasing power petered out. Many people had borrowed to invest in the get rich quick scheme and panicked at the prospect of lenders leaning on them for the lost loans. Many debtors departed the city in droves.

As people's spending power decreased suddenly *Flower Power* made a comeback to The Kingdom. Free and simple pleasures, such as stopping and smelling the roses grew in popularity.

Like so many others Innocent had put most of her gold coinage into this broken basket and now she was seriously short of spending power. Within four months her Privy Purse would be empty and without a pittance she would become destitute. Just as she had started to feel good about life again, it all fell apart with a mighty carriage crash.

She had never had to worry about money before. Throughout her entire life she had possessed a perpetually plentiful Privy Purse from her parents. Except for her brief tenure as a top earner at The Town Crier she had never gained gold from the fruits of her labour. Now as an investor in The Isle of Illusion, the idea of endless monetary means and mammon became mote.

Innocent convinced herself that if she just cut back on her expenses, and bide her time until her money was retrieved from the black hole, she would come out on top. She decided that cutting back on gowns and gems would help her greatly. After all, she had enough gowns to last her well into the next seven social seasons.

Her optimism came to an abrupt end as she received a knock on her door one day. It was a bill from her dress designer. Where once the prosperous designer had been happy to bill his clients every few months, his own lack of current capital caused him to collect charges immediately.

When Innocent looked down at her clothes bill she almost fainted.

Please pay promptly the princely sum of fifty gold coins. Failure to pay within the next week, will incur interest charges of 20%.

'Fifty gold pieces,' she screamed aloud! 'That is half of the money I have left! I can't possibly pay that amount.'

She dispatched a messenger to the dress designer telling tale of her tragedy and he agreed to a monthly repayment plan of ten gold coins of which 99% would be interest. Although she wasn't the greatest mathematician in the world, she was aware that she was getting royally ripped-off but relished the thought of a low monthly payment.

Just as she was feeling proud of herself for procuring a petite payment plan another creditor came knocking at her door. This time it was the landlord of her magical mews house. He explained that his own fiscal fiasco had forced him to increase Innocent's rental rate to the tune of fifteen gold coins per month – effective immediately.

From that moment on, a line of lenders anxious to recoup their losses made their way to Innocent's door. Grocers, dressmakers, gem-setters and even guitar players, all came with their cap in hand. Having made her staff redundant, Innocent was forced to open the door herself. She was shocked at how wanton her spending habits had been. She had been so free yielding with her Privy Purse in the past that half of the debtors knocking on her door she had no recollection of.

In fact her reputation for reckless spending was so well-known that a few crafty opportunists came to her door, fobbing off forged fees. None the wiser she added their bills to the accumulated pile of payment demands. The days of collective, cheap and cheerful credit were overwhelmingly over for everyone.

Innocent soon realized that she had not seen anything yet when the Big Bank came calling. Her *money not know-how* had led her to procure an account with the Big Bank a year earlier. She had entrusted a large portion of her coinage to their valuable vaults, which they had invested and made a 50% killing from. She had reaped 1% rewards from her endowment and her ignorance.

As Innocent's dear deposit had dwindled the Big Bank bosses had dispatched their tellers to keep an eye out for any opportunity to make up the shortfall.

Unfortunately the opportunity had arrived in the form of a banker's draft to a debtor that had taken Innocent's account a halfpenny overdrawn. In *open outcry* the tellers were dispatched at breakneck speed demanding recompense for her oversight. *Tell her* they were told, and towing banking rhetoric in their pockets they told Innocent that she would have to pay a bank charge. The barking bankers handed her a bill for twenty-five silver pieces for the halfpenny she was overdrawn. Innocent pleaded with the sheepish shysters to take into account all the money they had made from her previously, but to no avail. The charging charges left her more broke than before.

Innocent felt overwhelmed and overpowered by her payment demands. She did not know who to pay first or how to organize her debts and began ignoring the piles of payment notices. Every time someone came to her door she would hide and pretend she was not home. With the little money she had left, she would venture out at night to buy enough food to last her for a week of hiding out. Most of the food she purchased was sugary and sweet and provided the only comfort she had left. She packed on the pounds along with the interest.

She would often sob herself to sleep decrying, the injustice of it all. 'Why me? … It's not fair … I'm a good person … I don't deserve this …'

After two months of dodging demanding debtors she knew she had only one option left. She would have to return home to her parent's castle in the Borough of Look At Me.

Fearing debtor's prison Innocent put on her finest garments and face paint and faced her creditors, making arrangements to put herself on payment plans. At twenty-nine years of age, she was broke, depressed, still a single princess and heading back to live with her parents.

'Could life be any worse?' she cried and soon discovered it could. Her desperate landlord set fire to the mews house when she was out, hoping to secure a grand insurance payout.

By the time the flames were extinguished half of her belongings and clothes had gone up in smoke with the ensuing explosion. Innocent returned home literally with a bang, crying as she carried her last few possessions, payment plans and her remaining five gold pieces.

34
Innocent Comes Home

Innocent returned to her home castle a broken princess. She was eleven years older, had dark circles under her eyes and was unable to fit into her robes. Worst of all she was no closer to finding her prince than when she first ventured on her journey.

Her parents were away travelling for the social season. She was both grateful for the solitude and for having to avoid explaining her circumstances to the King and Queen. Innocent felt she had become a disappointment and embarrassment to her parents. After all, they were the only ones within their social peers who had not walked an offspring down the aisle.

In her room she found a note from her father that read –

My darling daughter,

I need to regretfully inform you that the gravy train that once filled your Privy Purse has now dried up. We will make arrangements to pay off all of your creditors, but will expect repayment when you are able. May I suggest that you now resort to getting a job until pensionable age? Your mother and I look forward to seeing you upon our return.

Always in love
Your adoring parents
xxxx

Innocent was aghast. It was now official she was no longer a freeloading royal but a *working royal!*

'Oh the shame, the shame,' she cried as she fell to the floor in floods of tears.

Convincing herself she would never be happy, Innocent began feeling depressed and hid herself away in her room. Ashamed and feeling like a failure as a Princess, she could not face anyone – particularly her old friends, most of whom she'd heard had found a marital match. She felt so bad that she thought seriously about changing her name to Princess Poor Me.

Often spending her days alone weeping, the only pleasure she allowed herself was her old hobby of reading the Fairy Tale Land Press reports on pretty princesses in The Kingdom. Pleasure quickly turned to pain, as the princesses of the press made her feel even worse. Innocent often felt jealous as she read about their fantastic princes, their perfect rubinesque figures, their designer robes. Why didn't she have those things? Where did she go wrong?

She began a reverie of regret, recalling and reviewing the recent events of her royal life. Surely she was not to blame for all her misfortune. Maybe some evil magician had cast a curse on her. Maybe some jealous princess had somehow used magic to cause chaos in her life.

'If only that Princess Easy had not lured Prince Bad Boy from me, I would be happily married to him now.'
'If only the Cracker Sellers had been locked up in the dungeon, Prince Rescue Me would have not required rehab and would have been ready to propose marriage.'
'If only Lord Lie-A-Lot's wife had let him go.'
'If only my parents had been richer royals.'
'If only … If only … '

Innocent came up with hundreds of *if onlys* about her life. She spent days going over and over in her mind all the people whose fault it was for her predicament, until she felt even worse than before. She suddenly felt an affinity with Vicountess Victim and wanted to change her name to Princess Woe Is Me.

This woeful worrying went on for weeks and weeks, until spring turned to summer and her room became unbearably hot. To cool off, she decided to go for a walk in the castle grounds. As soon as she stepped outside she noticed the fragrant flowers in full, floral bloom. She had forgotten how beautiful the castle gardens could be. After spending hours in the gardens that day, she was surprised at how much better she felt when she returned to her room.

The next day she went out for another walk, this time for longer. Once again the walk lifted her spirits. Pretty soon she was going for longer and longer walks every day. Innocent noticed that her robes began to fit her again. She also noticed the melancholy that she had felt was easing slightly, and she found great comfort in her walks.

Sometimes she would sit under the largest pine tree in the garden and soak up the sun. Somehow sitting under that great tree gave her a peaceful feeling. She remembered what Chief Eagle had told her about the healing power of nature and she felt comforted knowing that she could seek solace under the beautiful tree.

Innocent's thoughts began to change as she sat under the Great Pine Tree. She began a reverie, recalling and reviewing the recent events of her royal life. Her *if only* was replaced by *why did I do that*?

'Why did I move to the South of It Is What It Is and why did I buy all those robes, most of which I never wore?'
'Why did I jump into the royal bedchamber with Prince Bad Boy so quickly?'
'Why did I do so much for Prince Rescue Me?'
'Why did I quit my job at The Town Crier?'
'Why did I …'

Innocent went through hundreds of *why did I's* until she felt very stupid and embarrassed. The more she thought about these things, the more she was convinced she should change her name to Princess How Could You Be So Stupid. Her sadness was suddenly replaced by anger. She became angry with herself for becoming a Master of Misguided Mistakes. Every morning she would stand in front of her chamber mirror and curse to herself saying no prince would want to marry such a dumb princess.

This became very exhausting and often when Innocent visited the garden she was so tired from being angry with herself that she fell asleep.

She decided that being angry was a complete drain of energy, so her thoughts began to change once again. She sat under the Great Pine Tree and began her reverie, recalling and reviewing the recent events of her royal life. Her thoughts became more gentle and kinder. This time *why did I do that* was replaced with *I did it because I cared.*

'I did it because I cared about Prince Bad Boy.'
'I did it because I cared about saving Baron Booty from a life alone at sea.'
'I did it because I cared about Prince Rescue Me's life.'
'I did it because I cared about my appearance and that is why I spent all those gold coins on my robes.'
'I did it because I cared about Lord Lie-A-Lot's happiness and believed I could make him happier than his wife could.
'I did it because … '

Innocent went through her list of *I did it because I cared* until she started to feel proud about the things she had done. She started to realize that she was a kind and loving Princess who only ever had good intentions. The anger towards herself that she had felt started to fade and was replaced by a feeling of pride. Every morning she would look at herself in the mirror and feel proud of the kind woman she was. She would tell herself that she was a lovely woman with a big heart and that is why she sometimes got herself into trouble.

Innocent developed a spring in her step as she took her walks in the castle garden and she started to feel pretty good about herself.

Visiting the familiar pine tree, her thoughts changed once again in her infinite wisdom. *I did it because I cared*, was replaced with *If I hadn't experienced what I did, I would never have learned.*

She remembered Master Love telling her that life was a collection of experiences and that one often got the experience one needed for one's own personal growth. She had retrieved the Eagle Feather that Chief Eagle had given her and fashioned a pen from it. As she sat under the comforting arms of the Great Pine Tree, she began to list all the meaningful events and people she had encountered. Under each of those experiences she wrote down the lessons learned.

From Prince Bad Boy I learned:

1. *One cannot live by looks alone.*
2. *If it's too good to be true it usually is.*
3. *The more one chases after something, the faster it slips through one's fingers.*
4. *Introductory lovemaking.*
5. *Every girl loves a bad boy!*

Moving to Joie De Vie I learned:

1. *Wherever you go so do your choices.*
2. *People perform the same everywhere.*

From Countess Confidence I learned:

1. *Confidence is truly Queen.*
2. *Capture Confidence and you capture the world.*
3. *Confidence is a woman's best friend.*
4. *Confidence is beauty personified.*
5. *A true friend sticks by you through good and bad.*

From Baron Booty I learned:

1. *Wild abandonment.*
2. *A lover does not change because you want them to. If you cannot accept their terms and conditions do not enter into a contract of agreement with them.*
3. *How arousing making love in a dark, dingy dungeon, can be.*
4. *The definition of an orgasm.*

From Captain Unavailable I learned:

1. *The pleasures of big yachts.*

2. Casual means casual.
3. It Is What It Is!

From Marchioness Mostess I learned:
1. All that glitters is not gold.
2. Beauty does not guarantee happiness.
3. Living to impress can make one severely depressed.
4. An unconfident woman will eliminate any competition.
5. The hostess-with-the-mostess is full of neurosis.
6. Pedestal placement can be precarious.

From Lord Lie-A-Lot I learned:
1. What a clever conversationalist I could be.
2. Accepting second best is soul destroying.
3. That the line: 'But he would never cheat on me,' is the stupidest sentence a mistress can utter.
4. A liar never changes his lines.
5. Having a mistress instead of a divorce decree is a definitive sign of weakness.
6. That the statement 'Let them Eat Cake' is a rallying cry for the Society of Married Men for the Prevention of monogamy.

From Prince I-Only-Mean-What-I-Say-At-The-Time I learned:
1. The power of compassion is a gift you give yourself.
2. A person's potential is only the way others want them to be.
3. Daily actions ring truer than protestations and promises.
4. You should at least wait for conception to occur before naming your children.
5. Living is preferable to planning.
6. Do it now or you will never know what you are capable of.

From Sir Us and Them I learned:
1. It is preferable to be a 'them' rather than an 'us'.
2. Staying silent shows acquiescence.
3. Better-most people don't hang around with bigots.

From my friendship with Princess True I learned:

1. A true friend is someone rare and special.
2. To keep a true friend one must be more like her.
3. Friendship is about quality of time spent together, not quantity.
4. Life is a bitch and then you become one.
5. Pride cometh before that fall!

From Sir Sorry I learned:

1. It is unfair to try and makeover people the way you want them to be.
2. If you take responsibility for the world's woes it will wear you down.
3. Instead of apologizing to the world for his existence, Sorry should be apologizing to himself for failing to recognize his own value.
4. Sorry doesn't always make it better!

From Baron Press I learned:

1. Learning to listen is one of the most important life lessons.
2. Expanding one's mind with new experiences is exhilarating.
3. You can be in love with the idea of love and marriage.
4. How pressed for a timely engagement I actually was.

From Plain Shane I learned:

1. Some love is for but a fleeting moment, but lasts forever.
2. The precious gift of living in the moment.

From Prince Apron Strings I learned:

1. If a princess's main competition is from a prince's mother – forget it – you can't win!
2. Oedipus Lives!

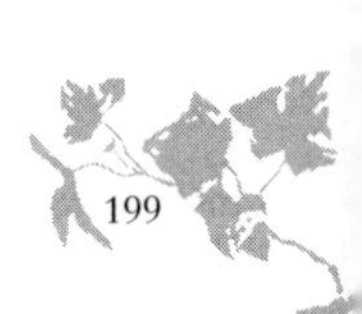

From All The Best Princes I learned:

1. Some people make better friends than lovers.

2. You cannot run away from yourself.

From Prince Fear I learned:

1. There is nothing in a dark room to fear, but Fear himself.

2. How decidedly difficult and scary living with Fear can be.

3. I would rather take the long journey home alone, than with Fear as my travelling companion.

4. If Fear puts on a suit of armour for protection he will probably attract an arrow.

5. Fear's thoughts can take form and become real.

From Prince Teach-Me-All-You-Know I learned:

1. Life must always be in balance.

2. Instant gratification is gone in an instant!

3. Princesses like trophies too!

4. Hey, I still got it!

From Baroness Booby Trap I learned:

1. The most important gift in life is good health.

2. The beauty of blazing a health trail for others.

3. Taking care of oneself is the most valuable lesson in life.

4. If you are being your body's best friend, it will be your best friend for life.

5. How letting it all hang out can be good for business.

6. Boob spotting is a mesmerising male hobby.

From the Magical Musical Troubadours I learned:

1. The music of love is truly all you need.

2. What a terrific team differing talents can make.

3. I love them, yeah, yeah, yeah.

From Chief Eagle I learned:

1. The Garden of Eden exists in our own back forest.

2. It is preferable to be a Human Being than a Human Talking.

3. The art of listening is sadly only an ancient art.
4. How liberating not wearing clothes can truly be.

From Prince Rescue Me I learned:
1. There is nothing sadder than a person's potential.
2. A talented taker gladly gravitates to a giver.
3. A habitual giver gravitates towards a taker.
4. The only person you can rescue is your own royal self.
5. The Royal Constitution protects the rights of all citizens to screw-up their lives – without interference.
6. I am not a vet and he is not a pet who needs to be fixed.
7. There were definitely three of us in that relationship – me, him, and the Crummy Cracker.
8. The definition of enabler.
9. I had an immense need to care for others!
10. The definition of denial.
11. Rescuing cannot buy me love.

From Master Tao I learned:
1. To listen to my body.
2. How to talk to my body.
3. To understand the burden of taking on the pain of others.
4. The power of Lucky 8!
5. I have the power to heal myself.

From Prince Good I learned:
1. If you see the good in people they won't let you down.
2. If you see the worst in others the worst will come out of you.
3. If you believe something to be true – it will be.

From eating cake I learned:
1. Cake will not fill up your heart only your bloomers.
2. I would choose chocolate cake over a beef cake any day.

From the Help Yourself Movement I learned:

1. *You need to help yourself.*
2. *You have to be ready to want to help yourself*
3. *It is an expensive hobby.*
4. *To beware of false prophets bearing all the answers.*
5. *It is only when we stop searching for the answers that they find us.*
6. *One answer does not fit all.*

From the Friendly Friends' Fraternity I learned:

1. *No-one is better or worse – only on a different journey.*
2. *If the friendship slipper doesn't fit, get another one that's more comfortable!*
3. *You can only see things in others that you have inside of yourself.*

From Queen Resolute I learned:

1. *The gift of having an older and wiser friend.*
2. *Love can be found anywhere, even on a park bench.*
3. *The best things in life are free.*
4. *I travel the good path*

From Master Love I learned:

1. *I am the creator of my life.*
2. *I create what I focus on!*
3. *Everything I do should be in truth and love.*
4. *The power of joy and appreciation.*
5. *Chaos is an exhausting form of self-expression.*
6. *Everything I need to be happy lies within!*

From losing my coinage I have learned:

1. *Throwing money in a black hole will make it disappear.*
2. *A Privy Purse is a privilege.*
3. *There is no quick way to make money.*

From living my life up until now, I have learned:

1. *To cherish moments of joy with another, understanding our time in their presence may be all but fleeting.*
2. *Appreciation of the treasure that is experience.*
3. *To embrace joy, laughter and love.*
4. *Detach and watch this space!*
5. *When one is truly ready for the responsibility of being oneself, they will draw to them all that they need!*

As Innocent reviewed each of the lessons she had learnt, she felt exhilarated knowing that each one was an amazing accomplishment – a stepping stone on her life's journey. Without those events she could not have grown into the happy, contented woman she now was. She might be broke, but she finally had abundance in her life. Her experiences had made her life rich and interesting. She marvelled at how a new perspective could change everything!

She amazed herself at how she had amassed such a wide, nutty net of people. Her life was full of charming, crazy characters – much like she was – she admitted, laughing to herself. 'What a rich tapestry my life has been,' she reflected out loud.

She was proud of all the different sorts of people she had attracted into her life and felt a new sense of gratitude for them. She could now see these experiences had bestowed a beautiful blessing upon her. Suddenly all the past hurts, hang-ups and horrors, left her heart – replaced by love, liking, lightness and laughter for those she affectionately named her *Lifelong Learning Partners*. Her heart was so full that she felt it might explode.

She decided to thank all of her *Lifelong Learning Partners*, by penning what she termed I LOVE YOU NOTES, on small parchment papers.

These notes were so named as they expressed her new appreciation for the supporting players who had performed so perfectly in her life. She wrote *I Love You*, vertically on her parchment paper and beside those words wrote new ones –

I
Learned
Overcame
Valued
Experienced
You
Opened up my
Universe

Then for each of her *Learning Partners* she picked the primary treasures they had provided for her.

Countess Confidence from you –
I
Learned how beautiful confidence can make a woman.
Overcome my sorrow of losing Prince Bad Boy.
Valued your words of wisdom
Experienced Joie De Vie
You
Opened up my
Universe

Prince Bad Boy from you –
I
Learned about the De-flowerment Arts
Overcame my unfamiliarity with the male anatomy
Valued the fun we had together at Pink Palace Performances
Experienced blossoming into a wonderful wanton woman
You
Opened up my
Universe

Prince Rescue Me from you –
I
Learned the joy of laughter
Overcame my fixing fetish
Valued our time together in The City of Love
Experienced the joys of motherhood
You
Opened up my
Universe

Innocent went through her entire list of life lessons, writing *I Love You Notes* to all the people, places and situations she had written about. She found the experience positively liberating.

The maturity she demonstrated from this exercise gave her a new sense of self-respect. She felt more grown up than she had in her entire life. Every morning she would stand in front of the mirror and repeat out loud again and again: 'It's okay to make royal mistakes, as it's only by making them that we learn. Each lapse in judgement means we are one step closer to where we should be.'

She suddenly remembered the great inventor King Courage. She had met him when he came for an interview with Sir Shake and Peer at The Town Crier. He had spent almost twenty years working on a formula to help torches glow brighter and longer. He had cut down hundreds of trees and performed over 2000 experiments to perfect his formula, each of which had failed. Everyone in The Kingdom had said it could not be done and he was often ridiculed by the court jesters, during their shows.

'There goes King Courage,' they would say, 'twenty years and 2000 tries later and he still can't get it right – someone should tell him to get a *light*.' That punch-line always got the most laughs.

The jesters joked, 'Have you heard about poor old King Courage? Last night he received a warning from his forest manager, saying that due to his experiments his borough had now run out of trees. As a result his castle had been overrun with chipmunks, squirrels and birds, looking for new places to live. Not only was it the last *straw* of wood for the royal borough but it became the last straw for his wife, who ended up running off with the head woodman. It seemed the lack of tree work had left him with lots of time on his hands which led to lots of hands-on time with the Queen.' This story usually had the audience rolling on the floor in fits of laughter.

King Courage, however, got the last laugh. When abandoned by his Queen and down to his *last* tree, he suddenly struck gold and the twenty-four hour burning brightly torch was created! Never again did anyone anywhere have to stumble in the dark. The torch became a worldwide wonder and King Courage became a legend.

When asked how he struggled on after years of failed experiments and ridicule by the entire kingdom, King Courage answered that he loved his work and got very excited every time his experiments failed, for he knew that meant he was one stride closer to succeeding. With every attempt he got more inventive and more creative. It taught him what didn't work, until all that was left was what did! He couldn't find that magic tree recipe until he had explored the whole forest. There was never a time when he viewed his 2000 experiments as failures. Instead he always looked upon his invention as a 2000 stride process.

Innocent always admired King Courage and sitting comfortably under the Great Pine Tree, took inspiration from his words and began to pen with excitement her life story. Her list of life lessons started to take shape into an autobiographical treatise, telling tale of her trials, tribulations and triumphs – an acknowledgment of her journey.

Innocent found her voice and she had something important to say. As the words unfolded onto her parchment paper, she felt positively invigorated. As if by magic, all the creativity she had buried deep within her began to bubble to the surface. She slowly began to recapture her lost love of writing, which had departed her when her most influential mentor, Sir Shake and

Peer, disappeared from her life. Suddenly the process of writing became just as important as the words she was penning.

All the creativity she was born with had been used up in her princely pursuits. She had become the consummate Drama Queen, expending her creativity on creating new ways to make herself miserable. Recalling Master Love's words, she realized she had been stuck in a revolving door, only rehearsing life by reliving the same drama over and over. With her innate creativity spent, living life as a Drama Queen became her only means of self-expression.

Recalling the performances she used to give as a child to the household staff, she wondered on more than one occasion if she had actually been a frustrated actress who perhaps should have pursued a career on stage. Perhaps now her book was a means to entertain folk – with a few life lessons thrown into the mix.

Innocent's pen became like a paintbrush as every word was like an explosion of colour. As the words strung together to tell the tale of a colourful life, she became the artist she was born to be. From that moment on, life opened up in ways that she had never imagined. It was as if she had been given the privilege of living life over again, this time with a new perspective and a fresh understanding.

As the pages soaked up all her dramas, Innocent began living *the easy life*. She felt content, centred and happy. It was not the exaggerated highs of happiness that one always felt when they were in the early throes of love – she knew the difference and hated coming down from those highs, usually with a mighty crash. It was not fleeting happiness but a sweet serenity deep within the soul where one could be anywhere or nowhere, do something or nothing, have everything or anything, and yet still experience the feeling of completeness.

Innocent felt as if she had struck gold. Happiness no longer became part of a package, nicely wrapped up in a new love, a new job, a new place, a new item, a new indulgence. It was deep within her, a gift she had given herself, and it became her constant companion.

She thanked the stars every day that her journey had taken her to this place and she blessed every experience that had come before. For the first time since childhood, Innocent had truly come home.

35
Innocent Dates Innocent

Innocent was happy being prince-free! She relished every moment she spent alone, either going for long walks or spending her days making edits and rewrites to her book. Innocent's creativity could not be silenced as it bubbled forth bringing her a real sense of accomplishment. She always had difficulty keeping interested and focused on one thing for any length of time and her foray into writing had proven to her that long-term focus was now a possibility in her life. Innocent felt that she was pushing her own boundaries and was getting to know herself for the first time. She wished she could speak to Sir Shake and Peer telling him that she now fully understood the power of the pen.

In Look at Me, appearance was everything and Innocent's quiet reflection was noted by others as a sad state of affairs – especially for a daughter of a Head of State. Observers felt that the Princess's only hope for happiness lay in finding a partner. Matchmakers were dispatched by not only her friends, but friends and associates of her absent parents.

Every day while Innocent went for a walk or sat sipping tea in town, she was greeted by a series of sentences:

'*Don't despair* you will discover your prince soon.'
'Can't you ask your parents to buy you a Prince?'
'Don't be so fussy Innocent, after all beggars should not be choosers.'
'Miracles can still happen! Ladies of your age have been known to walk down the aisle – and even having offspring!'

Ouch! When did I become a woman of a certain age and what's all the rush? She wondered.

It seemed everyone she met was on a mission to rescue her from her solo status. Everyone seemed to know a prince or a duke who would be perfect for her. They might not want *their* daughters to end up with these particular potential partners, but they would do for 'the desperate damsel' they deemed Innocent to be.

She found their meddling matchmaking amusing, especially in light of the fact that she appeared happier than they were living in wedlock. Innocent observed how miserably married, most of her matchmakers were. They often complained about useless husbands who had horrible habits. Lazy consorts who spent most of their time sleeping. Emotionally absent spouses who had never quite lived up to their potential and kings and princes whose idea of happily-ever-after, was an assortment of mistresses.

One wearisome wife spoke of her husband's dreadful habit of fiddling with his porcelain teeth and broken gold crowns. As he removed his teeth and crowns, she would often get *off her rocker* chair in disgust and leave the room, seriously questioning her own judgement.

'My husband's *cracked crown* really says it all about the sorry state of our amalgamations. Sadly our princes never did live up to all their happily-ever-after hype.' She surmised as all her friends nodded in agreement.

They seemed to be locked into unsatisfactory unions and the term wedlock now took on a whole new meaning for Innocent. She wondered what their husbands thought about them and concluded that it takes two to tangle a wedded web.

Coming from a balanced and blame-free way of being, Innocent concluded that the initial heady rush from romance was only fleeting. A happy and balanced union could only be sustained by a foundation of mutual self-love and an understanding that a spouse could *never* be all things to their partner. That is why one had other avenues of life – children, friendships, work and past-times. It seemed to Innocent that the *expectation* of making another responsible for one's happiness was a futile exercise.

As she sat solo in the café, Innocent was approached by more than one prince. Despite their keen interest in her, she politely declined, and was more than content to cultivate the blossoming romance she was having with herself and her book.

36
Innocent Catches Up With Old Friends

Innocent loved sitting in the local café, which was situated on the slow side of the street, where cars and people could move at a more leisurely pace. Almost down to her last gold coin, it was the only form of entertainment she could afford.

Her life had been a whirlwind of activity for the past eleven years and she relished the new experience of living life in the slow lane. She had a favourite table where she would sit and watch all the people pass by, as she worked on her beloved book. She discovered it was also an advantageous vantage point for happening upon old friends and new chapters.

One morning, a litter carrying a rather large woman suddenly stopped in front of Innocent's table. 'Why Princess Innocent, is that really you? It is I, your old school friend, Princess Princess.'

Innocent looked up to see her old friend being carried by four sturdy footman, each of whom had beads of sweat on their foreheads.

'Why of course it is, how lovely to see you, how have you been Princess Princess?'

Innocent immediately regretted asking that question as in one extended breath the Princess Princess proceeded to tell Innocent *all* about the last eleven years of her life.

'And of course I achieved my goal of marriage, children, a big house and more money than I know what to do with. Alas I never expected it all to be so much hard work. But my dear you wouldn't know much about that would you? You never married or had children? It must be sad for you and your parents.'

Before Innocent could answer and assure her that she was content with her life, Princess Princess had excused herself and was carried off on her litter.

Innocent laughed. 'Why I remember that litter, eleven years hence and the poor dear still hasn't got off her royal arse. Some things never change,' said Innocent to herself, shaking her head.

She was suddenly overcome with a sense of pride. After all she had a nice arse and by getting off it she had experienced so much in her life. She might not have achieved what she had originally set out to but had gained so much and her book wasn't even finished yet!

Innocent ran into another old friend from school, Queen Routine. Her parents were good friends of Routine's mother and father. She had always been one of the most good-natured girls in school. They used to spend hours together reading the pages of the Fairy Tale Land Press. They reminisced about their favourite princess who had traded life with seven little *domestic gods* for one Prince Charming – restoring her lily white reputation in the process.

Routine had a particular penchant for playing it safe. She lived in the land of *Never-Never:* never venturing beyond what was familiar to her. She had never in her life left the Borough of Look At Me – preferring to explore the world via the printing press. She was an avid reader who liked nothing better than to read about all the adventures she would never take. She had married her school sweetheart at eighteen and by the time she was twenty-three, had three children.

Happy to see each other the old friends hugged. They had been inseparable as girls and used to enjoy the same things, yet Innocent couldn't help but notice how very different their lives ended up.

'Innocent, I have followed your exploits through our parent's friendship for years. You are always doing new and exciting things. I do admire you. You have a great spirit and have achieved far more than most – more than I ever will. Life has not always been easy for me. I have often wondered what my life would have been like, if I had searched for greener pastures, as you have done.'

'You admire me? But look at what you have achieved – a husband, a family, all the things that I had searched so long for. I have spent years wondering what greener pastures would be gained from a life lived like yours, if I had met my *One True Prince* at a young age, like you.'

'Forget Prince Charming, my dear, I would trade my Prince in for any one of those seven little Domestic Gods we used to read about … Oh, for a cleaner a cleaner, my husband for a cleaner.'

As they giggled together like the schoolgirls they use to be, they both realized that the lawn was not always greener in their neighbour's castle. As they spun and unravelled the yarns of their lives, Routine finally got to experience an adventurous life and Innocent a taste of a domestic one.

One afternoon with a few days later as Innocent was sitting in the café there was a clambering commotion as a driverless carriage careened down the street carrying a man caught halfway between the door and the wheel. He was hanging head first upside-down. His boot was caught in the carriage seat and was the only thing stopping him from being dropped from the speeding carriage onto his head.

A gallant knight had intervened and grabbed the reins and brought the horses to a halt right in front of where Innocent had been sitting. He helped the man disengage his foot and he fell to the ground.

Innocent looked at the hapless heap on the ground.

'I know that clumsy Prince. Rescue Me, is that you? It is I, Innocent, are you alright?'

Prince Rescue Me, looked up at her, 'Why In … Innocent my dar … ling,' he hiccupped. 'I have fallen off the wagon.'

Innocent shook her head, in both pity and *utter* disbelief that she had ever thought she could fix this broken Prince. All the anger she had once felt towards the feckless fellow had vanished. Now all she felt was an overwhelming sense of sadness at a wasted life.

While she was tempted to send his carriage straight to the Royal Rehab Retreat, she pulled back. She had learned to let go of her fixing fetish and replaced it with the serenity of acceptance.

'Let me help you to where you want to go,' she said lovingly to Prince Rescue Me.

'Home please,' smiled the Prince. With the help of the gallant knight she helped him back into his carriage and arrange for a driver to take him home.

She kissed Prince Rescue Me on his forehead and sent him on his long journey home.

Two days later she was in her favourite café again. She was in the throes of her writing when she heard a booming laugh. There was only one person that formidable laugh could belong to, Lady Laugh-Out-Loud. She was a Lady loved by everyone for her ability to always find humour in every situation. Innocent hadn't seen sight of her since they made acquaintance in Nous Parlons Pas Anglais at the glittering breakfast gatherings. Innocent remembered that she had taken leave in Nous Parlons Pas Anglais to study sketching, but became distracted by a dashing duke. Innocent always wondered what had become of her.

Innocent called out to her old friend, 'Lady Laugh-Out-Loud, it is I, Innocent, how fortuitous that both of us would be in the same café, at the same time, after all these years'

Lady Laugh-Out-Loud ran over and gave Innocent a huge hug. They sat down and caught up on their lives. 'What happened with you and that delicious Baron Booty you were bonkers over?' Innocent laughed, she had not thought of the Baron in years.

'Some men are simply seasonal lovers, but what a season it was,'boasted Innocent as the two friends giggled like school girls.

'And you my dear Lady, what happened to that duke you dropped everything for? What was his name?'

'Duke Deficit, who I discovered was a definitive dud. After sweeping me and my Privy Purse away, he impregnated me with two beautiful children, who thank goodness took after me. If it wasn't for the fact that I had been faithful I would be doubtful that he actually did the job. After eight years of enduring his dereliction of duty and deception I dumped him decisively and returned to It Is What It Is.'

'You must have found it very hard,' said Innocent.

'No not very, that was the problem,' and with those words Laugh-Out-Loud and Innocent began their laughing frenzy. They laughed about every situation that had ever befallen them and their dubious choices.

When Laugh-Out-Loud laughed Innocent became hysterical. Eventually even the smallest things set them off and they heaved with hilarity, crying tears and tittering uncontrollably. When Innocent snorted it set them off even more until the manager of the café asked them to vacate the premises for causing a disturbance. After two hours of non-stop laughter Innocent's cheeks had cramped up and her stomach was full of stitches. She could no longer move and had to send for her carriage.

Innocent had never had so much fun in all her life and decided that laughter was the new orgasm. Lady Laugh-Out-Loud had an idea.

'I have taken up my sketching once more, which has satisfied me to no end. Won't you sit for me and let me sketch you as my personal gift to you?' Innocent said 'yes' immediately as she had never been sketched before.

Laugh-Out-Loud spent an entire day sketching Innocent in various states. As she took her work extremely seriously there was no fits of laughter. Instead Innocent had four changes of clothes and one change of undress. She smiled and pouted at the canvass as her friend swiftly swept her pencil rendering perfect portraits of the Princess.

Finally when she was done, Laugh-Out-Loud showed Innocent her work. She could not believe how perfectly her likeness had been captured. Innocent looked over all the sketches and for the first time in her life she saw a beautiful, grown-up, sophisticated, happy woman, starting back at her.

'My Lady what a fine artist you are. These pictures are positively beautiful,' gushed Innocent.

'No my Princess, it is you who is truly beautiful. My sketch only reflects the subject!'

'But I look so different,' said Innocent staring at the sketches.

'No my dear, you have always been beautiful, but you did not choose to see it. This is the real you. Please allow me to introduce you to my friend, Princess Innocent. She has been waiting to meet you for a long time.'

Innocent beamed. 'I am so pleased to meet such a bright and beautiful Princess, you and I are going to be the best of friends.' And from that moment on, she connected to the beauty she had both inside and out.

'This has truly been one of the greatest days in my life,' Innocent gushed. 'For the first time ever I can truly see myself, and, if I had known how beautiful I was I wouldn't have slept with any of those damp squibs.' And with that the laughing frenzy began again.

Three hours later Innocent returned home with her precious sketches. She put them around her room as a reminder that there was always a beautiful princess close by – and thus she would never be alone!

Catching up with old friends was like finding a cherished item that had been forgotten in a bottom draw. As Innocent revelled in rediscovery her mind wandered to yet another old friend, Princess True. Although she had come to regret little in her learned life, she had to admit that losing True was not one of her finest hours.

Before she had left the Chiefly City, she had heard that True had opened a very successful Ye Shoppe called *Bead Therapy*. She had cornered the market in therapeutic beads work, which proved popular for people looking for their next fix-me-up fix.

Innocent knew that she was responsible for the frightful falling out and decided that she needed to put it right. She was determined to contact True and apologize for her brash behaviour. If True refused to speak to her it would be nothing less than she deserved –

My dearest True

This is a humbled voice from your past. With age comes wisdom and I wanted to share mine with you. I behaved terribly towards you, as I broke our friendship over a RVSP refusal. I regret my folly and ask your forgiveness. Although you may feel the apology has come too late, please accept it anyway as a sign of the deep love and respect I will always have for you and our time together.

Your found friend always
Innocent xoxoxo

Within a week Innocent received a reply –

My dearest Innocent

My heart leaped with joy when I received you correspondence. How I have missed you over these last few years. There is no need to apologize. When can we meet? We have what seems like a lifetime of catching up to do. I will come immediately to see you as soon as I receive the word.

Your devoted friend always
True xxx

Innocent wept with joy and sent word for True to come and see her ASAP. She arrived a week later. As she stepped out of the carriage they both cried tears of joy. They spent three days catching up on all that had transpired in the missing years. It was as if no time had ever passed between them. Both led parallel lives with the same weird assortment of courting characters.

They hyperventilated in hysterical laughter as True told tale of her courting woes with Prince Possessive whom she had met at the Crystal Ball. Like Innocent she lasted no longer than a few weeks with the fatally attracted pursuer. They pondered what their lives might have looked like if their paths had crossed at the Crystal Ball, if Why Me had not intervened. As much as she liked to attend every ball of note, she avoided that one like the plague knowing that Us and Them and his terrible cousin would be in attendance.

She was glad however that things conspired as they did, as back then she would not have been ready to take responsibility for her rubbish. For Innocent, learning came just in time in relationship to whom, and where she was. She became conscious that even with the passage of time they could pick up just where they had left off. Older and considerably wiser, the two Princesses parted company looking forward to their future as mature friends.

37

Innocent Goes Back To School

Innocent was down to her last gold coin and decided that she could no longer live just by happiness alone. She desperately needed a paid position to top up her Privy Purse and repay her parents. She hadn't held down a post since her appointment at The Town Crier. She wondered what a Princess in her position could do. She went down to the local job posting message board and searched for suitable positions. Halfway down the board she found a notice which perked her interest. The position read:

> *CHILDRENS TUTOR REQUIRED*
> *Do you enjoy being around young children? Do you have the patience of a saint? Do you have high tolerance to noise and mayhem? Can you handle stress? Can you deal with incessant questioning? Are you comfortable making a fool of yourself? Can you deal with immaturity?*

—'This sounds like my love life,' Innocent joked to herself.—

> *If you answered yes to all of these questions you may be just who we are looking for. Come join the fun at The School of Joy and Happiness*. All *enquiries should be made to the Director, Duchess Delegate, via messenger.*

She dispatched her messenger and upon meeting the Director, was hired immediately. Within two days Innocent took up her position at the School of Joy and Happiness. It was a renowned school which had been instigated by the Intelligencia of The Kingdom. It put into practice a revolutionary technique of raising children. The Intelligencia had been deeply concerned about the happiness levels in The Kingdom. It Is What It Is, had always come in last in the Happiness Index of International Kingdoms.

The group of bright minds concluded that citizens were severely lacking in know-how in this department. After several royal commissions and research studies, it was concluded that more guidance was needed. They released their findings in a paper called *A Guide to Gaining Glorious Happiness, Gut Instinct and Great Grounding in Your Own Garden*.

An idea to instigate intensive intervention in infancy was enacted. The School of Joy and Happiness was thus established for two to seven year-olds. There was a long waiting list for admission to the school. The only requirement for acceptance was a child with a neutral name. The school did not approve of lifelong labels.

On the first day of introductions, Innocent was entranced by her young charges.

There was Young Master Jack, a jovial little fellow with the greatest giggle Innocent had ever heard. She loved hearing him breakout into a giggle explosion every time excitement entertained him.

Young Mistress Grace was a little lady who insisted on being carried whenever the group went walking. She was a Drama Queen in the making and would wail and weep whenever she didn't get her own way. For such a little mistress she had one mighty moan.

Little Lord Owen was the most gentlest and sweetest of children who overflowed with love and affection. He always greeted Innocent with a giant grin.

Joining them was young Master Billy, a bashful boy with a broad smile and little Duke Daniel, a child protégée of Meticulous

Mathematics. He taught Innocent about figures and fractions. She had wished that she could have met him before she had invested in the Isle of Illusion fiasco. There were sixty children in all, each of whom was unique and loveable in their own way.

Although Innocent loved all the children, she developed a special place in her heart for Young Master Marshall. He was just three and had a gallant twin brother named Galen. Marshall's beautiful blonde mother had given birth to the boys prematurely. As a result, Marshall had been born, smaller with less lung capacity. The physicians had told his parents that they did not give him much hope of living longer than a few days. However the little boy with the big heart fought back and decided he had important things to do in the world – gaining strength on a daily basis. The physicians labelled Marshall a miracle.

Young Master Marshall often struggled to breath and moved slower than the other children. Despite his size Marshall had a huge heart. He was full of love. Innocent was convinced that he had taken the decision in the womb to be the one born with difficulties, thus sparing his beloved brother.

Every breath Marshall took was laboured and he was watched carefully by the adults around him. Innocent marvelled at the marvellous Marshall. She was extremely fond of him and for the first time in her life experienced maternal feelings towards a child.

Watching Marshall manoeuvre his way around the school, Innocent felt slightly ashamed of how much time she had wasted on her wooing worries. She conceded that a gift of good health was the most precious possession she had and that as long as the blessing continued she could rise above any challenge. Innocent realized that she had indeed come back to school, only this time she was learning something useful.

She thought back to her own early childhood and recalled how happy and carefree she was running around the castle grounds. Like most people in The Kingdom childhood came to an abrupt end at five, when entry to educational establishments was enacted. In a quest for quiet conformity, creativity, individuality, uniqueness, happiness, laughter, playfulness, self-awareness, self-esteem, curiosity and confidence was quashed.

In the world of academia, excelling in the subjects of *Obsolete Algebra, Science Tables and Experiments You Will Never Have Use For*, *Enhancing Insecurity, Coping with Crummy Characters as Classmates* and *How to Survive NOT Being Teacher's Pet* took precedence over all.

As a result, Innocent like most of the populace, grew up proficient in the art of performance while practicing poverty of the person. As childhood became a distant memory, royal role-playing took even greater precedent over *being*, *knowing*, and *acknowledging* oneself.

With the creation of the School of Joy and Happiness, the Intelligencia sought to counter catastrophic outcomes by perfecting a progressive programme of personal awareness, personal best, politeness, positivity, productivity and profound happiness. Innocent thought how lucky these children were to be in such a model place.

She had been immediately welcomed by the seasoned staff. Duchess Delegate, the school director was a kindly jovial lady, who always had a funny tale to tell. She composed the duty roster ensuring staff were not derelict in their duties.

Baroness Blunt was a wonderful teacher who did not mince her words. She was strict but nevertheless a loveable lady who used her bluntness to help both parents and children to blossom.

Princess Practically Perfect was a mother herself of two young masters. She could do most things perfectly and particularly excelled in painting, cooking, flower arranging, parenting and sharing. She treated most of the children as if they were family and bought in tasty treats for the school staff and thus became affectionately known as Aunt Practically Perfect.

There was Marchioness Multi-Tasker who was a talented Master of The Madly Dashing Around Arts. She had three of her own children and had the ability to complete ten tasks at once. With sixty students to maintain, this talent came in handy.

Countess Spick and Span was responsible for germ control, ensuring the health of her young charges was protected at all times. She kept the school surfaces so shiny and spotless that they glistered and gleamed, saturating the school in a sheen of light.

And finally there was Gregory the Good, who was in charge of curriculum planning. Even though an adult, Gregory had not quite grown up yet and thus had never taken a royal title. He had a charming childlike disposition and loved making the children laugh. His enthusiasm and genuineness were an asset to the school and its young charges.

Innocent loved working with the staff. She relished being around people who she didn't have to perform for. She could just 'be' Innocent and they loved her for it. In turn she loved being with people who were grounded in who they were, and gave love freely, without the drama attached.

Excelling as a pre-school tutor, Innocent loved watching her young charges dress up as grown up princes and princesses. As they role-played she noticed how the *little princesses* loved to boss the *little princes* around, and in turn, the princes liked to tease the little princesses they had taken a shine to. Innocent laughed out loud, thinking how grown-ups still enjoyed playing childhood games.

At the School of Joy and Happiness laughter was the main pastime. Innocent couldn't help but notice how many times a day one of her young charges would laugh. They would laugh at the simplest of things; when they were in the play area shooting down the slide, as they fed the horses in the stables, as they frolicked in the grass, as they baked biscuits, as they sang songs and shared treats. Innocent wondered at what age adults had learned to stop laughing. When did life become so serious?

She also noticed how often the children asked her questions: *Why* was their favourite word. They loved learning by asking. *Why* opened up the children's world.

When did adults stop asking questions and decided they knew all the answers, Innocent pondered. That is why she and many others had simply stalled in life. Children appreciated the treasure of possibilities held in a question, while adults appreciated the treasure of being right about all the answers. She decided that these children were the real teachers.

One of the best-loved activities Innocent arranged for the children was bubble-blowing. She would prepare soap suds and an assortment of blow sticks which produced glorious bubbles in all shapes and sizes. As the children ran around outside trying to catch the floating bubbles, she compared the experience to her own quest for her perfect prince, as elusive to capture as a bubble in a child's hand.

Innocent's nights were filled with writing her life's lessons. Now that she was an *open princess*, she learned a new lesson almost every day.

She decided to try her hand at writing a children's story, and penned a humorous tale about a brave little princess who rescues a prince from an awful munching dragon. She read the story to the children who were captivated. They asked her to read it again and again.

Innocent was a hit with both the children and staff. When the biggest benefactors of the school, Queen Creating and King Structure, came to visit, they called for an audience with her.

The King and Queen had lived in wedded bliss for over thirty-five years. They were leading researchers, looking how route planning could form structures to improve people's lives.

The King explained, 'After our darling daughters had their own daunting journey of detours and disastrous dalliances, we decided to look into how we could make their lives and the lives of other young folk easier. We thus set up the school as a research facility for raising happy children into well-adjusted adults. It is a satellite school for sharing navigational information on overcoming road blocks and dead-ends.'

The Queen smiled warmly, 'my dear, Duchess Delegate has told us a little of your life's journey. We would be honoured if you come and spend the weekend with us at our peaceful palace in the country. We would like to see if our research into route planning for royals on their road to riches could be of benefit to you on your own personal journey.'

Intrigued Innocent agreed immediately. She had become like a sponge and could see that here were two people she sensed she could learn even more from.

38

Queen Creating and King Structure's Classroom

As Innocent's carriage pulled up outside the palace she was warmly greeted by Queen Creating and King Structure.

'My dear you are most welcome. After you freshen up in your rooms, we will take you to our special garden.'

An hour later, one of the butlers escorted Innocent to the garden for an audience with the King and Queen.

The King bounded over to her with an abundant smile. 'Welcome to our Garden of Telescopes, where anything is possible.'

Innocent stood looking at the garden in wonder. There was a large terrace with over twenty large white telescopes with gold trim, fixed to the ground. They looked as if they had sprouted from the ground like the surrounding flowers.

'Do you like our beautiful telescopes?' asked the Queen. 'They are there to inspire us to move towards the beauty that is in front of us. Come stand by this telescope and look into the distance.'

She motioned to Innocent who moved toward the telescope. The King explained to her how it worked. She had never used a telescope before and adjusted her eye several times before it seemed to fit on the lens.

'You are now looking through the *Lens of Light*. Now move it until you can see the violet flowers in the distance,' instructed the King.

Innocent adjusted the lens until she spied the violet flora. The King continued.

'Are the flowers in range?' Innocent nodded. 'Are you so inspired by their beauty that you want to move towards them, capturing them for a beautiful bouquet?

Now move your telescope to the right. Do you see those stunning stallions? Are you so in awe of their sturdy strength that you want to walk towards them and leap upon their saddle so you can ride into the wind?

Now move your telescope to the left. Do you see that enormous pine tree with towering branches? Do you see that table underneath it, laden with the most scrumptious succulent lunch? Are you not hungry enough to walk over to it so you can fill your stomach?' Innocent was moving her telescope in all directions, in awe of the magical machine which brought everything into view. The King gently patted her shoulder and Innocent looked up.

'You see my dear child, most people go through life literally grabbing at things that show up along the way. Rather than be a creator of their life they become a receptacle for experiences that appear, usually generated by others.

'What would that relationship look like to you?' This is because they do not allow themselves to find out what it is their heart is searching for.

For example as you move through a meadow of tall grass, you feel the grass gently touching and tickling your arms. The pleasant feeling subsides as soon as you leave the meadow. But my dear Innocent, when you decide that you want to recreate that feeling of the grass touching your skin every day, you will make a deliberate journey to that meadow ever day.'

Innocent looked at the King slightly confused. Smiling Queen Creating continued.' My darling child what is it that you want to create in your life?'

Innocent had heard those words before from Master Love.

'I would like to complete my book and then experience a committed relationship with a compatible prince.'

'What would that relationship look like to you?'

Innocent was stuck for words, she had never asked herself or been asked that question before.

The Queen attempted to extract the answer by asking more questions. 'What kind of relationship do your parents have, my dear child.'

'I don't honestly know, my Queen. My parents spent most of their time away on royal duties. Although they each spent time showering me with love, we did not often spend time together alone as a family.'

Creating nodded her head, 'just as I suspected, you have never known what exactly it was that you were looking for. All you knew was that you wanted something to go away – that being your solo status. As a result you have spent your adult life trading your solo status for suitors of no substance or staying power. You dabbled in these unsuitable, unstable and unfulfilling dalliances to fill up the gap that was left by not having the knowledge of what it is you truly wanted.'

The Queen moved closer and lowered her voice, as if sharing a secret.

'What did all your suitors have in common my dear Innocent? Well just like you, they all had an inability to create a future. Your gaping gap of knowledge gave you more in common with those cads than you would care to admit.'

Innocent suddenly thought that the phrase *Mind the Gap* had now taken on an entirly new meaning.

Creating continued, 'I suspect that for lack of your own princely vision, you substituted the suitors of Fairy Tale Land Press. It is the same the world over, for all the young princes and princesses. Instead of intentional wooing they take the easy way out and grab the nearest thing to settle in front of them, and then bestow *Fairy Tale Land fantasies* upon their intended.

Unfortunately most of you young people never get to see the real truth behind the Fairy Tale Land Press stories – a marriage rocked by an unsatisfied princess who can't get the six men she used to live with out of her head … a glass slipper that is broken over the head of serial, skirt chasing, Prince Charming … a husband who bores his wife so silly, that she slips back into slumber for another hundred years … a prince who hates his wife's long hair shedding in the bathtub so much that he leaves her …

We have met them all, on our own journey of research. We have been asked by many to help them put their broken lives back together again,' concluded the Queen shaking her head.

As if being struck by lightning, Innocent had the *AH–HA* moment of a lifetime. Her life and loves suddenly played out in front of her, and at last she understood why she had never achieved her goal.

'But … but it seems so stupidly simple. Why did I not suspect it before?'

The King was thrilled by her revelation. After all his life purpose was to put people in the picture, enabling them to discover their AH–HA moment.

'Because my dear child, no-one ever teaches you to take a look at where you are and where you want to go. Most people only look to the past for guidance and reassurance, guaranteeing that they never move forward – thus they are destined to be *stuck* as they repeat the same mistakes over and over. That is why we set up the School of Joy and Happiness, so children could learn the structure and skills necessary to create a life that has meaning for them.'

You see dear Princess, our purpose in life is *not to be perfect*, it is simply to perfect the art of moving towards our goals from where we stand. It is through striving for our goals that we achieve *mastery*.

When we ready for a race, we have the structure of a start and finish line to guide us. That is what all of us need – both a place to start and a desire which drives us forward towards the finish line.'

The Queen smiled. 'Now my dear child let us move towards that lovely lunch that awaits us under the pine tree.'

As Innocent accompanied the King and Queen to the lunch table she felt a sudden spring in her step that was stronger than ever. She felt that Creating and Structure had given her the missing puzzle piece that she needed to become master of her life.

Along with the succulent lunch was a pile of parchment papers and quill pens laid out on the table. As the trio engaged in both eating and conversation, Innocent wrote down what she wanted in a princely partner and relationship –

I desire a lifelong prince as a partner and best friend, who adds value to my life. This prince is free of any past baggage and has the ability to love me. This prince will be a reliable, cultured sort, who I can have sparkling conversations and laugh out loud with. Together we will have a mutually passionate, respectful, loving, easy relationship.

When she finished her *Wish List* she showed it to Queen Creating.

'Wonderful, but be sure to write down when you want this relationship to occur. If we do not demarcate definite deadlines we will not fire up that urgency within which drives us to get things done,' said the Queen clearly.

Innocent nodded her head and thought about the deadline, but before she had a chance to write a date down the King interjected.

'Now, think carefully upon giving this date. Let us review where you stand now. Tell me about your life now, what is going on and how you are feeling about it. Write it down and then read it.'

She nodded to him and wrote a short story of her current situation, which she presented to the pair –

'Well my dear King Structure and Queen Creating, as you know I am a solo Princess working as a teacher with children that I love and who love me. I am experiencing a one year harmonious hiatus from the habitual demands of dating. I am learning to enjoy my own company and be responsible for replenishing my own Privy Purse. I am enjoying the company of old friends. But best of all, I am in the middle of writing a book of my life's journey and lessons which has given me far greater pleasure than any of my past princes,' she said with a saucy grin on her face.

'Just as I have suspected all along,' said the King. 'You have finally found pleasure in your own pursuits.'

Innocent nodded. As she gazed at the words she had just written, her life suddenly leapt up from the page and into her heart.

'Wow, I never realized how good life is for me at this moment. I want to continue the momentum without interruption. Let's see ... well I am only thirty and have plenty of time ... I will give myself another two years from today before I begin thinking about entering into matrimony.'

Innocent could not believe how peacefully she had verbalized her wish for a postponement of her prospective nuptials. She had spent the last few months thinking how happy she was taking a holiday from constant courting, but standing up in front of her two friends and declaring her decision out loud made it real.

'It's not that I don't want to experience wedded bliss – because deep down I know I do. But it has suddenly become crystal clear how much fun I can have finding out how fantastic Innocent can be.'

The Queen clapped her hands in delight. 'Good choice my dear Princess, I suspect your soul has been searching for Innocent all along. I hope that we will see great things from you, which when achieved will free you up to finally join with your *Perfect Fit Prince*.'

'What a great name for him,' giggled Innocent.

As the three of them laughed well into the afternoon, she could not help but study the perfect symmetry of the two bright minds in her midst.

The pragmatic Princess was glowing after her glorious weekend with Creating and Structure. They had truly added practicality to her life. For the first time ever, she knew that she had the tools to accomplish her aspirations, making them a reality rather than just a daydream. She had spent a great deal of her life talking about what she wanted, but deep down she had never really believed she could have it. Suddenly life took on a new exciting energy as she took action toward her future plans.

Remembering the importance of a starting line, Innocent began organizing her life and collected all the I Love You Cards she had written to her past suitors and friends. Rather than reading them, she built a large bonfire on which she threw them one by one. As she watched them burn and disintegrate into the flames, she drew a definitive line under the past. She had lived life pre-occupied by the past – recreating previous hurts and experiences – and the future – consumed with the outcome of marriage. It would be the present she would live for now.

Next Innocent began creating a beautiful garden underneath her beloved pine tree. She got her hands really dirty as she planted a beautiful bed of roses. In the middle of the yet to unfold flowers, she erected a telescope.

From the outside edge of her garden to the telescope she put down several small, square, concrete slabs – just big enough to step on. There were ten slabs in all, which provided stepping-stones to the telescope. On each one of these stepping-stones, Innocent drew large question marks, using white paint. These question marks would serve as a reminder to always ask questions of both herself and others along the route of her journey. Questions were a way to find solutions that allowed her to move forward towards her future goals and without them she would be stuck in the same position of always thinking she had all the right answers.

Around the edges of her garden she planted all variety of flowers. The contrasting colours of flora added real beauty, serving as a wonderful reminder of the multiplicity of life and people. How less colourful a place the world would be if everyone was the same, reflected Innocent.

She looked into the telescope, bringing all of the beauty of the castle grounds closer to her. She imagined doing the same in her life. She would first create a career and when that task was complete, she would bring into existence a mutually satisfying and fulfilling relationship with her Perfect Fit Prince.

And as she stood beside the roses that were just about to bloom, she contemplated to herself, *could life truly be any better*?

39
Marchioness Moaner

Innocent had set a one month deadline for completing her book. She visited her favourite café every day after work, putting pen to paper. Her writing gave her the best relationship she had ever had in her life. One afternoon, as she sat writing, she heard a familiar voice.

'Why – is that my incredible Innocent?'

Innocent looked up and saw her Great Aunt Marchioness Moaner. She had not seen her father's aunt in many years and learned she had just returned to Look At Me after a grand royal tour. When Innocent was a child she often spent time at her aunt's house when her parents were away.

'Aunt Moaner, what a lovely surprise to see you. How are you?' asked Innocent giving Moaner a kiss on the check.

The Marchioness sat down beside her and proceeded to talk about all her aches and pains including her husband. She then moved onto everyone's favourite subject – Innocent's singlehood.

'Don't be sad about your solo status, it is probably better that you have never married, as men folk can be maddening morons.'

Before Innocent could tell her how happy she was, Moaner was on to the next gripe. She suddenly had a flashback to childhood and remembered her Aunt having similar conversations with her. My word, poor Aunt has been moaning about the same things for over twenty years.

As Moaner moved on to the subject of government regulations Innocent felt herself getting drowsy. She desperately tried to keep her eyes open but failed and fell asleep sitting up. As her head bobbed from side to side, Moaner carried on oblivious to her niece's slumber.

Innocent slept for half an hour until Moaner got up to use the facilities. Startled she suddenly awoke and wondered how long she had been asleep. She felt so groggy that she felt if someone had put a sleeping draught in her tea.

When her Aunt returned, she made arrangements to meet Innocent for Sunday breakfast. 'I will bring my granddaughter so you can meet your youngest cousin.' As she waved goodbye Innocent suddenly felt wide-awake and alert.

On Sunday, Moaner brought her granddaughter as promised to meet Innocent. Although the little girl was only six years old, she looked as if she had the weight of the world upon her shoulders. As Moaner introduced little Princess Whiner, Innocent tried to kiss the little girl, who pulled away from her immediately.

'Who is this Grandmama? Why have we come here? I am hungry! I want chocolate cake for breakfast.'

My goodness what a feisty cousin, thought Innocent.

Moaner asked Innocent about her father, King Absent and then proceeded to moan about him for not visiting her often enough.

As Moaner talked, Whiner kept kicking the table which Innocent found most annoying. When she tried to make small talk with her little cousin, she was greeted with a pink protruding tongue.

'I want my chocolate cake now Grandmama. Why must I wait so long? I am bored. Can't we go home? I don't like her. She's wearing stupid clothes. Can I sit at another table? Where's my cake? Please get the waiter to bring it now.'

'I will go and see what is causing the cake delay,' said Innocent desperate to get away from winging Whiner. Innocent asked the waiter to get a particularly large piece of cake to keep Whiner's mouth preoccupied.

When the cake arrived Moaner continued moaning about the price of tea and cake and moved on to the weather, the waiter, and the water rates. Innocent started to yawn and felt a wave of fatigue flash over her.

'Grandmama, I want another piece of cake, this time with a cherry on top and more clotted cream. I want a bigger plate as well. This chair is uncomfortable. I want to sit in her chair.' As the waiter brought another slice of cake, Innocent was grateful for the few moments of peace if would procure.

Good grief, this little Whiner is a moaning mini version of Aunt Moaner thought Innocent, now yawning incessantly. She would be a good candidate for rehabilitation at the School of Joy and Happiness.

'Aunty, as you know I am a teacher at the superb School of Joy and Happiness. It is a wonderful place that could do wonders for little Whiner.

'My dear Innocent, we do not do joy and happiness,' said the Marchioness indignantly. 'When I joined in wedded partnership with your great uncle by marriage – Marquis Misery – I promised faithfully to uphold the values and traditions of unhappiness, melancholy and despair. Misery loves my company as long as I continue to uphold two hundred years of family history. Whiner is the next generation of Miseries and she is not to be messed with.'

She then moved on mercilessly to moaning about the Inteligencia and their radical schools. Innocent wished she had never broached the subject. As Moaner moaned and Whiner whinged, Innocent suddenly thought of her own parents. For the first time in her life she paused and reflected on how lucky she was to have been born to them. If not for an accident of birthright, *she* could have been sitting in Whiner's chair! While her parents may have been away a lot when she was growing up and her mother may have been overly concerned with image, they had always wanted her to have joy and happiness in her life.

Before Moaner could go off on another tangent, Innocent decided to make a quick getaway having learned a valuable life lesson.

'Aunty, please excuse me but I must bid you both a fond farewell. I have a long overdue letter to write to my mother and father.' She kissed her Aunt and dashed off just as poor little Whiner began to cry.

That night, Innocent put her book aside and wrote a letter to her parents telling them all about what she had learned on her life's journey and her recent encounter with Moaner and little Whiner. She closed the letter with the words –

I am so grateful for the gift of two parents who loved me enough to let me find my own path to the School of Joy and Happiness. I love you more than words can ever say.

Your loving and proud daughter
Innocent
XOXO

40
Sir Richest Brander

While working in the school, Innocent was approached by young Master Billy's father. He was a smiling chap with a sprightly spring in his step.

'Let me introduce myself, my name is Sir Richest Brander. I am a Master Brander who has made a famous name for himself. My boy Billy is taken by your story of the brave little princess and the dragon. You indeed have a talent for writing. With my management you may be able to make a brand name for yourself as a published writer. Let us meet and discuss being optioned.'

Innocent became excited. She had almost finished writing her book and had not yet contemplated how her works would be distributed to the discerning public. Here, as if by magic, was the *how to*.

'Me – a published author?' she replied, her pulse suddenly racing with excitement. 'How strange that you would broach this subject with me whilst I am currently writing my memoirs.'

'Providence,' said Sir Brander. 'I love it! I suspect that the fates have big plans for you, my dear!'

'Would you really be interested in helping me get published?' asked Innocent – the high pitch in her voice betraying her utter glee.

'My dear we will meet tomorrow and you will bring me your work to review.'

Life just got really interesting thought Innocent, grinning from ear to ear.

From that fortuitous moment onwards, her life would forever change. Sir Richest Brander loved Innocent's work and he went to task making her a brand.

'Well my dear, you are *no* virgin that is for sure, so we will have to think up a more appropriate branding for you. Let us see … um … ' he said pulling at the small beard on his chin.

'I have it! We can brand you *A Racy Royal*. It has a sharp edge to it, don't you think, my dear? I will have a contract of agreement drawn up for you to pen your princess signature on.'

Innocent had never thought of herself in those terms and she had to admit that it gave her a certain *Bad Princess* edge that she quite liked. Maybe it's time I change my image to go along with my new perspective she considered. And with a swift sweep of her pen, signed her signature on the dotted line.

She worked tirelessly to put the final finishes to her book. She decided to call it *Living with Feet Too Big for a Glass Slipper*. She felt a little like a pioneer whose crazy, difficult and amazing journey was blazing a trail for others – perhaps helping others to take less painful steps.

Instead of being *on the shelf* she now had a book on the shelf, as she became a published author. She dedicated the book to Countess Confidence, Master Love, Queen Creating and King Structure, the four people who helped her make *being* a published author possible. And of course her parents who had given her a wonderful starting line to live and learn from.

Sir Richest Brander loved the title and upon completion of the book went about planning the publicity. He arranged for Innocent's book launch to take place in the biggest, brightest, brashest City of them all – the Chiefly City of Chaos and Congestion Charges. He invited the entire kingdom's press to a conference in the Great Hall of his abode, Glitz Castle, to promote Innocent's work and her brand name. It was an elaborate affair with balloons, buskers, jugglers and jesters performing and where Innocent would make her grand entrance …

41
Innocent and the Press Conferences

'My lady, Sir Richest Brander welcomes you to his home, he has arranged a suite of rooms for you, if you just follow me,' said the footman as he took Innocent's bags. There awaiting her she found a huge bouquet of flowers with a note –

Well, my little Innocent, how far you have travelled.
It does me most proud to be here for your book launch.
I would love to see you before the proceedings.
Just say the word and I will come to Glitz Castle immediately.

Love always
Baron Press xx

She dispatched a message that she would be overjoyed to see him. He had been one of her greatest loves – for a few months anyway – and as she retouched her lip paint she looked at the reflection of the mature and confident woman in the mirror. Looking back to their relationship she realized how immature and desperate she must have seemed to him.

She heard a knock and opened the door to find the Baron beaming at her.

'Darling Innocent what a joy it is to see you. Not only have you become an accomplished writer, but I see you have achieved the impossible and become even more beautiful.'

Innocent smiled and kissed the Baron on the cheek. She ordered tea and as they sat down together Innocent shared all the things that had occurred in her life since they parted. The Baron listened intently to the mature and grounded woman before him and felt a profound sense of pride in his former protégée.

'When we parted ways you were barely more than child, now I see you have blossomed into a bright, worldly woman. How wonderful for the world that you have chosen to share your wisdom.

I was a fool for letting someone of your calibre go. Will you forgive my folly?' And getting down on bended knee, he pulled out a ring.

'Darling, won't you do me the honour of joining me in wedded bliss for the rest of our lives?'

Innocent was bowled over by the Baron's bold behaviour. She had often speculated over what might have been if she had not driven him away. But now years later, although it was lovely to catch up with such an old dear friend, she realized that her feelings and fantasies for Press had been fleeting.

She pondered the irony that now she had become the confident and strong lady that he had wanted her to be in the first place, she was no longer interested in going down the aisle with him. Timing was everything, she surmised. Innocent smiled gently at him and took his hand.

'My dearest Press, You enriched my life by teaching me much about life. Our relationship was but a marvellous moment in time, which we both chose not to take further. Our moment has now passed and we cannot go back.'

'My darling, that is what I regret. I should have married you right there and then. Instead I was living in the moment of my former miserable marriage. If I had let go of that memory, I could have created blissful, modern matrimonial moments with you.'

'My dearest Baron, please rise and refrain from all forms of regret. One can only live in the moment as the person they are, at that time. We both did the best we could do with who we were *being* at the time – you a dejected former husband, me a dejected solo Princess.'

The Baron stood up, 'Profound words of wisdom my dear Innocent. Won't you reconsider my proposal so we can start again fresh? Won't you be the centre of my world?'

'Press, your previous protégée has proceeded onwards and upwards. I am no longer the petrified Princess you once knew. At this moment I have my own centre and do not wish to share it with another. Won't you let go of our past and let us part as perpetual friends?'

Press's free speech stopped as resigned, he accepted the inevitable.

'I accept your proposal my independent Innocent. You know where to reach me if a need ever arises.' And with a kiss of her hand he was gone, leaving Innocent to rush around readying herself for her awaiting and adoring public.

Innocent was immensely proud of her stand with Baron Press, recognizing how far she had come. In the past she would have jumped at Press's proposal or for that matter almost *any* man's proposal.

As she arrived at the Great Hall she saw her parents who were proudly surveying the proceeding. With the book advance she received from Sir Richest Brander, she had repaid her debts to them. Innocent had succeeded in life far beyond their expectations. Before she sat down to be pressed by the press, her parents pulled her aside. Her mother the Queen gently took her hand.

'My darling child how positively proud your father and I are of all your achievements over these last twelve years. What an inspired and independent life you have had. Your capacity to pick yourself up from difficult situations has impressed us beyond measure.

There is one thing left, however, that you have not done and your father and I would like you to rectify the situation immediately!'

The Queen pulled out a familiar box.

'I was packing up your things when I came across this gift given to you long ago by Sir Steady. It is your *Love Scarf* which I believe you are *now* ready to wear.'

Innocent gasped. Years earlier she had thrown the gift from Sir Steady in the bottom of her draw where it had become lost and mixed up with her other things. Now like her it had been found. As she took the scarf in her hands she held it up to the light and admired its craftsmanship. As if looking at it for the first time she noticed how beautiful the delicate diamond encrusted scarf was.

Her father King Absent took the scarf in his hands. 'Allow me to help you, my darling daughter,' and he gently tied the scarf around her neck. 'It is a perfect fit,' he said proudly and kissed Innocent tenderly on the forehead.

'Your mother and I love you dearly, don't ever forget that,' said the King, his eyes welling up with tears. The three of them hugged and cried until Sir Richest Brander told Innocent it was time to meet her adoring public.

As she took her seat, she saw her old friend Countess Confidence in the front row. Confidence blew Innocent a kiss.

'Ma petite, how proud I am of the woman you have become. You are truly an inspiration for an entire generation of royals,' she gushed.

'Here! Here!' cried the audience.

Innocent had loved her book into being. She had poured her heart and soul into her creation. Now all her love, hard work, focus and dedication paid off as people were touched by her story and bought her book in droves.

As a writer, Innocent was regarded as a keen observer of the human condition. She became a cause célébrité who had set a royal precedent by suggesting self-love and self-achievement as a means of securing happily-ever-after. Subjects of The Kingdom had always been led up the garden path where they had been told that *happiness* was procured only as part of a package wrapped up in a title, marriage, a profession, status, power, prowess or a protruding Privy Purse.

Innocent had simplified the matter by suggesting a *No Strings Attached Approach* to life, where detachment from *having to have* was replaced by *wanting to experience*. Innocent proposed that winning at the game of life was simply a matter of *being happy* at the start of one's journey as opposed to being a *Happiness Hound* – constantly chasing after and hunting for happiness.

Innocent suggested Do-It-Yourself techniques that could be done in the comfort of one's home. She wanted to share skills that would empower her readers rather than foster dependency on either her or others. She provided people with practical and sustainable methods proven to assist with the attainment of successful results. They included:

1. *Dating oneself at least once per week.*
2. *Glass Slipper breaking parties, where groups of royals both male and female, could smash both the slippers and Fairy Tale fantasies to smithereens.*
3. *Writing I LOVE YOU NOTES, to significant people and experiences and then burning them on a big fire to demarcate the past from the present and future.*
4. *Decorating one's home with mirrors to demonstrate one is never alone.*
5. *Planting a telescope garden, with small stepping-stones, as a place to start an inspired journey.*
6. *Have musical statue parties, whereby the players, painted in white paint, could mirror the life of a statue by standing Perfectly Still for ten minutes after the music stops – providing a physical demonstration on the tiresome and difficult demands of trying to be perfect.*
7. *Innocent suggested carrying small butterfly nets as an accessory – a gentle reminder to always be on the lookout for opportunities to network. Sir Richest Brander took advantage of her suggestion by developing a book tie-in brand of portable butterfly nets named, Let Your Net Work for You.*
8. *Intentional thinking about what kind of life one wants to create and when they want to do it by.*
9. *Advertising in the local press and on local bulletin boards for a suitable partner with similar aspirations.*
10. *Asking at least two questions a day to acquire useful and progressive information.*

11. *Hugging a tree in awe and appreciation of being a part of Mother Nature's blessings.*

Innocent believed a healthy body held a healthy mind. She encouraged her readers to:

1. *Eat a hearty and healthy breakfast to hinder habitual snacking and to ensure one has enough energy to enjoy life.*
2. *Drink a large glass of water every two hours to flush the thirst and fat away.*
3. *Walk or dance for an hour every day.*
4. *Smile and laugh at least ten times per day.*
5. *Eat a handful of berries and vegetables twice daily.*
6. *Get some sleep!*

People found these techniques truly liberating. Her readers could not believe how simple and cheap obtaining happiness and health could be. The Racy Royal demonstrated a whole new way of being free. Her demos were dubbed DEMOCRACY as an acronym for DEMOC (Do Enjoy My Own Company) as suggested by RACY.

With freedom came responsibility and Innocent inspired people to get off their royal behinds to attain their aspirations. She was so effective that even Princess Princess got up from her blooming buttocks and obtained liberty from her litter.

Innocent was a magnificent Motivational Princess who moved many to their satisfaction in life. She roamed around It Is What It Is, lecturing on her lessons and eventually spread her message to the surrounding kingdoms.

One morning, after lecturing to a large group of women, Innocent was mingling among the mesmerized masses when she accidentally dropped her handkerchief. As she picked it up, her eyes caught a beautiful pair of bright red shoes before her. As she stood up, she was face to familiar face with a fan. As Innocent flashed back through her memory files she recalled a young woman wearing a pair of red shoes in the Under-the-Ground Carriage System. The shoes might be different but the beautiful face had remained the same. Innocent's own face turned the colour of the red shoes as she recalled her jealous jaunt in the transport tunnels many moons ago in the Chiefly City. How greedy and selfish she had been by not wanting another to share her beauty with the world.

As she stared at the young woman in front of her she was met with a magnificent smile. Innocent recognized the veneer of vulnerability exuding from the young woman. Her heart melted. How could she have judged a jewel so jealously? How many other jaded women had directed their ugliness at this weary woman, to fill up their own lack. She might be beautiful but it did not exclude her from having to navigate the pitfalls of life, just like everyone else.

She reached over and gave the young woman a hug and in front of the cheering crowds told the young woman how happy she was that she'd been blessed with such a rare beauty. There had never been such a plucky princess so public with protestations of another's beauty before. The tide turned as the trend for treading, trouncing and back stabbing, was turned on its princess heel and traded in for the practice of venerating and appreciating others. In fact, contests were enacted throughout The Kingdom to see who could create the largest lists espousing the qualities of another.

Innocent remembered another beauty from her past and got back in touch with Queen BBB. She wanted to rectify her recklessness with BBB's feelings and invited the Queen to talk about her work with horses. People everywhere gained a new appreciation for BBB's internal beauty and she gained a new audience and a new generation of admirers for her activism.

All the politicians wanted Innocent to appear in their public portraits hoping that in the process, they would be painted with the same brilliant brush. Famous actors such as King Cool liked to stand next to Innocent during her lectures, sharing the spotlight as she illuminated the stage with her presence.

No-one was more surprised than Innocent at the adulation she received.

Who would have ever imagined that a princess with feet too big for a glass slipper would have found happily-ever-after, she thought to herself, humbled by her good fortune.

42
Innocent Changes Her Name

For the first time in her life, Innocent came to understand how much she mattered in the world. It wasn't so much what she said that mattered the most to people – it was *how* she was saying it. By *simply being* an ordinary titled person who overcame obstacles, others could then see that they too had that possibility in their life.

She had spent most of her adult life feeling that she wasn't enough and was driven by her mantra *please love me*. Now content to love herself she was free to give love unconditionally to others. She had already obtained the happiness she had always been seeking, and anything else that came into her life now, she considered a bonus.

What made this Motivational Princess so popular with the people was both her humility and honesty. She did not believe in all her publicity and remained a *real princess* with failings that everyone could relate to.

From her friendship with Marchioness Mostess she had learned how perilous being the hostess-with-the-mostess could be. Although she was flattered by all the attention, she did not want to become lost in her sparkling new image. She had already spent a lifetime acting out various roles and she had no intention of taking on a new role of *Grand Guru* to the masses. Role-play was decidedly a drain of precious energy.

Innocent reigned in her royal ego by reminding herself that her *job* as a writer and speaker in the spotlight didn't make her more special than anyone else – just different. The world wasn't in need of another book or another guru, Innocent had simply *decided* that she had something to say to bring a little light and joy into the world. Through her writings she'd at last found a new way of *expressing herself* which added value and fulfilment to her life.

Innocent also reminded herself that she needed to keep on asking questions as she didn't have all the answers. To keep herself on the right track she hired the renowned kindly coach, Count Questions. He was a pusher of pragmatic planning who prodded and primed people with questions so they could come up with their own solutions. He helped Innocent think outside the *Glass Slipper Box* by asking her the right questions so she could keep ideas flowing.

The day after a session with Count Questions, Innocent was brushing her hair, when she suddenly found herself looking intently into her eyes reflecting back at her in the mirror. All at once she had an epiphany!

'I am ready to let go of Innocent and simply let her story be a book,' she declared out loud.

Innocent's story had come to a close. She no longer *had* to do anything. All that was left was to simply *be,* and with that she officially changed her name to ***Queen Be.***

EPILOGUE

After a year of accolades the new Queen Be – formally known as Princess – decided to get away from it all to prepare for her next publication. She decided to write an authorized biography on the life of Prince Rescue Me, in the hopes of shedding light on the darkness of addiction.

Just as she was about to leave, she received a message from the Politician's Pocket Fund. Apparently all the lost money from the Isle of Illusion investment had been recovered and sorted and readied to hand over to the rightful owners. It had been over two years since Be had seen her money and she had stopped worrying about getting it back a long time ago. Now after letting go, it suddenly appeared.

She had obtained such a large amount of gold coins from her book sales and lectures that a new bank was specifically built for her own Privy Purse. Now that she had a new gargantuan fortune, she wanted to put her old fortune to good use. She contacted Queen Creating and King Structure and together they decided to open up an additional school of Joy and Happiness for older teenagers who were a year away from leaving their home castles. They all agreed that a little knowledge could provide great preparation for a pimply pupil.

Be retreated to the south of Joie De Vie for relaxation and quiet reflection on her new publication. She found a charming café by the water's edge and sat there writing the outline of her new book. Her concentration was suddenly interrupted by a familiar voice.

'It's Princess Innocent, isn't it? Or at least that was how you were known when we first met.' She looked up and saw a bespectacled man smiling down at her.

Though he looked familiar, Be couldn't quite place him.

'It is I, Prince Nice Guy, we met many years ago in the South of It Is What It Is. Do you not remember me?'

Be had a vague recollection of meeting him at the first ball she attended. She suddenly remembered that he was the first man she had ever met after leaving her home castle. She also recalled her brash behaviour and felt slightly embarrassed.

'Of course I remember you.'

'How fortuitous that our paths have crossed again for a third time,' the Prince said.

Be smiled, but was slightly confused. 'A third time – I thought this was only our second meeting?'

'You are right dear lady that this is only our second face to face meeting, but I was also number six on your Speed Princing list, but alas you never called on me.'

'Really, I had forgotten all about that. I had given up after Prince Number Five. I am so sorry – please do not think it was anything personal,' said Be, blushing.

She could not understand why her cheeks were suddenly flushed and why her pulse had started to quicken. As Prince Nice Guy sat down beside her, her palms started to sweat.

Still smiling he proceeded to ask Be all that she had done since they had first met. The conversation continued for an entire two weeks. He wanted to know everything about her, what she thought, how she felt, what she liked. Be had never experienced a man who was so content to listen to her speak of *her* hopes and dreams.

She learnt that he had made a fortune in windows. He had developed a new type of glass that was so crystal clear that it brought amazing views into one's living room and one's life.

'If truth be told, I owe much of my success to my dear former wife, whom I married not long after meeting you for the first time. Despite the love and affection I lavished upon her, after two years of marriage her head was turned by another – Prince Bad Boy. They ran off together and left me pondering my inadequacies as a husband.'

Be's eyes widened upon hearing her old lover's name as she recalled her own folly with the fickle Prince Bad Boy.

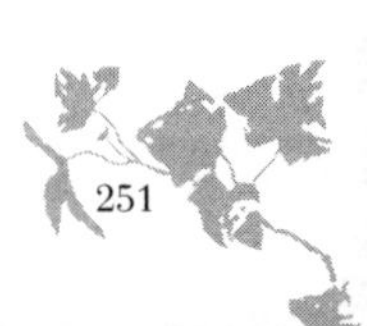

'When she left me, I put my love and affection into my work and became hyper-focused on my windows.'

As the days unfolded, Be grew fonder of the gentle Prince Nice Guy. She found herself becoming conscious of her attraction to him both physically and emotionally. Beneath those spectacles was a super-man full of strength, integrity, decency and humanity. For the first time ever she felt completely safe and cherished in a man's presence. Being with the Prince was so effortless and drama free.

The Prince asked her permission to continue calling her Innocent. He told her it reminded him of the first time they had met and the first time she touched his heart.

She had experienced feeling deep love towards many of her past sullied suitors, but she had never experienced one of them loving her as deeply in return. It wasn't that they had not tried to love her to the best of their ability, but their capacity to love her was closely connected to the love they could give themselves. Here was a rare breed, a man comfortable in his own skin. He was what he was, and thus a *true prince amongst men,* in It Is What It Is.

'You never changed your name?' Be asked curiously.

'I never felt the need. To be honest I was always content to simply *be* Nice Guy. I had nothing to prove other than to myself to remain the man of integrity my parents raised me to be. After all, I was no Bad Boy in the looks department and only had my great personality and affable nature to fall back on,' said Nice Guy grinning.

Be shook her head and laughed. 'Why did I let you go all those years ago?' His answer made her fall in love with him even more.

'Darling Innocent when I first met you, you were so young and eager. You had princes and worlds to conquer. I was equally young and had little experience to offer you. I was not what you needed at the time. You required the taste of forbidden fruit in order to find yourself. You still believed *happily-ever-after* only came from a handsome prince and I was still the frog. We were two different people then and were not ready to be together.

Besides, it was fortunate that we did not get together sooner as you would have taken a different path and the world would not know you as it does now. Our time is now my love.'

And with that he got down on one bended knee and with no ring prepared, asked the question:

'My love, will you marry me?'

She had been living in *unwedded bliss* for almost two years – ever since she had returned to her home castle and started writing – and no longer *needed* to be a wife. Be had accepted and embraced the life that she had created. She had detached herself from any notion of what she *should do* and was happy to simply *be free*.

She realized that up until now, she had never fully been ready to commit herself for more than a short time to anyone, and that is why her *Perfect Fit Prince* never appeared to her. Now life was giving her an opportunity – a learning experience – to live in a committed and mutually loving relationship.

Be looked at Prince Nice Guy and studied his gentle eyes as he waited anxiously for her answer. She stood still taking a few precious moments to say goodbye to her single life.

'Yes I will be your wife,' she said smiling, 'not because I need to, but because I want to.' And with that, they kissed and made love for the first time.

Be was more than pleasantly surprised. It seemed that her Prince was able to hyper-focus on more than just his work. She would never again judge a book by its cover.

'Shall we plan a large wedding to declare our love to the world?' asked the Prince holding his beloved Innocent closely in his arms.

'No,' she said, 'let us rejoice by allowing our love to just *be* between us. Let's find a Master of Marriage Ceremony and declare our love only to one another, with only the ocean as our witness.'

'Are you sure my love? This will, after all, will be your only wedding.'

'I have never been so sure of anything in my whole life,' she responded, gazing adoringly at her Prince. And well within her two year mark for matrimony set in Queen Creating and King Structure's garden, she wed her *Perfect Fit Prince,* with a plane gold band.

On the last day of her honeymoon, Queen Be went on a morning stroll on her own, having thoroughly worn out her Prince. As she walked on the promenade she noticed a beautiful young girl, no older than eighteen, sobbing uncontrollably on a nearby bench.

Be walked over to the girl to see if she could be of assistance.

'You seem troubled about something my dear. Do not worry, this too will pass …'she gently reassured the girl. And it did …

Prequel

The story of It Is What It Is began when, in the year 2000 B.R. – Before Reason – a travelling troupe of Nordic Entertainers took a wrong turn and inadvertently ran into a terrible storm. Their ship, damaged beyond repair, ran aground on the shores of the new found land.

Shipwrecked, the Captain railed the entertainers to accept that they might be there for a very long time, and thus it would be advisable to make the best of things. He named their new home It Is What It Is, in reference to the reply he gave to the frequently asked question: 'Why have we ended up here Captain?'

It wasn't long before the castaways discovered the only inhabitant of the land – a wise old sage who lived alone in a cave. No-one was quite sure how he ended up there, as he showed little interest in mixing with the new immigrants.

The recluse spoke their language that he aptly demonstrated when on the rare occasion he did surface, he stood upon the beach, and with his long beard and white robes blowing in the wind, predicted:

'You are all *doomed … doomed* to 2000 years of self-imposed suffering. But have no fear, *Drama Kings and Queens*, as light will *finally* arrive in the blessed age of 1 A.R. – At Reason, when you will be ready for enlightenment and an easy life. But until then you are *doomed … doomed … doomed!'* he lamented, shaking his head and shrugging his shoulders.

Finding the sage thoroughly depressing – as well as unsettling – the *settlers* decided to move to a new beach and leave the eccentric alone with his opinions. As a departing *gift* the old sage gave them a large scroll on which he had intricately drawn out a spiral calendar demarcating the years from 2000 B.R. to 1 A.R. which he had highlighted.

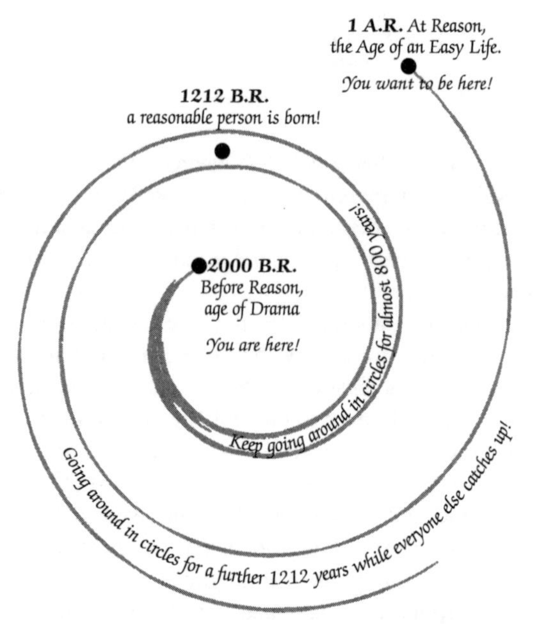

However it was not long before his prophecy began to take shape. When the Nordic Entertainers first landed they found themselves free from conventions of their Nordic land, laws and playwrights, and within weeks lost the plot. The urge to perform was the one constant that remained from their homeland as they took comfort in staging monthly plays. Sadly, it did not take long before many members of the performance troupe began competing for the title of *Lead Actor in a Performing Role*. The right to be pride of place on the stage became the *raison d'être* as all reason went south when the non-competitive members of the troupe built a new boat and sailed off into the sunset, tired of all the drama.

The remaining inhabitants were to discover that when it rains, it pours in The Kingdom. Within a year, other troupes had arrived on the shores of It Is What It Is. Invited to the performance, it didn't take long for the new arrivals to become infected by the *Lead Acting Bug*, as they nominated their own *Best Actor* for the precious position. A bloody war of words began in the peculiar pursuit of the powerful prize – as people became lost in a sea of character roles. Troupes turned to *Flower,* picking blossoms as an emblem to wear as they fought their fraught cause.

After the unwinnable Wars of the Roses, the Lilies, the Pansies, the Gladiolas and the Daisies, it was finally decided by the powers that be, that the only solution was to separate The Kingdom into a series of drama districts where each troupe could be trumps and the show could go on!

As a result, It Is What It Is was made up of 200 Royal Boroughs, each with their own *Best Actor* and *Best Actress* – responsible for the administration of the district. To keep the peace and to keep insurrections at bay, everyone was given the opportunity to *feel important* as the title of *Best Actor and Actress in a Supporting Role* was bestowed on everyone else.

For all premier performers, a sense of entitlement emerged alongside their enormous *egos*. Eventually the '*e*' did go in *entitlement* and all that was left was *title*.

Indeed, in The Kingdom a noble name was the norm. There were more titled ladies and gentlemen per capita in It Is What It Is than in any other kingdom in the world.

Life amongst the *Drama Queens and Kings* was bloody hard work and continued that way for generations. It would not be until centuries had passed when the population finally got some light relief from the heaviness of having to constantly perform.

Almost 800 years later in the year 1212 B.R., The Kingdom was blessed by the birth of one of the most reasonable citizens to ever grace the land – Princess Innocent. Little did anyone know at the time, that the beautiful baby sleeping peacefully in her bassinet would one day give rise to a new paradigm for The Kingdom …

To the reader

If you have picked up this book you will have proof in your hands that dreams do come true. It has taken me two and a half years for It Is What It Is Chronicles to come to fruition! I began this journey in a difficult time of my life: my relationship was ending and with it my desire to continue rescuing people; I had lost all of my money through a series of bad investments and recklessness; but far worse, I watched my brother's rapid deterioration from cancer.

As I kept asking myself how I got there, I began to laugh at some of my dubious choices and decided that it was just part of my journey and learning experiences. I began to put pen to paper and as my life as I knew it was deconstructing, a new one was emerging – as a writer. If I could laugh, then things were never that bad and if I could share my story, maybe someone would make the decision to pass up on the next Prince Bad Boy.

I had always been inspired by Jonathan Swift's *Gulliver's Travels* and Antoine de Saint-Exupéry's *The Little Prince* – fascinated by their ability to create children's books with deep meaning and profound observations of life that resonated with people of all ages. Perhaps the popularity of those books reflects better than anything that we are all children at heart and that a return to simplicity is the order of the day. I hope my own fairy tale can capture the essence of that message.

I currently live between London and Vancouver as a writer and motivational trainer.

Every day is a new chapter!

Thank you for taking the time to read my first novel: Living with Feet Too Big for a Glass Slipper. Please log onto my website at www.lynnetapper.com and share with me your own stories and insights.

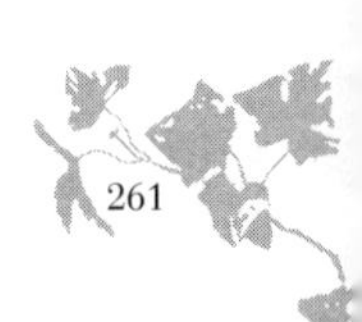

Learning To Live With Feet Too Big For A Glass Slipper

CHARACTERS IN ORDER OF APPEARANCE

Princess Innocent
Queen Appearance
King Absent
Grand Duke Diabolical
Sir Orator
Sir Steady
Prince Nice Guy
Prince Bad Boy
Countess Confidence
Baron Booty
Captain Opportunist
Captain Unavailable
Marchioness Mostess
Sir Lamb
Lord Lie-A-Lot
Lady Denial
Prince I-Only-Mean-What-I-Say-At-The-Time
Queen Panache
Lady in red shoes
Sir Us and Them
Vicountess Victim
Lady Why Me
Lady Lack
Princess True
Sir Sorry
Sir Show Me the Money
Queen Rumour
Baroness Bitter
Baron Bombastic
Lady Haughty
Sir Short-Comings

Baron Press
Sir Shake and Peer
Plain Shane
Prince Apron Strings
Queen Umbilical Cord
Prince Tight
Prince Possessive
All The Best Princes
King Cool
Prince Buff
Prince Fear
Prince Teach Me All You Know
Baroness Booby Trap
Magical Musical Troubadour
Chief Eagle
Prince Rescue Me
Queen Compensation
Master Tao
Prince Good
Count Cut and Paste
Friends' Frenzy Fraternity
Queen Resolute
Lady Everything
Princess Harried
Master Love
Princess Princess
Queen Routine
Lady Laugh-Out-Loud
Kids and Teachers from the School of Joy and Happiness
Queen Creating and King Structure
Marchioness Moaner
Princess Whiner
Sir Richest Brander

It Is What It Is Chronicles
Book Two

Prince Rescue Me's Ride to Ruin

Book two in the It Is What It Is Chronicles charts the life of Princess Innocent's former lover – the Crummy Cracker addict, Prince Rescue Me. From within this twisted tale of his riotous road to ruin we learn that Crummy Crackers are but one of many addictions people perpetuate in the kooky kingdom of It Is What It Is.

As Rescue Me struggles through life committing *crime against Crackers* at every turn, the laws of addled attraction ensure he encounters characters struggling with their own addictions. As the story unfolds and characters cope with cravings from the sublime to the ridiculous, we can see that in It Is What It Is, some people have definitely lost the plot!

Coming soon – please go to www.lynnetapper.com for release dates and orders.

It Is What It Is Chronicles
Book Three

Pandora Havoc One Helluva Highway-Woman

Book three in the series follows the life of Prince Rescue Me's lover Pandora Havoc. The beautiful bandit causes chaos on the highways as she pillages Privy Purses. As her notoriety spreads throughout the land the *anti-cinders* – as she is hailed – throws all convention out the window of what a well brought up lady should be.

Pandora becomes the first ever *Rock and Roll Star* of It Is What It Is – rocking polite society by rolling people over. Bewitched by her beauty every king, prince, knight, baron and lord of the kooky kingdom wishes they could be her next victim.

Living life through a kaleidoscope of excess, she becomes obsessed with fame and fortune. She can run from the authorities but cannot hide from the gilded cage she has created.

Welcome to the world of *celebrity*, It Is What It Is style!

Coming in 2012 – please go to www.lynnetapper.com for release dates and orders.

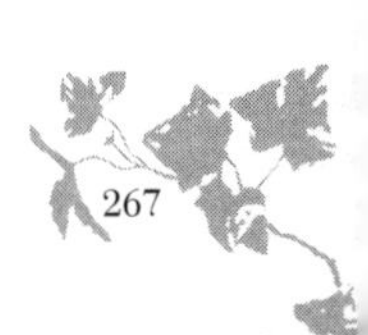

IT IS
WHAT
IT IS